RESORT
TO
MURDER

DALE KESTERSON

Jumpmaster Press
Birmingham, AL

Library Cataloging Data
Names: Dale Kesterson, 1950 -
Title: Resort to Murder / Dale Kesterson
5.5 in. × 8.5 in. (13.97 cm × 21.59 cm)
Description: Jumpmaster Press™ digital eBook edition | Jumpmaster Press™ Trade paperback edition | Alabama: Jumpmaster Press™, 2018. P.O Box 1774 Alabaster, AL 35007 info@jumpmasterpress.com
Summary: Lauren Kaye, reporter for The Daily Gleaner, checked in to an exclusive, Long Island resort, assigned to write her first Sunday feature story, while tasked to investigate a fatal scuba accident. Her suspicions deepen. Robert, her mentor, calls in his friend, police captain Danny O'Brien, who accepts Lauren's help to untangle the perplexing events at the new resort. Navigating jealous, romantic triangles, and evading precarious situations, Lauren must prove her skills to the veteran law officer and put herself in jeopardy to catch a killer, who has already proven the will to ... Resort to Murder.
ISBN-13: 978-1-949184-94-5 (eBook) | 978-1-949184-56-3 (paperback) |
1. Scuba diving 2. Murder 3. Poison 4. Jealous triangles 5. Drugged drinks 6. 1950 7. Reporter
Printed in the United States of America

RESORT
TO
MURDER

DALE KESTERSON

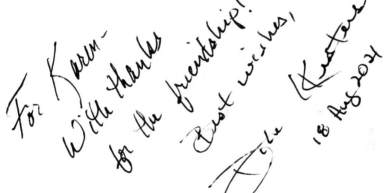

For Karen—
With thanks
for the friendship!
Best wishes,
Dale Kesterson
18 Aug 2024

This one is for Jim, who always understands,
for Heather, who always believed,
and for Anne, who always will be missed.
- DK

Acknowledgments

This book is very personal to me. A senseless death in the family hit me hard, and it seemed fitting to me to use this way of dealing with my grief.

The characters of Lauren, Robert, and Danny have been around for a long time. The first draft of my initial story for them, which I still have, is written in pencil on a legal pad! I would like to thank Gene and Kyle and the rest of the Jumpmaster Press team for giving Lauren a publishing home. My dream of seeing her in print has come true thanks to you. You welcomed me into the publishing family, and I appreciate it more than I can express.

I would like to publicly thank Gail, Yashila, Aubrey Stephens, and the late Robert Asprin for their encouragement to keep writing. I know Bob would be pleased as he predicted long ago that I could do this.

Above all, I would again like to thank my daughter Heather and my husband Jim for their patience, love, and support. I couldn't have done it without you!

1

The telephone's ringing bell, barely audible through my locked apartment door, taunted me like a naughty three-year old sticking out its tongue.

Listening to the jangling sound, I stood in the narrow, dimly lit corridor struggling to juggle full grocery bags and my oversized-purse, fervently wishing humans had three arms. A myriad of tantalizing odors wafting through the air reminded me I forgot to eat lunch. My stomach growled at me like a grizzly bear coming out of hibernation.

I got the key into the lock. My determination to enter the sanctuary of my apartment heightened when the infant in the apartment down the hall started to wail. Inhaling deeply through my nose in frustration, I concluded my neighbor across the hallway once again succeeded in scorching his dinner, which reinforced my decision to decline his standing invitation. The key to my new apartment stubbornly refused to cooperate. Exasperation mingled with the fatigue of the long week, making my Friday complete.

"Give up," I mumbled to my unknown caller, "I don't want any."

The ringing ceased as if it heard my plea. Encouraged, I put down the two grocery sacks and shed the roomy shoulder bag my coworkers swore could be used to smuggle a corpse. Unencumbered with my hands freed, I concentrated on getting the door open. My talents never extended to manipulating a brand-new key in an old lock. Finally, the mechanism yielded. I sighed with relief and gathered my bundles.

My peaceful respite lasted while I stored the first bag of groceries. The telephone shrilled again when I began to unpack my second bag of provisions. I glowered at the black instrument with its innocuous dial. My job with the local Long Island newspaper included answering my phone or I risked my boss' wrath; at home I exercised my freedom of choice. Ignoring the jarring sound, a finely honed talent, rendered a sense of satisfaction.

"I'm not playing," I blithely informed it, "so you may as well quit." I finished my task to the accompaniment of the intermittent annoyance. It ceased while I filled my tea kettle. "Thank you," I murmured politely in the restored silence. "I appreciate your cooperation."

I eagerly anticipated getting home on Fridays, my one calm evening alone with a pot of tea, whatever I could concoct from my pantry, and - above all - no telephone calls. It provided a precious break from my hectic schedule, giving me the chance to clear out the mental cobwebs life provided. I jealously guarded it. I sipped my tea contemplating what I could make with the least effort from my restocked supplies when Ma Bell's irritating contrivance once more made its presence known.

I gave up after the ninth ring.

"I am not here," I stated sharply and distinctly into the receiver. "You can now hang up."

"If you're not there, Lauren," a deep baritone voice reasonably inquired, "where are you?"

"I haven't decided yet, to be honest," I said, smiling while I settled into the comfortable chair conveniently positioned close to the telephone stand. "My mind could use a week in Tahiti, however I doubt my boss would agree since my body would have to go along."

Robert Mallory's cheery rich laugh came over the wire. I easily pictured his winning smile and twinkling eyes. "If that's the mood you're in, I'm surprised you picked up the phone. Or was my third attempt the charm?"

"You didn't want to talk to me before this, Mr. Mallory. It's been a hectic and frustrating week."

"Poor dear. I guess I don't have to ask how your job is going."

"Oh, the paper isn't the problem. Besides being finals week, moving into this apartment was exhausting."

I surveyed my small abode. The rental agent referred to it as an efficiency apartment. When I first saw it, I apologized for being unaware that *efficiency* now equaled a synonym for *tiny*. Unfortunately, she did not appreciate my sense of humor, but truth lay inside the sarcasm. I traded living in a single room with kitchen and bathroom privileges for this place, although it was barely larger.

It took me a full week to make the move. A delivery delay of my convertible sofa, purchased because the place could not house both a bed and a sofa, hampered my efforts.

Two bookshelves along the wall by the door dominated the main room and a fake oriental patterned area rug graced the floor. My eventual plans for the room included a dinette set I could not afford yet, so most of the rug remained bare. I admit my priorities took precedence when I unpacked my books with far more care than my pots, pans, and dishes. The apartment came equipped with venetian blinds which made curtains superfluous. The double window faced south, and my desk stood underneath it. I positioned the stand for the telephone next to the desk; I could reach it from either the desk or the kitchen. My extra chair, where I currently relaxed, could be moved around. An end table next to the sofa supported my radio.

No matter what I called it, I now occupied a one-room studio-type apartment with a small kitchen area and a tiny three-quarter bath (shower, no tub). Spartan quarters, but all mine. I could manage it on my own, a proud accomplishment for a young, working woman in the brand-new decade following the close of the Second World War.

"I hope you're not too tired to go out to eat," Mallory's voice in my ear re-garnered my attention. "I got back into town today and I'd like to take you to dinner."

"Now?" I gazed longingly at the sofa, my big extravagance. My original intention for the evening involved relaxing with my feet up, listening to the radio.

"Unless you'd rather wait until breakfast to have dinner, 'now' seems logical." His sense of humor matched mine, one of the foundations of our friendship. "Do you have anything on the stove at the moment?"

"No," I admitted, "I was trying to decide what to make when you rang."

"Ah! Good timing, then! I wanted to catch you before you started. You'll have a better meal this way, you know."

I chuckled. He knew the limitations of my culinary abilities. "I hate to turn down a meal I don't have to cook—" My voice trailed off and I sighed before continuing, "however—"

"Besides having an interest in seeing to your nutritional needs," he interrupted my objection, "there's something I'd like to discuss with you."

"Nothing tricky, I hope. I doubt I could handle anything complicated right now." I slumped in my chair.

"You can manage this, I promise." Sensing my continued reluctance, he reinforced his invitation. "I haven't been to see Susan in over a week. Please, Lauren, don't make me go on my own," he cajoled.

"All right. I'll take pity on you," I capitulated. *Still in my work clothes, why not? Besides, Susan ran a wonderful restaurant.* "What time shall we meet?"

"Why don't I pick you up? I'd like to see your new abode," he briskly said. "I'll be there in about twenty minutes."

I watched him survey my small apartment. In his early forties, Mallory smiled down at me from his height of over six feet, topping my sixty-seven inches by seven. His casually styled brown hair held a hint of deep auburn with no sign of grey. Always immaculately dressed, the light grey of his jacket enhanced his startlingly blue eyes. A very attractive and charming man, I knew Mallory usually chose to spend his evenings with one of any number of sophisticated ladies, yet he generally made a point of seeing me once a month. I could not tell whether or not he liked my new apartment. I suspected he would eventually let me know.

"I want to swing by a new Levittown-style development," Mallory told me once we were in his car, a late model Oldsmobile.

"Oh? I wasn't aware you were shopping for another house. A present for Julie?" I asked.

"Can you picture your best friend in her own home?" He chuckled. "I doubt that will happen until after she graduates. No, I'm scouting for a client of mine. His newly-married son wants to relocate out of the city.

Some of these single-family homes are quite reasonable."

"So I've heard. Very popular with some of the GIs from what I understand, even if they all seem to be based on the same floor plans. I'm glad the Glen has a few apartment complexes, though. I can't see me in a house," I remarked while he turned off the main road into a new subdivision. "Besides, I doubt I could ever afford the house I would like to own."

"Are you sorry your mother sold your home after your father died?"

"The old farmhouse? No, I'm not. Although it was a great place to grow up, it was too big for the two of us. I couldn't manage it on my own." I smiled and shook my head. "No, my dream home would be more along the lines of yours," I said, thinking of his beautifully decorated mansion. His library, which he called his office, came complete with floor to ceiling bookcases and a desk I would kill to own.

"You can't blame young married couples for wanting to set up in their own homes with yards, where they can raise kids," he replied, pulling up in front of a modest ranch-style house with a 'Model Home - Open House' sign in the yard. "Our school system is one of the best in the state, and new schools are going up to accommodate the growing population. Howard Johnson's is putting in a restaurant on the highway, and a friend of mine bought the land next to the new movie theater with plans to build a roller rink. The whole area is growing."

He got out of the car and came around to open my door.

"Well, you can certainly tell the new homes from the ones built by the old-money families. Those estates were established in our wilderness to escape the crowded cities. I recently heard one of the scions of a Hampton family complaining they were starting to feel cramped by the new suburban trends. He would have preferred to stop time and stay in the 1940s." I snickered. "Of course, he inherited his money and home."

He chuckled. "We are in a new era of progress. Northwoods Glen was always going to open up once the war ended. With Levittown as a prototype, suburban development here was inevitable, especially since we're centrally located on Long Island."

Following a tour of the slab ranch, Mallory drove to a small shopping center sitting off the main highway, home to one of the best kept secrets in Northwoods Glen.

Resort to Murder

2

Nestled between a pharmacy and a florist, an unobtrusive entrance opened into Susan's Place, the Glen's sole authentic Italian *ristorante.*

Deceptively deeper than wide, the cozy dining room housed a score of round tables and four long tables, each boasting immaculate linens, sparkling glasses, and flatware. One of the long walls consisted entirely of brick; on the opposite side, the bricks stopped at a chair rail with oak paneling above it. A few paintings of scenic Italian hills, villas, and coastlines graced the walls. Two alcoves sheltered by movable decorative screens flanked the doors to the kitchen: one served as the stand for water and trays, the other housed a table which could seat six.

"Mr. Mallory! We were hoping you'd come by this evening," Susan greeted us. "Gianni has been playing with the sauces, and he invites your opinion." She showed us to the table in the alcove generally reserved for family and friends. I exchanged questioning glances with Mallory. Susan usually seated us in the main dining area.

Gianni and Susan Gianello deliberately set an atmosphere of home-style service for their exquisite cuisine. An Italian immigrant, Gianello escaped from Mussolini's tyranny to the US in 1939 armed only with a true love of cooking and enthusiasm for his new country. At the end of the war, tired of being told what to make, he relinquished his job of under-chef at a five-star Manhattan restaurant in favor of starting his own elite eatery. He hired Susan, a native New Yorker and war widow, to be his hostess. They fell in love and married. Together they created an atmosphere of classic elegance, keeping the surroundings simple and relatively exclusive. The food won rave reviews from critics and customers alike. The chef contentedly presided in the kitchen while Susan ran the front with a small staff. Their regular customers never bothered with the menu. Susan flatly refused to show it to Mallory and he told me I would insult Gianello if I requested one.

"Lauren, have you been skipping meals again?" Susan's blue eyes took in my tall, slim appearance with maternal shrewdness, her lovely face framed by a hairstyle that would not dare become disheveled. In her late fifties, her petite stature matched the ambiance of the place: timeless and chic, not overwhelming. A colorful scarf used as a belt off-set her white blouse and full, long black skirt.

"Susan, I swear I don't do it deliberately," I said, attempting to look contrite. "I get busy and forget. The job keeps me busy."

Of course, I realized even if I wore a similar skirt and blouse, I would look dowdy. My body structure did not fit current trends because I lack curves and the Rulers of Style currently favored them. In the roulette game of fashion I figured builds like mine might someday become the vogue. Meanwhile, I consoled myself with the thought I felt comfortable in a utilitarian straight navy skirt and plain white blouse with my brown hair pulled back into a bun.

"And you keep going to those classes at night? Which means more meals skipped," she admonished, shaking her finger at me. "*Oy!* How are you ever going to catch a husband if you're just skin and bones?"

"Susan, stop sounding like the Jewish grandmother you are and bring us two of whatever Gianni is keeping warm," Mallory intervened, smiling at my discomfort.

Susan bustled off and I gave my host a mock glare. "You don't have to encourage her, you know. She's good enough on her own."

"Can I help it if she takes a proprietary interest in her customers?"

"I guess not. Her maiden name is Goldberg, and she takes it seriously. Somehow you don't expect that in an Italian restaurant."

"Here." Susan joined us long enough to deposit a basket of fresh breadsticks on the table and pour water into the waiting goblets "Start on these."

"Uh-oh. Something is wrong," I observed, frowning. "I only got one lecture."

"You're right. She forgot our drinks and she hasn't chastised me for not being here for a week or more. Watch out for storm warnings."

"Well, I'm certainly not going to ask for our drinks. If you want to risk it, go ahead," I said, reaching for one of the warm breadsticks Gianello baked daily from scratch. "If Susan is flustered enough to skip a scolding and forget beverages, storms are merely annoyances. It's time to dig a bomb shelter."

"I can agree with that!" He picked up a breadstick.

"Speaking of something being up, what did you want to discuss?"

"Julie's birthday." His voice reflected his uncertainty and I watched the usual glint of humor fade from his deep blue eyes. "She's going to be twenty-one and I'm not sure what I should do for the occasion. I'm hoping you might have an idea or two."

Knowing how self-confident he was with other aspects of his life, I chuckled.

"Stop the press! New forty-eight point headline! Robert Mallory, successful executive stymied by having a daughter coming of age!" I amiably ribbed my host. He started to comment and I put up a hand. "I apologize but I couldn't resist that. I assume the problem is not simply that she is having another birthday. Am I hearing the usual 'yelp for help' I get every year?"

"Precisely." His stiff shoulders relaxed while he sighed and sank into the comfortable chair. "This is one of the big ones. Is it time for a party?"

"I would say so. The last major one you did was for her sixteenth." I leaned back. "Three things need to be decided. First, do you want a mix of family and her friends or just her friends? Second, how many people will be attending? Third, we need a date." I ticked the items off on my fingers. "Once we have that, I can plan the other details like a theme and food."

"Hmmm. I may have to give that some thought. The one five years ago was strictly for her friends," he recalled. "Maybe we should open this one up to all ages. I know I've left this late. My only excuse is I've been in and out of town for the past two weeks."

"It is a 'rite of passage.' My only caution is if the guest list goes above twenty, we'll either need a caterer or you'll have to give your housekeeper a raise." I spotted the growing hint of panic in his eyes and relented. "Relax. Give me an idea of the guest list. I can work with Mrs. Fiddler once you give us some guidelines."

Julie, Mallory's only child and my best friend, was exactly three and a half years my junior. Following her mother's death eleven years ago, Mallory purchased the large house down the road from my parents' house and installed his daughter with a housekeeper. Originally his plan included a governess. Alice Fiddler, who grew up in England, decried that as 'stuff and nonsense', insisting that another woman would get in her way. Mrs. Fiddler ran the Mallory home with all the efficiency of a Marine drill sergeant coupled with the insight of a qualified psychologist. She embodied the combined tasks of cook, teacher, mother, and disciplinarian to Julie, who adored her. Mrs. Fiddler staunchly protected her charge, yet refused to coddle or spoil her, and meted it all out with love. She more or less adopted me as a fact of Julie's life because I persistently turned up. An only child living in the immediate neighborhood, I learned Mrs. Fiddler would always welcome me if I accepted and followed the house rules.

I quickly calculated dates in my head. "The 25th is a Sunday, giving us a little over two weeks, which should be enough time. It's June and your backyard terrace is lovely. We could keep it simple and make it an afternoon garden party. With luck, the weather may cooperate." I smiled seeing the relieved glint in his eyes when he nodded. "Let me know when you want to panic over her present, too," I continued, knowing from experience he would. "I have an idea which is decidedly traditional. She'll love it and you'll appreciate it because it's expensive."

He laughed aloud. "You know me. That sounds great. I'll start working with Mrs. Fiddler tomorrow."

I chuckled and watched all the remaining tension visibly drain from his face. Completely relaxed and at ease, he smiled. Susan came up to the table again before my chuckles ended. She brought our usual drinks: coffee for him and hot tea for me.

"It's good to see you both laughing," she approvingly nodded.

"Forgive me for being blunt, Susan, but what's wrong?" I asked.

"Now why should something be wrong?" she countered defensively, her face flushing.

"You only fussed at me once, you skipped scolding Mr. Mallory for not coming in last week, and you didn't bring our drinks when you brought out the breadsticks," I promptly detailed. "You're flustered."

"So why should it be something bad?"

"Your smile is not reaching your eyes," Mallory told her.

She glanced around, checking her two other customers lingering over after-dinner coffee. The Friday night rush, generally their busiest, usually started after seven.

"*Baruch HaShem*! Pardon me. Thanks be to the Almighty. I am so glad you are here tonight," she confided, sitting down with us. "We are both so worried I had to remind Gianni to use onion in the marinara sauce this afternoon."

"Is everyone well?"

"Everyone has their health, Mr. Mallory, thankfully. It is not sickness. It's—it's just—" Her voice faltered and broke.

"It's Arlene," Gianello supplied, coming up to the table with a small pitcher. He placed it on the table. "Susie forgot the milk for your tea and coffee."

"Your customers are getting up to leave," I prompted the chef, nodding in their direction.

The two diners approached the small, elegant reservations stand located off to one side near the door. He headed over to receive their compliments and payment.

Mallory stood when Gianello returned to our table. The two men shook hands and sat.

"Is Arlene in trouble of some kind?" Mallory asked, his eyes shifting between them. He and I knew their world revolved around Arlene, their nineteen-year-old granddaughter whom they adopted following the death of her parents.

"She's a good girl," the chef affirmed in his careful English, "but we think she's in a bad place. Things don't seem right where she is." About my height and stocky, worried dark eyes emphasized his swarthy skin, wavy black hair, and hooked nose.

"Can you elaborate, please? We can't help if we don't understand." I turned to Susan. "The last time I came in, you told me that Arlene would be returning to Long Island to work in a recreation camp as a swimming instructor. Did she?"

"Oh, yes. She's working at Northwoods Resort and Beach Club, the new place. It opened in mid-May before the regular summer season. Not a camp exactly, because they have both children and adults there. Some come for the day, some come for a week or more and use cabins. Families, couples, single people—not like the kids' camp Miss Julie used to go to."

"I've seen the advertisements in the Sunday section of the *Daily Gleaner*," remarked Mallory. "According to what I have read, they have everything from water skiing and swimming to the new sport of scuba diving, with an instructor on hand for all of it. So Arlene is working there?"

Susan nodded. "She's the water sports director since two weeks ago."

"I thought these places hire staff for the summer and open on Decoration Day," I said. "This is the second week of June. Job openings don't generally come up after the summer starts. Why didn't she start at the beginning of the season?"

"She replaced a staff member who was killed," said Gianello.

"Someone died?" Mallory and I said together.

"The girl who started as the swimming instructor died in an accident," Susan explained. "She and Arlene both applied for the job. When the girl died, the manager remembered Arlene's application. Such a nice bonus they offered if she would take the job!"

"Accidents do happen. What's the problem?" I asked the two grandparents. Gianello exchanged looks with his wife.

"You get their dinner, and I'll explain," she told him. "It's on the house tonight," she added to Mallory. "We have bad feelings about this, and we need your help."

"Susan, your instincts are usually right," Mallory assured her. "You say that Arlene is fine?"

"That's the good of it, thankfully, so far at least." Susan sighed.

"Start at the beginning, and take your time," I encouraged.

"Arlene applied for the job out there before her finals. The resort is less than an hour away and you know she doesn't like being away during the summer. She even got called back for a second interview. According to what the man told Arlene, she and the other girl had the same qualifications and it was a matter of deciding which one would fit with what he called his clientèle. Arlene found another job teaching swimming at the YMCA sleep-away camp in White Plains, but when she was offered the bonus to change jobs she decided to take the one she wanted in the first place. The pay is much better, and you know she's saving for school."

We both nodded when she paused. Arlene, going into her sophomore year of college, planned to major in physical education. Susan started to speak again when

Gianello interrupted her, serving two plates steaming with pasta, sauce, and veal smothered in cheese and more sauce. The aroma alone was tantalizing. He took the table's remaining seat.

"The place is nice. Once she got there, Arlene invited us to drive out one morning so she could show us around," he related while we dug into the enticing entrées. "It's just like the advertisements. We saw families on vacation, a few couples, and a few women staying there during the week with their kids while their husbands came out for the weekend."

"It reminded me of some of the resorts in the Catskills," put in Susan, "only not quite so rich-looking and not as large. The cabins are more like lodges than a hotel. Arlene showed us her room, which is comfortable, and we met the manager and the owner." She stopped and nodded to her husband.

"That's when Susan started getting uneasy," Gianello told us, taking over, "when we met the man and lady. The lady owns the resort, and he runs it. At first I thought it was foolish to be nervous, but you know my Susie." His face lit up when he proudly regarded his wife. "She has a good instinct for people." His gaze came back to us. "How is the veal?"

"Wonderful," I murmured, swallowing a bite. I nudged Mallory's ankle under the table, and he nodded. We both knew the sauce did not quite meet his usual standards—it was good yet not the normal great. We each cut another piece.

"What made you uneasy?" I asked the hostess. "Was it something specific you felt was wrong? Do you feel they are untrustworthy?"

"*Oy,* at first I thought it was only because I didn't like the man. Something about him catches me wrong. The lady owner is kind of flighty and she didn't think we were worth her time, but that's not enough to fuss over. The man told us he was pleased Arlene had taken his offer because it helped him. I think he meant it, yet it sounded like just words to me." She shrugged. "He reminded me of the *meshuggeneh* salesman, the crazy fool who tried to get us to buy a more expensive car than we wanted. Pushy, smooth, and a little annoying."

"Why are you worried?" Mallory asked her.

"To tell you honestly, Mr. Mallory, at first I was only concerned. It wasn't until I got Arlene's letters that I got worried. In her first one, she told us that she found out the other girl drowned and she was not supposed to ask any questions about it. Her second letter was short and full of nothing. Lots of words but saying nothing. Not like her letters from school, which were always full of what she has done, funny stories, and her studies."

"Could it be a matter of her being very busy?" A foot tapped my ankle and I cut another bite of veal.

"With classes, sports, and dating, she writes pages. With no classes, no dates, and her evenings free, she writes only one page of nothing?" Susan shook her head. "*Feh!* No, that's not my Arlene. The one thing she did say in her first letter was that the girl who drowned shouldn't have, that the accident shouldn't have happened."

"What do you want us to do?" Mallory asked, giving up the pretense of eating. He put down his fork and regarded them in turn. The pair exchanged glances, and focused on me.

"Lauren, you work for the newspaper," Susan said. "You do research and you write stories. I know this is a lot to ask but I have a feeling my Arlene may not be safe. Can you find out what's going on out there?" She gave a slight shrug and put her hand on her chest. "Forgive a grandmother's worry. She's all I have left—besides my Gianni."

The bells on the front door chimed softly admitting a family of four; Susan rose to seat them. Gianello stood, looking down at me. He hesitated.

"Arlene is mine, too, and if Susie is right, someone has to find out what is happening before anything goes more wrong." He shrugged and gestured with both hands; his accent, stronger than usual, made his simple words poignant. "I'm not saying this right. I'm not good with words."

Mallory rose and the men shook hands again. "We'll talk this over and let you know before we leave," he assured the worried chef.

"Garlic," I commented to Mallory after he sat.

"Garlic?"

"Susan reminded him to put onion in the sauce, but he also forgot the garlic." I caught Susan's eye and she detoured to our table. I handed her my unused spoon with a little sauce on it. She tasted it and I repeated, "garlic."

"*Oy!* You're right. I'll see to it." She made a face and headed to the kitchen.

"Other than the garlic, it's fine," Mallory remarked, cutting a piece of veal. I nodded while I twirled up a few strands of angel hair pasta. "What about their problem?"

"If Arlene isn't being her usual chatty self in her letters, it's possible that something may be sour. She's like Susan when it comes to feelings and I know they have grown very close over the past few years. A letter with—how did Susan put it?—'Lots of words but saying nothing' is not a good sign. Even the boy she dated twice last semester fueled three pages." I rolled my eyes. "I know because Susan showed it to me in the hope that I would get the idea and find a boyfriend of my own!"

Laughing, my dinner partner put down his coffee cup. Susan returned with a tray as he picked up his fork again. Rapidly collecting our plates, she replaced them with fresh ones.

"With garlic." She hurried off.

"You may have saved Gianni's reputation," Mallory said after he tasted the fresh sauce. "This is much closer to normal."

"This is Friday night, and we can't have bad sauce," I agreed, spearing a piece of the tender veal with more enthusiasm. "Any ideas?"

"One or two. Let's enjoy dinner first."

Diners came in, ate, and left during the hour and a half we took to leisurely eat our meal.

"I like your place," Mallory told me. "Small yet somehow it suits you. Have you met any of your new neighbors?"

"One. The guy across the hall and I have spoken a few times. Lawrence works at the Hempstead Bank. We met when he helped me juggle the bookcases after I banged one into the wall while trying to get it through the door. Three nights ago he invited me to dinner at his place and when I begged off he made it a standing invite any time I want to come by. He renews it whenever we run into each other."

"Sounds promising. Are you going to accept?"

"He's nice enough. He seems genuinely likeable even if he's a bit dull. However, before I go over there to eat, I may recommend cooking classes."

"Really?"

"Lawrence gets home earlier than I do, with his traditional banking hours. There hasn't been one night this week when I haven't smelled something burning."

"Oh? You're not great in that area yourself."

"I'm aware of that. That's why you and I eat out or you invite me to the house." I smiled when he chuckled. "I'm also smart enough to not invite company for dinner until I get better at it." I grinned.

"There's also the problem of somewhere to sit," he pointed out.

"What's wrong with a couch and tray tables? Besides, I'm not home much."

Mallory conceded it with a smile and a nod. "I could give you a dinette table for Christmas and four matching chairs for your birthday," he generously offered. "I might even let you pick them out."

"Gee, thanks. I could open one package in the morning and the other in the afternoon to lessen the confusion," I laughed, reflecting on my Christmas birthday. "Remember I won't take birthday presents wrapped in Christmas paper." I shook my head. "Seriously, you know while I appreciate the thought, I'd prefer to manage it on my own. Please?"

"All right, I'll back off for now. Let me change the subject. What did you think of the house we saw?"

"The construction is better than I thought it would be. I love the fact that although it is on a cement slab, the heating comes from hot water in pipes in the concrete. I hate putting my feet on cold floors during the winter. The furnace is oil-fired?"

"That's what the man said. I thought the floor plan was flexible. The kitchen is big enough for a table and the two bedrooms are decently sized. "

"Yes and the area off the main room could be anything from a third bedroom to a dining room or a library. The sliding doors to separate it are a great touch. Close them for privacy or open for more living room space."

"You only want someplace with a dedicated library," he teased with a chuckle.

"Guilty," I admitted, smiling. "I don't think I'll ever have enough book space."

Totally at ease, I realized spending time with Robert Mallory never disappointed me. No patronizing talk, no 'you silly child' admonitions, just two friends who enjoyed being together despite the difference in our ages. He rarely brought up the fact that the first time he laid eyes on me he caught me trespassing on his property. I regarded him across the table. Close to being leading man handsome and equally charming, his warm blue eyes provided my best clue to his mood.

Susan, making her usual rounds of the tables, stopped briefly to lay her hand on my shoulder. "Thanks for the tip about the garlic." She bustled off and we both chuckled.

Finally, I laid down my fork. "That's it, no more." I sighed, frowning slightly at the quantity of food remaining. I managed to eat only half of the serving. "Gianni is too generous and it always makes me look bad. I'll bet I'm in for another scolding. Oh well. It will be normal and Susan will feel better for having to do it."

Mallory laughed. Laying his cutlery across his plate, he grew serious. "Lauren, I can think of one way to check on what's going on out at the Northwoods resort."

"I have to go out there for a few days. I also thought about asking you to register for the weekend."

"Well, I wasn't going to suggest it, but I'd feel better if I did." He closely studied me, his blue eyes steadily holding my dark brown ones. "There may be nothing to this, yet if there is something amiss, I'd prefer you weren't out there on your own."

"I wonder if I could get Mr. Slater to agree to let me do an article on the place," I mused. "The paper hasn't done anything yet and he wants one. It's a plum assignment though, the sort of thing he'd usually assign to one of the older guys." I grimaced. "It's not exactly my area, however in the two years I've been there no one has told me exactly what my area is. It would be better if I could land a job at the resort but this is the middle of the season so that's out. I can't go out there as a guest because I can't afford to take time off, much less pay for my stay. I'll bet it's expensive."

"You could try asking for it. A profile article would give you leeway to nose around and ask questions. Bernie should stand you to your expenses, too. I can easily arrange to come out for a weekend. I can always use the break."

"When was your last vacation?"

"Last summer. Remember? I took Julie with me to London. I built a few extra days into the business trip so we could see some sights. When was yours?" he asked, smiling.

"What's a vacation?" I smiled back, blunting my cynicism. "Between work and classes, I rarely get the chance to do nothing." I saw him start to speak and I shook my head. "Please don't start the loan squabble again. Since you are determined to help me, I would happily accept assistance selling my boss on the article idea. I know you have some pull with him because you helped me get the job."

My mother passed away from cancer two years after my father died in the D-Day invasion, and four years ago I found myself on my own. I gathered over the years that my mother's brother, an uncle I never met, worked for the government in a hush-hush capacity. When she died, I wrote to Harry Daniels at the box address I found in Mom's Christmas card list. I got a telegram of condolence and regrets signed "Harry" for my effort.

Before her death I promised my mother I would finish college, yet money got tight after her medical expenses. To honor her last wish, I switched from full-time school to evening classes at Hofstra College and put in applications anywhere I thought could use a good English/Journalism major. After settling for office clerical work for two years, I landed a job with our local paper. The editor of the *Daily Gleaner* took me on as a general assignment writer, which roughly translated to 'anything no one else wants' for stories. I could not afford to be picky. About six months ago a staff member made a sarcastic comment, prompting me to make surreptitious inquiries. I discovered my boss offered the position only after Robert Mallory intervened on my behalf. Neither of them ever admitted it. I suspected the intervention occurred because I refused to let Mallory loan me the money I needed for tuition or co-sign a loan with me. He continued to offer both once every six months.

"How did you? Oh, never mind," my host waved his question away. "Yes, Bernie may need some coaxing, so I'll see what I can do. Why don't I meet you in his office on Monday? Meanwhile, let's tell the grandparents we will check into this." He signaled Susan. "We'd like our salads now."

3

Leaning back in his well-worn office chair, my boss regarded me over the top of his horn-rimmed glasses. File folders in precarious stacks, like unsteady dominoes, covered the over-sized desk in front of him. I figured the desk would groan under the load if given a voice. Seated on the other side of his desk in a squeaky wooden chair, I noticed the files challenged the phone for space; they already encroached on part of the blotter. The closed glass door separating his office from the paper's city room cut off the clatter from the half-dozen typewriters currently in use.

"I agree we need a story on the place. We haven't done one yet. *But.* I am not thrilled with the idea of sending you to a nice resort to snoop around on the basis of a grandmother's instinct." Bernard Slater straightened up. "When we do the piece, I want a major spread. I'm saving it for the lead in the Sunday section of the July Fourth weekend."

"I understand," I acknowledged, fidgeting in the paper's *hot seat* opposite him, "but Boss—"

"Don't call me Boss." His eyes briefly closed while he fiddled with the pencil he held. "It's also not something I'm inclined to assign to a junior staff member. I admit you have done well with what I have given you and I've been waiting for a larger piece for you to try. However, this is not simply larger, this is major. I'm not sure you are ready for it."

"Please give me the chance at it, Boss, not simply for Arlene's sake, either. I'm ready."

"Don't call me Boss," he repeated while he regarded the point of his pencil. "I refuse to send you out there to determine if an accidental death was anything sinister. Lauren, this would be a make or break assignment for you. *If* I send you out there, I want a real profile piece on the place." He stared at me. "Photos, attractions, activities—the works. I need complete coverage."

Slater unsuccessfully strove to act intimidating, a futile effort. He did not possess the face or temperament for it. Not a tall man, he looked exactly like a journalism professor who got tired enough of teaching to try his hand at his calling in the real world. Four years ago, he purchased a local weekly gossip and advertising sheet. Acting as publisher and editor, he transformed it into a respectable daily in less than two years. Current office rumors indicated he wanted to ease someone else into the publisher spot so he could focus on editing, his first love. Balding with a round face and a surprisingly spare frame, he absently doodled with his pencil on his ever-present notepad, an indication we did not hold his rapt interest.

"I realize that, and I can handle it."

"I could let you have a day on location to get the material you need for the article."

"Boss, I'd want more than one day. To fully cover a place like this, I'd need to spend the night." I steadily met his attempted glare.

"Now you're asking that I send you out there for a couple of days?" Slater protested, abandoning the effort of staring me down. "What about your night classes?"

"This is the break between the spring semester and summer session." I diplomatically swallowed the urge to add, "Nice try."

He grimaced as if he heard my thought. "Robert," he complained, glancing over at Mallory, "I could use some help here."

Mallory, standing in front of the office window facing us, folded his arms over his chest. I suspected the straight face he wore required effort while he watched the exchange.

"Sorry, Bernie. I can't help remembering the expression on Susan's face when she was telling us about it. Both Susan and Gianni are worried sick about this. Gianni forgot to put onion and garlic in the marinara sauce on Friday."

"*What?*" The statement stopped the pencil. We had his full attention.

"When Lauren and I were there on Friday, Susan told us she had to remind him to add onion, and *we* had to tell Susan to have Gianni add garlic. That's how distracted they are." Mallory paused and sat in the chair next to the desk. "Susan feels Arlene is in what she calls *a bad place.* Maybe there is something which should be checked out."

"Let's not get carried away. Before we go any further, let's see what was reported." Slater reached for his phone, punched an internal line, and asked for the news file on the death at Northwoods Resort and Beach Club. "There may be nothing to it."

The single file folder contained three clippings. The dates indicated the incident happened at the end of the resort's first week of operation. A short summary taped to the inside of the folder read:

The body of Vera Campbell, water sports director at the Northwoods Resort and Beach Club, washed up on the new facility's private beach Friday, the 19th of May 1950. A fully qualified Water Safety Instructor diving alone at the time of her death testing new equipment,

Campbell was twenty-five. Autopsy revealed water in her lungs. Investigation determined her air tank was empty. The coroner's report assumed she became disoriented from lack of oxygen and ruled the incident a simple drowning accident. Verdict: death by misadventure.

The articles in the file provided no other pertinent details. We each read them in turn. Last in line, I handed the folder back to my boss.

"Comments? It seems straightforward to me," stated my editor. "We are not in the habit of raking up scandal. This is not a yellow sheet anymore, and I don't want to start back in that direction."

"Relax, Bernie. No one is suggesting anything like that," soothed Mallory. He turned to me. "You're a certified lifeguard, Lauren. What do you think? Is this just hot air?"

I shook my head. "There may be something to it. This woman was a certified Water Safety Instructor. They teach life guard classes. The one thing emphasized throughout the lifeguard course is *safety*. In the water, the first rule of safety means 'with someone.' The idea a WSI would go diving alone with unproven equipment in open water when she had a pool handy is close to ridiculous nonsense. I don't dive, but I would have thought she'd test her gear in the pool." I shifted my gaze from Mallory to my editor. "Susan's instincts may be spot-on. We need a way to find out one way or the other, if only out of respect for the Gianellos." I took a deep breath. "Boss, please let me do this."

"Don't call me Boss," he automatically retorted and sat back in his chair. "How would you go about it, if—and I mean *if*—I agree to it?" Slater gazed from me to Mallory and back.

"Why not send Lauren out to do a full profile story on the facility? Have her stay for a few days to really get the feel of the place." Mallory suggested. "She can ask questions and take photos without raising suspicions."

"The manager should jump at this, Bo—, er, sir," I hastily corrected myself. "It would be great publicity for the resort, especially after the accident." I refrained from saying more, although I considered it.

Slater sighed. "Are you going to be a part of this?" he asked Mallory.

"I thought I'd book in for the weekend to be on hand," Mallory replied. "I told Lauren I can use the break and it won't be hard to arrange to be away from the office."

"I promise I'll come up with a decent Sunday piece on the resort," I told Slater.

"I haven't agreed to it."

I ignored his comment. "Before I go out there, I'll nose around to see what there is on the background of the people involved," I said, musing out loud. "More importantly, though, I'd like to meet Arlene in town, say on her day or evening off, and ask her some questions to give me a better idea of what I'd be getting into."

"You have to admit, she's thinking," Mallory said to his friend.

"I grant you she's great at research. Let's arrange the meeting with Arlene before I make a decision," replied Slater. "I'd like to be present." Spotting the elation on my face, Slater hastily added, "Lauren, this does *not* mean I'm buying into any theory of something amiss *or* handing you the assignment. Got that?"

"Yes, Boss." I did my best to seem abashed. "Sorry, it slipped out."

Mallory grinned. "It sounds like this means another trip to Susan's. How about tonight?I'm up for it if you two are. Six o'clock? I'll even buy!"

"Mr. Slater, Mr. Mallory! And Lauren! From my mouth to the ears of the Almighty—such wonderful friends are a good thing to have! I told Gianni all would be well." Susan greeted us with a big smile and escorted us to the back table Mallory and I occupied the previous Friday.

"Susan, you might have the grace to act surprised," Mallory bantered. "Nothing is settled yet. Bernie wanted to talk to you, and Lauren wants to consult Arlene. Would that be possible?"

"This is fair," she conceded. "I'll phone to see if she can come now. Her evenings are mostly free. Meanwhile, try the chicken. I'll be right back with the breadsticks and your drinks."

"Hard to resist one of the natural forces of the universe, isn't it, Bernie," observed Mallory. "She assumes we will do what needs to be done, and that's that."

"She's a grandmother who thinks her grand-daughter is in danger. To my mind that *is* a natural force in the overall scheme of things," I quipped.

"So now what do we do?" asked my editor.

"Simple." Mallory and I stated it together.

"Simple?"

"Sure," said Mallory with a wink to me. "We try the chicken."

About half-way through Gianello's version of chicken cacciatore, which had plenty of onion and garlic, Arlene entered the restaurant and made a beeline for our table. She sat down in an extra chair and picked up a breadstick.

"Gran said you wanted to talk to me." Arlene Hancock, attractive and intelligent with a warm personality, looked worried. Short, curly dark hair framed her pretty face, yet her brown eyes showed no signs of her usual bubbling spirits. She toyed with the breadstick without eating it.

"Your grandmother is concerned about the situation out at the Northwoods Resort." Although Slater kept his tone factual, I noticed Arlene's discomfort affected him. "What can you tell us about it?"

"All I know for certain is what I've heard, that the gal I replaced as water sports director drowned when she was diving by herself. It was ruled as an accident caused by misadventure. That's the trouble." She started tearing the breadstick into little pieces. "I met Vera when we both interviewed for the job. While we were waiting, we talked about swimmer safety. We agreed that safety in the water absolutely comes first."

"It wasn't just talk?" Slater asked.

"I don't think so." Arlene frowned. "Vera told me about an incident last summer, when she was a guard on the ocean side of Jones Beach. She had to rescue someone who went in without a buddy and didn't know how to handle the undertow. She called the guy an idiot. I don't think Vera would have gone down alone in open water to begin with, and certainly not without thoroughly checking her equipment in the pool first." Arlene gazed at each of us in turn. "Scuba is new sport. It's wonderful, but every diver I know realizes your life is only as good as your equipment. A test dive in the pool would have been a breeze."

Mallory nodded his agreement. "I've been down a couple of times, and my dive coach really laid it on thick about safety. The ironclad rule is *never* dive alone. He told me it is much stronger than the well-known axiom *don't drink and drive.*"

"When I first reported to Northwoods, the manager took me into his office. After the usual orientation spiel, he explained there had been an accident. He told me he didn't want me listening to rumors or loose talk, and he wanted me to hear about it directly from him."

Arlene picked up the torn pieces of her breadstick, put them onto a small plate, and brushed her hands together to shake off the crumbs. Moving the plate aside, she folded her hands together on the table in front of her and sighed.

"That's a reasonable notion," Slater said. "There must have been a lot of gossip about it and he wouldn't want it to continue."

"What's he like?" I asked.

"The manager?" At my nod, Arlene considered my question before replying. "Edward Thompson is good-looking, kind of sophisticated, and self-confident."

"Is he someone you can trust?" questioned Mallory.

"I don't particularly trust him, but he's okay. He thinks he's a real ladies' man, which can be annoying, but he knows his job from what I can see. Everyone seems to like him. It's a nice place to work, or it would be, without this odd feeling hanging over it. The pay is better than most summer places, and the staff is better treated than at other camps. It's definitely classy."

"What about the rest of the staff? What are they like?" Slater asked, playing reporter.

"For most of the jobs, like waiters and housekeepers, they hired college kids. They're a nice bunch with the usual cliques, nothing nasty. A few older people were hired for other jobs, and everyone gets along."

"Your grandmother mentioned a woman who owns the resort. What's she like?" I asked.

"The owner doesn't mix with the staff at all," Arlene offered, wrinkling her nose. "She's a real snob in my opinion and treats us like peasants. Mrs. Constance Ambrose."

I happened to glance at Mallory when Arlene pronounced the name. He hesitated in the act of cutting a bite of food for a second or two before continuing, something out of character for him. I made a note to check on it later.

"Mrs. Ambrose?" I echoed. "She's married?"

"She's a widow. I only met her briefly when I filled out some forms the day I started. Mrs. Ambrose is rich, beautiful, and her clothes are stunning, I'll give her that." Arlene paused. "I get the impression she considers Mr. Thompson her personal property, although he certainly doesn't act that way."

"Why aren't you happy with the idea that the girl died by accident? Even professionals make mistakes," Slater pointed out. "Is there something specific?"

Arlene looked around, and lowered her voice. "When I first got to the resort and heard about the accident, I wanted to be sure that none of the other gear was faulty. Six new sets of regulators and tanks were purchased for the resort. The set involved in the accident was taken by the police. I found," she said, bowing her head slightly, "that some of the remaining equipment had been tampered with."

"Tampered with? How?" I put my fork in my mouth because it looked silly in mid-air with chicken on it.

"One of the regulator hoses has a tiny hole in it. Another won't seat completely on the tank. It all looked good at first, though. I took everything down into the pool. The leaky hose isn't a big deal because it's on the exhale side. I discovered that the regulator with the faulty seating would be good for about three minutes before the air would billow out." She stopped when Susan came up to the table again carrying a soft drink for her.

"Lauren," Susan's voice carried warning tones I recognized. I quickly took another bite of the chicken and smiled at her while I chewed. She left, chuckling.

"Did you find anything else?" I asked Arlene once I swallowed.

"No. Everything else checked out. I put it all back, but I marked the bad sets. No one has asked to go diving, which is good because I got busy so I haven't had time to get repairs done."

"Could it have been manufacturing damage?" my editor, a natural skeptic, inquired.

"I don't think so."

"Do you have anything else to go on?" Mallory asked.

"No, not really," she replied, shaking her head. "That's part of what makes the whole thing scary. It's just a feeling. Nothing I can put my finger on and say, 'That's it!' I can't help feeling something is funny out there."

"Well," said my boss, "if it wasn't an accident, and I am not saying I agree, do you have any idea why the girl was killed?"

"None."

"Did she have any boyfriends, fights with any of the staff, that sort of thing?" I questioned.

"Not that I know of. From what I can gather—and remember, I can't ask a whole lot of questions—Vera was a bit of a loner but well-liked. One of the housekeeping girls, who has a crush on Mr. Thompson, thought that Vera spent too much time with him." She shrugged. "That's just gossip."

My boss looked at me, then Mallory, and back at me.

"Lauren, this would be a newspaper assignment, not a police investigation. If I send you out, you will be there as a reporter. Period. Can you remember that?"

"Boss, I will ask routine questions, take photos, try to be social, and do my best to stay out of trouble," I earnestly told him. "However, if there is something out of line, I intend to find it."

"I'm concerned, not convinced," said the ex-journalism professor, regarding me the way he would a recalcitrant student with a discipline problem, "and I want you to know that. The police won't thank you for interfering either. Their case is closed. They would not appreciate you trying to stir up trouble or attempting to create a case out of thin air."

"I know that, and there may not be anything to find." I held up a hand when Arlene took a breath to speak. "Let me nose around."

"You're not Nancy Drew, Torchy Blane, or even Bobbie Logan. There's no Ned Nickerson, Steve McBride, or Bill Street coming to rescue you, so you will have to be careful," he admonished, his voice solemn. "No scandal. I don't want any legal repercussions. Also, if there *is* something fishy going on, I definitely don't want a story about a dead reporter showing up on my desk." He gave me the sternest stare he could muster—his face never cooperated—and finished, "Got that?"

"Yes, sir." I kept it meek.

"Then we go?" Mallory asked his friend.

"Yes," said my boss.

Arlene got up and headed for the kitchen. A moment or two later, she came back followed by her grandmother. Arlene sat down; Susan stood between me and Robert Mallory.

"The good Lord will watch over you, Lauren." She gave my shoulder a squeeze and turned to Mallory. "You watch over her, too." She made it an order.

"I will do my best, I promise, once I am out there." He turned to Arlene. "Until I get there, will I be able to reach Lauren by phone?"

"Yes, the cabins have phones. Individual rooms in the Lodges don't have phones, but there is one located in the lobby of each building." Arlene smiled for the first time; it lit her face and put a sparkle in her eyes. "You're really coming?"

"It looks that way. I can't say when, hopefully it will be soon," I told her.

"Arlene, I will call the manager tomorrow and ask if I can send a reporter out there to do a profile piece on the resort, making arrangements for her to stay a few days. Since it would be good publicity for such a new place, he's bound to agree," Slater assured her. "I'll try to set it up for this week, hopefully beginning Wednesday."

"When Lauren does arrive," Mallory spoke up, "it would probably be a good idea if you two acted as if you didn't know each other."

Arlene and I nodded.

"Okay, that's settled. However, I can tell you this," volunteered my editor. "Nothing is happening until I finish dinner. This is delicious!"

My boss called me into his office late Tuesday morning.

"You have a reservation out at the resort for Wednesday through Sunday," he informed me. "You know what I want. Don't disappoint me." He gave me the once-over. "Take the rest of today to get yourself organized."

"Yes, sir! Thank you! I want to see if there is any information about the people behind the resort, and I'll need to pack. I've got two cameras, my notepad—" My voice trailed off, overrun by my thoughts.

"Lauren, I hate to bring this up but from my talk with the resort's manager I have to ask. Do you have suitable clothes? I gather the resort is fairly high-end."

"Oh! I didn't think of that. I'll talk to Julie Mallory. Her background for a place like this is better than mine and she's good at that sort of thing."

4

One phone call later, I pulled into the Mallory drive. Julie never drove anywhere, so I picked her up and took her to my place to discuss clothes for my five-day stay. I assumed she would have a few objections to my wardrobe. Sadly, I completely underestimated her reaction.

"Nothing here will do. We are going shopping," she decreed following her inspection of the contents of my closet, "and I will choose what we buy."

"Hold a moment!" I protested. "I can't afford the things you pick out!"

"Well, you can't go in these," she countered, gesturing at my clothes. "You'll be expected to change every night for dinner, at the very least."

"I'm doing a story, not auditioning for Miss America! I don't need new clothes," I insisted. I watched her lips become a thin line and hopefully offered a compromise. "Maybe one new outfit?"

She ignored me. Picking up my phone, she dialed a number. Recognizing it, I felt a sinking sensation in my stomach, knowing I already lost this encounter.

"Daddy? Lauren got the assignment and she needs clothes. I want to take her out to buy a few appropriate ensembles and she's arguing with me about money."

I heard his deep laugh come over the line. Julie held the phone so I could hear his words.

"Tell her we can't have her showing up in rags and the wardrobe is on me. No arguments allowed. Don't forget shoes."

"Don't worry." She hung up and turned to me with a triumphant grin. "So there," she said firmly, nodding her head. "Shall we go?"

Book stores drew me to them like magnets attract iron filings. I tended to ignore department stores. Shopping for clothes ranked very low on my list of things to do, only marginally higher than letting a dentist drill my teeth without anesthesia. On this occasion, Julie's bubbling enthusiasm more than made up for my lack of it. Three hours later, back at my apartment with assorted bags and boxes, I pulled out my suitcase.

"No. Absolutely not. It's too small and seedy." Julie smiled at me while her eyes gleamed. "Let's go back to my house and I'll find one to loan you."

"I give up," I told her, recognizing the futility of further discussion. "Let's get this over with."

We bundled all the purchases back into my car and returned to her home. She kindly allowed me to watch while she carefully packed my new wardrobe into her suitcase. She added a few pieces of her jewelry for good measure.

"There. You're all set," she pronounced, closing the case. "Don't forget your mother's pearls."

"I'm not sure how much of this was necessary, but thank you," I told her with a smile, grateful for her assistance. I gave her a hug. "You realize I'm not Cinderella, you're not my fairy godmother, and I'm not meeting a prince."

"Maybe not but you could end up at a ball." Julie's blue eyes, similar to her father's, danced with laughter. Shorter by about four inches with shoulder-length dark auburn hair, she possessed all the curves I lacked.

"You thoroughly enjoyed this, didn't you!" I stated accusingly as I rolled my eyes.

"Of course I enjoyed it! I love shopping just as much as you don't!" Her expression changed from delighted to slyly mischievous. "Umm, Lauren? Double trouble, fire and light," she chanted, referring to a childhood oath we made up for sharing secrets. "Daddy has wanted to do this for you for a while and we knew how you'd feel about it. This gave us the excuse."

"Just between us, honor bright," I completed the rhyme with a grin. "I guess I've been totally out-maneuvered. All right, I won't mention you told me."

She picked up the suitcase and carried it to my car. Her smile faded. "Lauren, be careful. Please? Daddy is worried that there may be something going on out there."

"I will do my best." I got behind the wheel and started my car. "Thanks for your help!" With a wave out the window, I pulled out of the circular driveway.

I would be well-dressed with the proper accessories even if I might be walking into an angry hornet's nest.

Wednesday morning, with Slater's warnings to stay out of the obits ringing in my ears, I set out. Armed with maps, notebooks, a folder full of background information, and two cameras (a Kodak Retina kit and a well-hidden Minox), I headed deeper into the wilds eastern Long Island in my 1948 Triumph roadster. The two-year old car could be cranky but I loved it. Since I memorized the route I would be taking due to my lousy sense of direction, I relaxed and enjoyed the drive. A light breeze stirred the leaves on the trees along my route, pleasantly adding to the sunny, summery day.

All the preparations ate up the time I wanted to study the files. I hoped to find the opportunity to read them once I got there. My thoughts momentarily focused on Robert Mallory. His reaction to hearing Constance Ambrose's name aroused my curiosity. The one time I tried to bring it up he sidetracked me. At the time I did not push. It now topped the list of questions I compiled.

Susan mentioned the drive out took less than an hour from the Glen proper. With the word "beach" in its name, I figured rightly that it lay on Long Island Sound. However, the roads leading to it gave the definite impression of being in the country. The area, thus far evading the wily grasp of real estate developers, included some farms. I even heard a rooster crow during my drive.

I missed the final turn onto a dirt road leading to the resort. Thinking some nasty thoughts, I maneuvered a U-turn and gave it another try. The mysterious Mrs. Ambrose might believe the stylized concrete pillar with a small brass plaque engraved "Northwoods Resort and Beach Club" gave off an air of sophistication. Possibly it did. To me, it seemed an inadequate signpost for a turn. A bush blocked it. The resort needed a bigger sign or a smaller bush, or both. The ruts in the dirt road leading up to the main entrance strained the shock absorbers of my car. I bounced like a hard India rubber ball all the way to the entrance. Another negative point on my score card. Hopefully it conspired with the pitiful sign to keep out the riff-raff, but by the time I got to the gate I felt like I had been traveling in a cocktail shaker.

A guard came out of the gatehouse in the middle of the widened area of the entrance, and approached with a clipboard. He looked fairly typical for the job: older, slightly bored, and only as helpful as necessary. He leaned down and spoke.

"Name?"

"Lauren Kaye. I have an appointment with Edward Thompson."

"Let me see," he mumbled, running his finger slowly down the page. "Yeah, it's here. Park in front of the office." He trudged back to his chair without inviting further conversation, so I did not waste any.

When I pulled up to the office, the door opened and a man stepped out. Arlene correctly described Thompson as good-looking. Above-average in height with wide shoulders and slim hips, his short-cropped wavy hair was almost black. He wore sunglasses, so I could not see his eyes; I bet they would be brown. Apparently he tried to dress casually, yet the blue silk shirt, tan slacks, and Italian leather loafers looked expensive. He radiated welcome while he evaluated my carefully coordinated outfit of tailored slacks (thank you, Katharine Hepburn), an equally tailored blouse (no shoulder pads, apologies to Joan Crawford), and a cardigan sweater over my shoulders. I wore flats, which Julie recommended because heels might make me too tall. I went along with it because driving a sports car in heels did not work well.

"Miss Kaye?" he inquired in a nasal voice. He offered a wide smile and showed white, even teeth. "I've been looking forward to meeting you. I'm Edward Thompson, the manager." He opened the car door, and I climbed out.

"Thank you, Mr. Thompson."

He extended his hand and we shook. He tried to make it firm, except his soft hand scotched the intention. It felt more like foam rubber than muscle and bone.

"Shall I move my car?" I asked, nodding at the sign in front of my car that read "Temporary Parking".

"If you will leave your keys, I'll have someone attend to it and take your luggage to your accommodations." He smiled, extending his hand for my keys.

"The transmission can be a bit tricky," I demurred. "I'd prefer to move it myself, if that's all right. Where shall I park?" I smiled back at him because it seemed expected. Only one other person drove my car occasionally, and certainly never a stranger.

"Not a problem at all," said Thompson smoothly, still—of course—smiling. "Come inside and I will give you our brochure, which has a map of the entire facility. I'll show you where to park, and you can move your car later." He opened the door and allowed me to pass inside.

My first impression was "posh." The office interior resembled a sitting room more than it did a business office, not like a hotel lobby at all. A registration book sat on a small desk; a large frame with a layout of the resort hung on the wall above it. Other furnishings included a bookcase with a variety of novels, a table with some pamphlets and brochures, and several smaller tables with two leather chairs each. Ashtrays imprinted with the resort's logo lay scattered around on various surfaces. One interior door remained closed.

Thompson removed his sunglasses, revealing the brown eyes I anticipated. After offering me a cigarette from an initialed gold case, which I politely declined, Thompson handed me a brochure. He motioned me to sit in one of the leather chairs. I opened the beautifully printed advertisement while he leaned toward me and spoke. Apparently, he considered it more intimate that way.

"We are proud of this resort, which is also a day beach club. The emphasis is on water sports: swimming, water skiing, and scuba diving. We offer memberships so local people can enjoy the beach or pool during the day. We provide cabanas and lockers for their use. We have ten cabins and two lodges for overnight guests. Members and their guests are welcome, however, we give precedence to our members and they receive a discounted rate should they decide to book a cabin or a room." The well-rehearsed, smooth sales pitch flowed. He kept smiling and I began to wonder if it might be his only facial expression. His brown eyes matched his cultivated tan, and I guessed his age around late thirties or early forties.

I studied the brochure. "You mentioned lodges and I see two on the map. What are they?"

"Those are for guests who prefer to stay in a room rather than a cabin. One is for men, the other for women. We keep them separated because the bathroom facilities are common in each building. The dormitory-style arrangement lets our singles feel less isolated, and of course, it's less expensive than renting a cabin. The cabins are more for our families." The smile, which faded slightly for a moment or two, came back. "We try to provide a full range of activities. For families, we have play areas: two swing playground sets, a croquet field, six holes of miniature golf, and a wading pool next to our full-size pool in addition to the beach. We have a full-service restaurant offering a breakfast buffet in the morning with hot dogs, hamburgers, and sandwiches during the day. Our chef offers a choice of two entrée specialties for dinner in addition to a few standard options. We have our liquor license and we serve beer, wine, and liqueurs at meals. We also have an open bar for our evening activities."

"What activities do you offer for evenings?"

"We try to have a group activity each night, such as music, dancing, games, live entertainment, or adult-only evening swims. I'm considering setting up a piano bar and letting guests sing while a professional plays. We are striving to provide a get-away-from-it-all vacation spot close to home. A resort here on Long Island, incorporating a beach club that can be used daily by members, is a new concept. We're not looking to make this overly large, either. My philosophy is keeping it small makes it more intimate." Thompson leaned closer, exuding earnestness. "We're not the Catskills, but then we aren't trying to be." He chuckled; it emphasized the nasal quality of his voice.

The interior door opened and I caught a glimpse of a private office. A woman entered; Thompson jumped to his feet. Not to seem churlish, I stood.

I faced a slim, tanned woman dressed in a pink silk blouse that tied at the neck, gorgeous white wide-leg slacks, and high-heeled sandals. Immaculately made up and an inch taller than my sixty-seven in those heels, her bleached blond hair and dark brown eyes completed the picture. She wore several rings, bracelets on both wrists, and earrings that matched her pendant necklace. If genuine, her jewelry could pay my rent for three years. I found it difficult to judge her age through the thickly applied makeup. My best guess put her in her early thirties.

"Mrs. Ambrose," Thompson extended a hand towards her, not quite simpering, "this is Lauren Kaye from the *Daily Gleaner*. She's here to do a profile on our resort."

She acknowledged my presence with a nod in my direction. She made no move to come toward me.

"Miss Kaye, I was delighted to hear that the *Gleaner* is *finally* going to do a story on our resort. So far, the only publicity we've had has been our advertising." Her voice, low-pitched and sultry, struck me as bored. Before the long ashes on the cigarette in her holder fell off, Thompson grabbed an ashtray for her. She did not blink, much less thank him; to me it indicated a practiced routine. "I understand you will be staying with us through the weekend."

"Yes, ma'am, if that is acceptable. I want to do a full profile on all your facilities and activities, complete with a photo spread. My editor is planning on using it for the cover story in the Sunday section for the July Fourth special edition."

"I don't believe I have seen your byline in the Sunday section. Eddie," she continued, in the same low voice, "where are we putting Miss Kaye? Lodge Two?"

He nodded. "I thought that would be the best way for her to see the facilities."

"Thank you," I wondered how he liked being called Eddie, a nickname more suited to a carpenter or plumber. It clashed with the image he attempted to project, including his soft hands.

Mrs. Ambrose turned without another word and went back into her office.

"Mrs. Ambrose was foresighted enough to see this concept of a resort would work and put up the money for the land and construction. I'm happy to say she takes an active role in the day to day operation. Although she owns an apartment in Manhattan, she spends at least four or five days a week out here. She has a cabin reserved exclusively for her use, and she likes to say she wouldn't ask anyone to stay somewhere she wouldn't enjoy herself." His smile widened to emphasize that important concession on her part.

I decided 'so she enjoys slumming' would not be diplomatic. It took bucks to own, rather than rent, an apartment in Manhattan. The difference between her apartment in town and my studio place in Northwoods

Glen would be analogous to a comparison of a millionaire's yacht to a Central Park rowboat. I nodded with a smile. "Do you live on the premises?"

"Of course," he replied, with another nasal chuckle and a flash of his gleaming teeth. "I wouldn't dream of not being available to our guests during the season. I have a small apartment in the city and I'll move back there after we close for the winter." He rose and extended his hand. "Let me take you on a tour. Have you had lunch?"

"It's a bit early yet and I do have to move my car," I reminded him. I ignored the hand and stood in front of the framed layout. "The Residents' Parking Lot? I see it marked."

"Leave your luggage here," he suggested. "I'll have someone take it to the Lodge."

I brought my suitcase into the office and moved the Triumph. I re-entered the office. My suitcase remained precisely where I put it. Thompson motioned to the door, apparently forgetting his offer to have someone take it to my room. He, of course, would not deign to do it himself, which I considered very unchivalrous although I smiled when he turned to me. I picked it up and followed him to the Lodge Two lobby.

"I'll let you get settled. Why don't you meet me in the clubhouse in, say, a half hour?" he asked. "Men are not allowed past the lobby here and likewise women aren't allowed past the lobby of Lodge One."

"That sounds fine," I agreed.

I got my key from the concierge. She wore resort livery: a green polo shirt embroidered with the resort's logo and a simple khaki A-line skirt. Her name tag read *Dorothy*. The description of a dormitory fit. The lodge consisted of a long hall with rooms on either side, the concierge lobby in the middle, and communal bathrooms on each end.

I found my quarters smaller than the foyer in Robert Mallory's home in the Glen. Decorated in rustic wood with pine paneling, the furnishings included two twin beds, a vanity dresser with four drawers situated between them, a small desk and chair, and a closet. I hung my new clothes after checking to make sure all the price tags were off and proceeded back to the lobby area. The phone on the counter did not have a dial.

Following the map in the brochure, I made my way to the clubhouse, which apparently hosted all major activities. My first glance around noted some tables and a library nook with a sign posted stating the availability golf putters, croquet mallets, and board games. Discreetly marked rest room facilities on one side faced a large area separated from the rest of the building by movable partitions, marking the dining area which included a fireplace. Thompson awaited me at the inside entrance, although I noted an outside door which opened directly onto the terrace bordering the pool.

"What would you like to have for lunch? My treat," he added with his chuckle. "I'm going to have a chicken salad sandwich, which comes with a pickle and potato chips."

I checked the posted menu. It included prices, which surprised me for some reason.

"I'll have a hot dog with a coke, thank you."

He gave the order to one of the waiters. "It's a nice day. Why don't we eat on the terrace?" he suggested, indicating tables outside with umbrellas.

"That's fine."

"Pool side or beach side?"

"Let's enjoy a view of the Sound."

"Did you bring your bathing suit?" he asked once we were seated.

"Definitely. I love swimming," I admitted. "It was one reason I asked for this assignment. I hope it will be acceptable to use your facilities. I would really like to try scuba diving."

Thompson chuckled. "You'll give us a better write-up if you're happy," he observed. His smile faded. "We did have some unpleasantness earlier in the season, but that's past."

"The diving accident. The *Daily Gleaner* reported it," I told him. "It was a tragedy—she was so young."

"Vera was a lovely young woman," he said. "However, life must go on. We have a new swim instructor, Arlene Hancock, who is quite good. In fact," he lowered his voice and leaned towards me to make his next words more confidential, "she was the one I wanted to hire in the first place."

The waiter brought the lunches to us with our drinks.

Thompson leaned back and picked up his sandwich.

"I'm curious. If you wanted to hire Arlene in the first place, why did you hire the other girl instead?" I started on my hot dog.

"Constance, that is, Mrs. Ambrose, insisted; she wanted Vera." Thompson chuckled again; the nasal sound began to grate. "Both girls were qualified, and it was a matter of personality. Mrs. Ambrose felt Vera would fit in with our guests better, nothing against Arlene. After the accident, it made sense to offer the position to Arlene." He leaned in again, his face serious. "I hope you won't mention it in your article. We had enough trouble with it at the time and I don't want to lose more business."

"Mr. Thompson, the case is closed," I assured him. "I'm simply here to do a profile of the new resort. My editor likes to see anything new in the area get a nod."

"We appreciate that, especially after the incident," he acknowledged with a smile and another chuckle. "How do you want to handle this? I can take you around and introduce you to the staff if you wish."

"I've been giving that some thought," I honestly told him. "I think the best way for me to get a sense of the resort's facilities would be to let me explore it on my own. If I need help, I'll ask for it. Would that be all right?" Slater had suggested that approach.

"Certainly! You can experience the resort as a guest!" His smile became even more enthusiastic, which I found hard to believe. "My only request is if you interview any of the staff for publication, I'd like to know. Mrs. Ambrose would also like to see your piece in advance."

"I believe that can be arranged." I flashed a smile of my own, what Mallory called my sincere one. "The *Gleaner* is a respectable daily now with an expanding circulation. I'm simply here to do a profile piece."

"Let me know if there's anything I can do to make your stay more enjoyable," Thompson finished his lunch and rose. "Ah, that hit the spot." Smiling, he offered his soft hand to shake. It still felt like foam rubber.

"Thank you, Mr. Thompson," I told him. "I will certainly do that." I took my last bite of hot dog and swig of soda.

5

I strolled back to my room and pulled out the file of background information. I barely started reading when I heard a knock on the door. I called, "Come in!"

Arlene came into the room wearing a resort shirt and khaki shorts, her version of the uniform.

"Hello," she greeted me, winking. "I'm Arlene Hancock, the water sports director here at Northwoods. I understand from Mr. Thompson you are interested in learning how to scuba dive."

"How thoughtful of him!" I exclaimed, returning the wink. "As a matter of fact, I would love to know more about diving. Come in and sit down." I got up and closed the door. "I was going to search you out."

"I'm so relieved you're here," she told me, sinking onto one of the beds. "What do you think of Mr. Thompson?"

"Mr. Smoothie Smile? His teeth would be a stellar advertisement for any dentist." I grinned. "He welcomed me yet wouldn't lower himself to carrying my suitcase. I've also briefly met Mrs. Ambrose. I doubt she rates me very highly."

"You're not a man," she said with a slight grimace. "Wait until you see her meet Mr. Mallory."

"Mr. Thompson did mention something I found interesting." I related his comments about preferring Arlene to Vera.

"That's odd. When I got here and was filling out my paperwork, Mrs. Ambrose told me the exact opposite: she wanted me originally and it was Mr. Thompson who insisted on hiring Vera."

"Very strange," I murmured. "Would she have said that to make you feel more welcome?"

"I doubt it. She's not that friendly," Arlene said, shrugging.

"I know it's a small point yet that makes it more than odd—"

Later, after I changed into shorts, a top, and sandals, I wandered around the grounds, eventually steering towards the office. The inner door stood open, so I called out.

"Hello?"

Mrs. Ambrose appeared in the doorway. Her automatic smile faded when she saw me.

"Miss Kaye, may I help you?"

"Mrs. Ambrose, I have been enjoying your facility so much I forgot to ask how I can make a telephone call out." I smiled. "I should let my editor know I have arrived."

"Oh. I suppose you'll have to," she peevishly muttered. Her phone rang. "Excuse me."

She stepped back into her office, leaving the door open. Unobtrusively, I edged closer and listened.

"Good afternoon. Northwoods Resort and Beach Club. How may I help you?" She paused. "Yes, we do have vacancies for the weekend, either in one of our cabins or a room in our dormitory-style Lodge. May I have your name, please?" She paused again and her whole attitude completely altered. "It's entirely up to you, Robert. Personally I would recommend a cabin for more privacy." Her cooing voice dripped like sweet maple syrup over a stack of pancakes.

Privately, I decided Mallory, who preferred to make his own calls despite his efficient secretary, would agree to a cabin rather than a cramped dorm room. After some back and forth conversation, including rate information which made me glad someone else would pay my bill, Mrs. Ambrose confirmed his reservation for a cabin.

"Oh, Robert," she gushed at the conclusion of the call, "I am *delighted* you are going to be *my* guest for the weekend! It has been *too* long! See you tomorrow!"

Once she hung up, she returned to the outer office and found me standing by the desk, carefully studying the display map on the wall.

"We are staying busy yet we're not full," she told me, her face glowing from her phone conversation. "I am hoping your article will help create interest."

"It is a lovely place," I told her honestly, "and I'll do my best. May I use the phone?"

"Oh, yes, of course." She led the way to her domain.

Slightly smaller yet more richly decorated than the lobby area, her wide window overlooked the lawn and enclosed pool area. She sat and indicated the phone on the desk. I reversed the charges.

"I didn't get lost," I said once connected with Slater.

"Congratulations. Robert Mallory should arrive tomorrow, and he'll take care of getting any extra information to me, if and when it does come up."

"Got it."

"Give me a good story, and be careful."

"Yes, Boss," I meekly acknowledged.

"Don't call me Boss," he told me, hanging up. Short and sweet.

I replaced the handset onto the cradle and turned to her.

"Mrs. Ambrose, do you have a few minutes free? I would like to discuss your role here and what you see as the benefits of a resort such as this. You're breaking into new territory." She nodded and invited me to sit on the chair opposite hers. "Thank you." I tried to be disarmingly cordial. "Before we start, however, you mentioned earlier that you don't recall seeing my byline in the paper, and I'd like to be honest with you," I told her with a shade of hesitancy.

"You *are* with the *Daily Gleaner*?" she challenged, chagrined.

"Yes, ma'am," I hastened to confirm. "I've been with the *Gleaner* as a general assignment reporter for two years. If I may speak candidly," I paused while she nodded, "I specifically requested this story. My editor wanted to send out one of the older reporters to cover the resort. I felt a younger, more active person would do a better job showcasing what you have to offer." I smiled, doing my best to ooze sincerity. "Now that I'm here, I'm certain I can do it justice."

She regarded me shrewdly, measuring me. "I see. Then is your first big assignment."

"Yes, and that makes me all the more eager to do a great job."

"I see," she repeated, relaxing a bit. She took out a cigarette, inserted it in her holder, and lit it. "As Eddie already informed you, we are creating a new type of recreational alternative."

"I understand. Your resort offers something that the large Catskills and Poconos places do not. It's innovative to offer the opportunity to spend an afternoon or evening without having to book in overnight, yet it's not a country club." I had my small notepad out although my memory generally served. "I noticed there are cars in the day parking lot."

"We've been pleased with the way our members have embraced the day and evening program," she related, a self-satisfied smile playing on her face. "That was my idea. We also have had a good response from our members on weekends for day visits. Weekday business is lagging, but we seem to be catching on. Schools are still in session, and we hope once they let out business will pick up. We welcome families."

"I would imagine that word of mouth from your members is a major factor. Do you allow your members to bring guests?"

"Of course, and when a referral joins, we give a voucher for two complimentary dinners to the sponsoring member. The restaurant is also open to the general public."

"I would be interested to know how all this came about." I glanced up from my notes. "First, though, I would like to compliment you on the grounds. They are a good blend of natural and planned. Did you use a professional landscaper?"

"Thank you, and no. As a matter of fact," she said with pride, "once our construction for this phase of the development was completed, I designed the grounds myself."

"The layout is impressive. Do you have a background in designing gardens?"

"Not exactly," she said with a genuine smile. "I grew up on a large estate and I helped sketch out the gardens there."

"What made you decide to start a resort?"

"Oh, it was Eddie's idea. I was looking for something new and I had some money to invest, what I inherited from my late husband. When I met Eddie, I liked the concept he outlined and he told me I would be welcome as an active participant in running the resort." Her face shaded with a slight frown. "Eddie's very well-organized but he didn't have a lot of advantages as a child. He told me he was looking for a partner who could help him design, build, and run a place like this."

"I see." I translated her words to mean he did not have the built-in class the place needed; I could have been wrong.

"We had an idea of what we wanted to offer. He and I traveled around and stayed at several resorts before we finalized our plans for Northwoods. He found the property and I purchased it. Our next phase of development will add more cabins along with walking and hiking pathways on the additional land we already own. We're also considering a tennis court."

"You already have a good variety of activities for a small resort, besides the water sports. Mr. Thompson described some of your evening offerings."

"I wanted to make sure we offered enough to attract guests of all ages," she admitted. "Being on the water, it would have been foolish not to have boating and skiing in addition to the beach and pools. Eddie suggested adding scuba diving."

"Do you swim?"

"Not really." Her unenthusiastic reply rang a defensive note.

"I didn't mean to offend you, and I apologize if I have," I quickly said. I wondered about the full story. "I assumed with such a strong emphasis on swimming and boating that you did."

"I'm trying to. I—I had a bad experience as a child," she hesitantly explained, crushing the remains of her cigarette in the ashtray on her desk. "I'm getting over it with Eddie's help. I spent a lot of time on my late husband's boats, but I never felt comfortable."

"I have a confession to make. I almost applied for the water sports job myself. I certified as a lifeguard."

"We wanted a water safety instructor. You wouldn't have qualified." She put it firmly without being harsh.

"That's what stopped me." I gave her my most disarming smile to show no hard feelings. "I have met your water sports director, Arlene. She seems very capable."

"Arlene gives swimming lessons and oversees the water sports equipment. Eddie says she can also teach water skiing and scuba diving. Eddie wants me to learn how to dive and, once he thinks I'm ready for it, he wants to teach me himself."

"I love the water, although I haven't been diving yet."

Mrs. Ambrose nodded while she got out another cigarette. I got the impression her interest in the interview waned to the point of boredom. Thompson walked in and saved me the trouble of working out a way to exit gracefully.

"Here you are, Miss Kaye," he greeted me, stepping up to light his partner's cigarette with impeccable timing. "I was wondering where you had gone."

"Mrs. Ambrose generously gave me a few minutes of her time for some background on the resort," I told him. Rising to my feet, I turned to her. "Thank you. I know you must be busy."

"Perhaps we could continue another time," she murmured politely, "if you think it would be helpful."

"The three of us could have dinner together," Thompson suggested with his usual smile to me.

"That won't be necessary." Abruptly, Mrs. Ambrose's demeanor changed, like a switch flipped. No longer welcoming, her manner turned cold and patronizing. "I think Miss Kaye would find it more informative to dine among the rest of our guests."

"I agree. Is there a dress code for dining?" I asked, noticing how quickly and completely the change occurred. She blocked his suggestion with more force than necessary.

"We request you wear something other than shorts or bathing suits—dresses and skirts for the women and nice shirts with slacks for the men." Thompson smoothed over her reaction. "Sport coats and ties aren't absolutely necessary for the men, although some of our members choose to wear them. We want our guests to be comfortable, but we feel that some decorum is needed." Thompson smiled at Mrs. Ambrose seeking her approval. She gave him a slight, imperious nod. I got the impression I no longer mattered.

"Do your staff members mingle with your guests?" I inquired, thinking of Arlene.

"Not generally, although there are occasional exceptions," the manager said. "It's not something we encourage."

I nodded. "I understand. What time is dinner served?"

"The restaurant is open from six to nine; serving stops at eight," he said.

I thanked him politely for the information and returned to my room with the intention of reading my files.

My reputation in the reporter's pool stressed my penchant for thorough research. Before coming out to the resort I spent a couple of hours digging up available information on the resort and its primary staff members.

The first file I read belonged to the chef. Thompson lured him to Long Island from a high-end place in the Adirondacks. Although I knew how badly the Gianellos spoiled me, dinner would be more than acceptable.

Resort to Murder

Preparing for dinner my first evening, I selected the simplest outfit Julie coordinated for me. I donned a nice beige blouse with embroidery on the collar, a full dark brown skirt with a petticoat, and a wide belt. In the store, Julie decided the warm tones enhanced my dark eyes and brown hair. I took my ponytail and worked it into a bun. I wore my new sandals because I figured heels would be needed for the weekend.

"Lauren," Julie's words echoed in my mind, "I know you don't like to fuss, but you'll have to blend in. Daddy won't be there until Thursday so you'll be on your own Wednesday evening. Don't forget jewelry!" Her advice came back to me when I reached for my doorknob. I returned to the dresser and dug out my mother's pearls and matching earrings. I knew a girl could not go wrong with pearls.

I waited until after six-thirty to walk to the main building. The dining area appeared more formal. The tables sported tablecloths, cloth napkins, flatware, and glasses along with small vases of flowers. The host seated me at a table for two by the window on the pool side. A menu card lay where my plate would go; it listed appetizers and described two entrée specialties with options for things like a ground beef patty smothered in mushroom gravy. The chef's choices for this evening consisted of a seafood casserole or a roast turkey platter.

"Good evening. I'm Jim and I will be your waiter for dinner." A young man, outfitted in resort livery with a khaki apron, introduced himself. He stood next to the table with a pitcher of water. Of average height with sandy blond hair and blue eyes, Jim waited patiently until I nodded before he poured.

"Good evening." I smiled. "I'd better admit up front that this is my first visit. I'm not familiar with your procedures."

"Welcome to Northwoods!" He returned my smile. "Have you come for the evening or are you staying overnight?"

"I'll be here through Sunday, staying in Lodge Two."

"I'm sure you will enjoy your stay. I'm happy to hear you'll be with us for the weekend. Tomorrow night is Italian night, one of our most popular dinner nights. For now, though, what can I get you?"

"I'll have the seafood with a house salad. Turkey is not my favorite."

"Would you like wine with your dinner?"

"No, thank you. Water will be fine."

"Would you prefer your salad as an appetizer or with the main meal?"

"I think I'll skip an appetizer and have the salad with my entrée."

He left to turn in my order. I reflected that someone properly trained the wait-staff. The options echoed the choices Susan insisted on at her restaurant, although Mallory generally requested our salads after our entrées.

I scanned the room. Twenty-five tables of varying sizes, some round and some rectangular, filled the area, although it would hold more. Guests occupied only about ten. I saw a family of five; the kids appeared to be about seven, eight, and nine. Single women sat at two. Couples sat at several. I spotted one table, large enough for four but set for two, situated in a prime location near the fireplace. I speculated it belonged to the owner and her lapdog. At seven they arrived and sure enough, the host showed them to it. Thompson nodded to me, and I noticed Mrs. Ambrose frowned. I recalled Arlene's comment that she treated him like her personal property.

My line of sight included their table; I had them in profile. Constance Ambrose leaned towards her dinner partner, occasionally touching his hand. He conscientiously attended her, lighting her cigarettes. Her long holder threatened him once or twice, forcing him to lean back to avoid getting knocked in the nose by the glowing tip. After another waiter took their order, Thompson got up and visited all the occupied tables, stopping at each for a word or two. I noticed he spent more time with the women than he did with the family of five. The owner's eyes followed his every move like an owl watching a mouse prior to swooping down.

"Miss Kaye," he greeted me with his ever-present smile, "I hope you will find the food satisfactory."

"I ordered the seafood. I looked up your chef before coming out here," I confessed, "and his resume is very good. I do have a question: is there a charge for the meal, and if so, how do I pay for it? I didn't see prices listed."

"We decided to charge for meals because of the day memberships, otherwise bookkeeping would be a nightmare. The prices are listed on the back of your brochure in the bottom corner. Add your dinner to your room tab," he suggested, leaning down. "Our day guests pay cash and overnight residents generally put it on account."

"That makes sense." I gazed past him. "You'd better get back to your table. Mrs. Ambrose appears to be getting lonely."

He wasted no time. Thompson glanced around the room every now and then to check on the progress of the guests. Mrs. Ambrose, on the other hand, ignored us as unimportant and beneath her notice.

Whatever else occurred at Northwoods Resort, I confirmed their chef lived up to his credentials. The seafood casserole, artfully presented, tasted wonderful. The flavor of the shrimp and scallops was enhanced rather than smothered. Served over rice, the entrée included steamed vegetables on the side. The crisp salad came topped with dressing that tasted fresh not bottled. Jim, attentive without being intrusive, approached a moment or two after I set my knife and fork across my plate.

"I enjoyed that," I told him while he picked up my dishes.

"We have a choice of cheesecake or blueberry pie with vanilla ice cream for dessert," he informed me with a smile much more genuine than Thompson's.

"After that dinner, I think I'll pass. I'm not used to large meals."

"We also have a selection of liqueurs. I could get you a small scoop of vanilla ice cream with a shot of crème de menthe over it. That would be light but refreshing."

"That sounds good."

Jim returned in record time. He set down a small sundae dish of ice cream and green liqueur, complete with a dollop of whipped cream and a cherry on top, presented on a small plate with a doily. I picked up the long spoon.

"Fancy!" I exclaimed. "Jim, are you a student?"

"I was. I am taking a year off so I can work to save enough money to go back to school."

"Is this your first waiting job?"

"Yes," he admitted. "I was afraid I wouldn't be good at it, but it was the only job I could get without experience. Too bad it's only for the summer." He smiled. "Enjoy your dessert."

I did. When I finished, I gave Jim my name and room number, instructing him to put the meal on my account. The owner and manager, busy with entrées, looked up when I reached the door. Thompson smiled and I nodded. On the door, I saw a posted notice there would be a bingo game later in the evening once the dinner crowd finished. I left.

A clear sky greeted me, deepening from blue to dark navy with stars beginning to glimmer against the darkening velvety background. The warm evening enfolded me with an occasional breeze drifting to shore from the water while I strolled down to the boathouse and the dock. Arlene looked up from snapping the cover on a small speedboat.

"Hi! Are you done for the day?" I asked.

"Almost. I was putting some of the equipment away. We use the boat for water skiing," she explained, double-checking the tie lines. "I generally have one of the cleaners or waiters act as my lookout when I have someone up on skis."

"What other kinds of boating do you offer?"

"We have canoes and rowboats." Lowering her voice, she added, "Come see the faulty scuba sets."

"May I see the canoes?" I asked, more for cover than curiosity while a couple walked past us and nodded a greeting.

"Sure!"

We went inside the boathouse, which housed them and boasted a ramp to the water. I counted four aluminum canoes, two aluminum rowboats, and a sailing board. One of the canoes looked like it could be adapted for a mast and sail. An equipment rack held paddles and oars next to a larger one for water skis. One set of hooks held life jackets of different sizes. Arlene explained the large locker stored the net and balls for water volleyball.

"My desk is in my office, which is where I keep my records of who is using the equipment," she indicated a locked interior door. "I store the scuba gear in here, too."

"Do you fill your own tanks?"

She nodded. "There's a small outbuilding behind this one that has the compressor and water tank I use for filling the air tanks. Vera got all that set up. The alternative would be hauling the equipment to the nearest fire station." She unlocked the door and we entered a neatly organized room.

Arlene handed me a regulator with a marking on one of the hoses. I spotted a mark on the metal plate of another unit where the hoses joined the actual unit.

"What did you use to mark it?"

"Chalk. It's all I had."

I inspected the two faulty ones. "I suggest we write down the serial numbers of the two that are bad. That way, if anyone erases or changes the chalk mark, we'll be able to tell which ones shouldn't be used." I heard her gasp. "Arlene, it may not come to anything, but it can't hurt to be cautious."

"I guess not." She took a sheet off her clipboard and wrote the numbers as I read them off.

"The leaky hose is on the regulator with serial number 3721-2867-4538. The one that won't seat properly is serial number 4217-1840-2332."

She hung the five regulators on padded hooks. "I did find an air tank that leaked. It needed a new O ring."

"I thought all this equipment was new. Do you have the ring you replaced?"

She showed me a small ring with a tiny dark line. "It's cracked, which is why it held for a couple of minutes."

"I do want to learn how to dive," I told her, handing the faulty ring back to her. "Scuba has always fascinated me. I know Mr. Mallory has taken classes. Besides, if there was anything funny about Vera's accident, I want to be able to take care of myself in the water."

"That's easy. How about meeting tomorrow morning at ten by the pool?" She made a note on the reservations clipboard and locked the inner door when we stepped back into the main boathouse. She locked the outer door.

"Do you have the only key?"

"No. There are three others. Mr. Thompson has one, there's one at the main office, and the head housekeeper has one."

"Bother! That's too many to be useful in eliminating opportunity." I inhaled deeply before slowly letting it out. "Arlene, I really hoped there was nothing to this, yet the O ring, the hose, and second regulator make this suspicious."

"I know. When is Mr. Mallory coming out here?" she asked while we walked along the beach.

"He reserved a cabin beginning tomorrow. I don't know exactly what time he's going to arrive."

"I want to thank you for believing me," she said, scuffing a bit of sand with her sneaker, "since I really have nothing concrete to go on."

"I know you and your grandmother well enough to figure that when you two share an uneasy feeling, it's wise to take a closer look." I stopped for a moment. "I forgot to ask Mr. Thompson something. What time is breakfast, and where do I get it?"

"It'll be set up in the main building, buffet-style. Monday through Thursdays it's from seven to nine; Friday and Saturday it's from seven to nine-thirty, and Sundays it's more of a brunch from nine to eleven."

We walked up the path to the terrace on the pool side of the big building and parted ways.

My nose came up out of my files when I heard a knock on my door. Putting the folder aside, I rose to answer it.

A young woman, possibly a year or two older than me and wearing resort livery, smiled. Her name tag read *Janet*.

"You have a telephone call, Miss Kaye," she informed me. "You can take it in the Lodge lobby."

At the desk, I took the receiver from her, conscious of her attentive presence four feet away.

"Hello?"

"I see you got there in one piece," Mallory said.

"You had doubts?"

"Absolutely not." He started to say more; I cut him off.

"This place is lovely." I tried to frame my warning. "I'm in Lodge Two, which is basically a women's dormitory. My room is nice and there's a phone in the lobby so I didn't have to walk all the way to the main office to get your call." *Who knows how many ears are on this line!* "You'd like it out here. Boating, water skiing, rustic furnishings, and a good chef are all available for your slightest whim. I've even signed up for basic scuba diving instruction! Right now, though, I'm reading."

"I see," he said, picking up my implications. "I'm calling to let you know that a friend of mine will be arriving out there tomorrow. I hope your reading is going well. Have you taken photos?"

"Not yet. You know I always bring my camera on vacation."

"Good girl. I'll leave you to it, then." He hung up.

I put the phone back on its cradle. I shrugged and smiled at Janet. "One of these days I'm going to have to remind someone that vacation means no calls from him."

Janet chuckled. "Somebody wants you to take photos?" She returned my smile. Cool composure set off her appearance. Light brown, carefully curled hair barely touched her shoulders and framed her intelligent-looking face. The green resort shirt emphasized her hazel eyes.

"An old friend of my family. I think he wants to see if he'd like the place enough to come out here himself. I don't mind, since I'll be taking pictures anyway." I smiled. "May I ask a question? I'm curious. This telephone doesn't have a dial. Is it an extension?"

"Yes, it is. Calls to the general resort number are answered at the switchboard in a small office in the clubhouse, and the operator transfers the calls to whatever extension is needed. The reservations number goes directly into the manager's office."

"It sounds complicated."

"Not once you get used to it," she replied. "I'm learning how to use the board. Mr. Thompson told us he wants a couple of extra people trained on it in case someone gets sick."

"That sounds like a good idea." I smiled. "Thank you for coming to get me."

"Are you going back to the clubhouse for tonight's bingo game?"

"I think I'll pass. I'm not much for games and I want to get an early start on those photos."

7

Thursday morning, I followed through on my decision to get the outdoor photos for my article. Wearing the sundress Julie insisted I needed, I set out immediately after breakfast with my Kodak Retina. One of the regular shutterbugs at the paper privately told me my eye measured up to professional standards, one of the reasons Slater suggested I get the pictures myself. I took shots of the beach and boathouse, a few of the pools and terrace, one of the mini-golf course, one of the croquet set-up, and a few of the cabins. After winding back and labeling the exposed film roll, I inserted a new roll.

Although I made my bed prior to my photo shoot, I noticed other things in my room seemed out of place. Nothing major, just little things like my pajamas moved to the other bed and my hairbrush repositioned. I strolled down to the lobby.

"Good morning, Janet," I greeted her with a smile, surprised to see her still on duty. "I'd like you to make a note that my room doesn't need cleaning or tidying, if that's possible?"

"Of course. That won't be a problem," she answered. "Our housekeepers haven't been around yet but I'll let them know."

"Are you certain? Someone has been in my room this morning."

"No one that I know of," she cautiously responded. "Is something missing?"

"Oh, no. A few items were not quite where I left them. I assumed that someone had been in to straighten up."

"Excuse me," a voice said, "I beg your pardon. That was me."

I turned and saw a petite girl with dark hair in a ponytail, vivacious brown eyes, and a slightly olive complexion standing behind me. Her name badge read *Carmella*. Her eyes uneasily shifted back and forth between me and Janet.

Nervous, I mused.

"Carmella, you've already started?" Janet asked.

"Yes, ma'am. I saw Miss Kaye walking across the grounds and I wanted to get a start on my assignments," she replied. To me, she timidly added, "I hope I didn't upset you."

"No, you didn't. I'll be here until Sunday and, if it's all right with you, you can skip my room. I'm used to taking care of myself." I smiled at her. "I'll keep it neat, I promise."

"Yes, Miss Kaye." She looked at Janet. "Is that okay with you?"

"I'll make a note on the housekeeping schedule, and you won't get into trouble," Janet assured her. "It'll be fine."

Carmella relaxed. "If you need anything or want me to clean, please just ask me."

"I will." I walked down the hallway beside her. "It's nothing personal against you or any of the other housekeepers. I'm a writer and I usually have notes lying around. If you were to tidy them they could easily get out of order." *Oh well, it sounded plausible.*

"I understand. I'm like that at school. If my research papers get out of order, I go crazy." She smiled.

"You're a student?"

"Yes, I'm going to Hofstra. I'm a music major trying to get through all the other courses I have to take." She grimaced. "I'm going into my junior year this fall."

I laughed. "I know exactly what you mean. How did you end up working here?"

"I needed a summer job and my mother suggested I try for one here. My family lives in Merrick, and I wanted to be close." She hesitated for a moment. "Mrs. Ambrose is related to my mother, but Mr. Thompson hired me."

"He seems like a decent guy," I remarked.

"She thinks so. According to her, he's good at keeping things organized."

"Running this place must take a lot of logistics. I know I couldn't do it."

"Me neither," she said, wrinkling her nose.

"From what I have gathered, she owns it and he runs it."

"Oh, it's more than that. It's a partnership. I was cleaning the lobby and heard them talking. If anything happens to her, he gets the resort," Carmella confided. "Thanks for making sure I won't get into trouble if I don't clean your room, and don't forget to let me know if you need something." She left.

I entered my room and sat down on my bed to think about the very interesting piece of information Carmella handed me. I hoped she would not realize exactly how interesting it might prove to be.

I met Arlene poolside at ten for my scuba lesson. A few spectators watched her curiously while she unloaded a cart full of equipment. She laid out a couple of masks, a set of fins, and a snorkel in addition to a backpack with a tank and regulator.

"Good morning, Miss Kaye," she greeted. "I'm glad to see you have a tank style suit. The backpack works better with one. Your hair in the pony tail is good, too."

"What's first?" I asked, intrigued.

"I know you said you're a lifeguard, but I'd like to see a few things for myself. I want you to do a length of the pool in a crawl, another in the approach stroke, then dive to the bottom and swim another length. When you surface, tread water, using your arms for a minute followed by another minute with your hands out of the water."

I spent the next few minutes performing the assigned tasks with no problem. Once I finished, she called me over to the side.

"Very good! Have you used any equipment before?"

"Just a mask."

"Put the mask on. Do you know the trick to keep it from fogging?"

"No. I do know how to clear water from it by tipping sideways and gently blowing out of my nose to push water out."

"Good. Here's the other trick." Arlene demonstrated the art of spitting into the mask and swirling it around. "Don't ask me why it works, but it does." She laughed at the expression on my face. "This is how to attach the snorkel." She demonstrated slipping the snorkel under the mask's side strap. "Make sure you come up far enough to clear the snorkel with a sharp breath, otherwise you'll end up taking in water instead of air."

"That makes sense. I tried fins once. I didn't like them."

"You'll quickly get used to them."

"If you say so," I mumbled.

"You'll be fine," she encouraged, handing me a pair. "Now do two laps around the pool, using the snorkel to breathe. Kick from your hips, and don't use your arms. Put them out in front of you."

I swam around watching the odd shadows cast on the bottom of the pool by the few clouds. I kept wanting to stroke with my arms; I quit only after I discovered that it actually hampered me. When I completed my laps, she instructed me to do a surface dive to the bottom, swim under water for a width of the pool, and come up far enough to clear the snorkel. After my first attempt resulted in coughing because I did not clear the surface properly, I caught on.

"Very good! You're a natural in the water," she complimented me when I did it twice with no spluttering. "Take a minute and relax. We're through with the preliminaries."

I sat on the edge of the pool and watched a few more people gather, including Thompson and Mrs. Ambrose. The latter, seated at the edge of the terrace, seemed to be paying attention, something I did not expect.

"Does this usually draw a crowd?" I asked Arlene.

"I really can't say," she whispered, bending down. "You're my first victim."

"Oh, swell." I grinned. "Okay, coach. What's next?"

"We gear you up and you go scuba diving, all the way to the bottom of the pool. You can leave the snorkel on the deck."

"I've heard the term scuba, and wondered where the name comes from. I've also seen all the letters capitalized sometimes when it's written. Is it an acronym?"

"Yes, SCUBA stands for self-contained underwater breathing apparatus." She helped me into the harness and backpack.

"It's heavier than I thought it would be," I told her while she adjusted all the straps on the equipment.

"It won't be in the water. Move your arms as if you were swimming."

I did and she double-checked the straps.

"The harness should be snug, not overly tight. This looks fine." Arlene grabbed a mask for herself. "Pull your mask down, put the regulator's mouthpiece between your teeth, and breathe through your mouth. One hose allows you to breathe in air, and when you exhale, that air goes out the other hose."

I felt the air flowing. I inhaled and exhaled. She nodded and smiled. "Ready? Keep your breathing slow and easy."

I nodded, breathing. *This is going to be a cinch!*

"Now we get wet." She put her mask on. "Walk down the steps. When you're ready, go under. I'll be with you. If I want you to surface, I'll use a thumbs-up hand signal."

Walking in swim fins gave me a new appreciation of feeling awkward. I made it to the steps of the pool without tripping over them although they acted like big clown shoes. Carefully maneuvering down the four concrete steps, I glanced up at her before I submerged into the five-foot depth of the shallow end. Arlene came down, spotting alongside me while we went deeper. After two minutes, she gestured up. We surfaced.

"Are you used to skin diving?"

I nodded and took the mouthpiece out. "I'm good at it."

"I can tell. Let's try this again."

We submerged. After another three minutes, she signaled again and we rose.

"We have a problem. Go back to the steps and rest. I need to get something from the boathouse."

"Okay." I sat on the steps, wondering what she meant by a problem.

"Are you having difficulties?" inquired a voice I knew well.

"Apparently," I answered, "although I don't really know what it is. My instructor went back to her office to get something. Do you dive?"

"I've been down a couple of times," he said. He moved into my line of sight, pulling one of the chairs closer to the edge of the pool. "I'm Robert Mallory. Forgive the questions. I don't mean to be nosy, I'm just curious." Casually dressed in navy blue slacks with a white shirt open at the collar, he exhibited all the natural elegance Thompson aspired to emulate. He raised his sunglasses long enough to wink at me, his eyes full of fun.

"Lauren Kaye." I felt silly introducing myself. "Here comes my instructor."

Arlene walked up carrying three webbed belts with chunks of metal on them.

"Arlene!" Mallory stood and greeted her with a big smile. "I didn't know you were working here!"

"Hello, Mr. Mallory," she returned with a shy smile. "Are you a guest?"

"I'll be here for the weekend. After seeing the advertisements in the *Daily Gleaner*, I thought I'd give it a try. I'm staying in one of the cabins."

Thompson left the table he shared with his lady boss to greet his new guest. "Welcome to Northwoods Resort! I'm Edward Thompson, the manager. I see you know our water sports director." He chuckled, and I managed not to wince.

"Robert Mallory." The men shook hands. "Yes, Arlene's grandparents are friends of mine," he said, "and I've known her for a while." He turned to Arlene. "Your pupil is having difficulties?"

"She's an experienced skin diver." Getting back into the water, Arlene shot me a big grin. "We were under for over two minutes and she never took a breath."

"What?" I stared at her, open-mouthed.

"Miss Kaye, the whole point of scuba is to breathe under water," she pointed out. "You didn't. You instinctively held your breath."

"Oh, bother! I didn't mean to be difficult," I apologized. "And please, call me Lauren."

"Like I said, it's an instinct. I'll bet you can stay down for over three minutes."

"Yes, I can."

"We're going down one more time. Stay toward the side at the ten foot mark. Remember: you have air. It's perfectly okay to breathe under water." She put her mask back on, gripped the belts, and waited for me to submerge. She stayed in the water just above me at the side of the pool, watching from the surface through her mask.

I knew I could breathe from the tank. I knew I *should*. I tried to use the regulator. I simply could not make myself do it. When I ran short of air, I started to head up. The instant she saw that, Arlene executed a beautiful surface dive, tackled me, and wrapped the belts around me.

I could not move. The heavy belts held me down. I struggled with her. I needed air and I wanted up. She held on to me. She blocked any move I made. Her eyes steadily held mine but she would not let me wiggle free.

Her masked face, inches from mine, mirrored concern. I began to panic. My ears buzzed. Darkness started to form around the edge of my vision, rapidly increasing to black.

Arlene tapped my mouthpiece.

Right on the verge of passing out, I took a breath. I exhaled the breath. I took another one and exhaled. It felt *wonderful*. My vision cleared and my ears stopped buzzing. Arlene hovered in front of me, grinning. She headed up to grab a breath of her own. I sat on the bottom looking around, quite happily breathing. I saw two men at the edge of the pool gazing down at me and I waved. One of them waved back. Arlene came back down, untangled the belts, and signaled me to surface.

"What was that all about?" I questioned, spitting out the mouthpiece. I removed my mask. "Honestly, I'm not angry, just curious. Those belts felt like lead."

"That's exactly what they were: lead weight belts. We use them to adjust buoyancy in the water. Your instincts as a skin diver had to be overcome," she explained, smiling. "The only way you were going to take a breath from the regulator was if you *had* to." She got out of the water. I stayed in; the tank weighed less that way.

I laughed. "Wow! Neat trick. Thank you!"

"Arlene, that was a terrible risk," Thompson berated. "It was dangerous!"

"No, it wasn't," I contradicted. "I wasn't in any danger. If I had passed out, she could have had me on the surface in less than five seconds."

"Truthfully, if you had passed out, you would have taken a breath out of the regulator. I would have made sure it was in your mouth." Arlene turned to the manager. "Mr. Thompson, I've seen this before. An experienced skin diver will put off taking that first breath instinctively because all their training tells them they can't breathe under water. It's a reflex. Once it has been overcome, once they have taken that first breath, there are no more problems."

"Mr. Thompson, I experienced a similar reluctance the first time I dove. Like Miss Kaye, I'm a trained skin diver." Mallory, standing protectively behind Arlene, joined the discussion.

"Did your teacher tackle you?"

"Not precisely, but close enough. A friend and I were snorkeling in a lake, and she asked if I would like to try scuba. We geared up and went under. I held my breath until I wanted to surface, exactly what Miss Kaye did just now. My friend dug into the bottom of the lake and grabbed my harness to make sure I couldn't get there." Mallory chuckled at the memory. "Same principle, different setting."

I decided I could live without knowing who risked the underwater wrestling match. Instead, I turned to Arlene and asked, "Can I go back down?"

"Sure. I'll hover over you on the surface." She slipped back into the water.

Arlene correctly assumed I would not experience more difficulties. Scuba allowed marvelous freedom in the water and I glided along, no longer forced to limit my down time to three minutes. Of course, the bottom of the pool lacked interest. I flipped over to watch the clouds through the slight ripple of the water's surface, and swam around some more. Arlene dropped in and signaled me to surface.

Once back on land, she helped me out of the harness. "End of lesson. Congratulations! You survived your first dive!" She returned the equipment to her cart and headed back to the boathouse.

Mr. Thompson hailed me from the terrace. "Miss Kaye, may I have a moment?"

"Of course." I grabbed a towel and wrapped it around me. "That is an amazing feeling! I thought skin diving was fun, but wow!" We found a table. I glanced around; no sign of Mrs. Ambrose. "Thank you for allowing me to try it. That was spectacular!"

"Diving? I agree—I love it." He sat down next to me. "Are you sure Arlene didn't put you in any danger?"

"Absolutely." I regarded him. "Mr. Thompson, I am a certified lifeguard. I've learned sometimes you have to take things from a slightly different angle, especially in the water. "

"Such as?"

"May I join you?" Mallory asked formally, pulling up a chair. "You're a lifeguard?"

"Yes. My lifeguarding instructor was a big man over six feet tall with a solid, stocky build and long arms. In order to certify, each member of the class had to bring him safely back to shore without endangering either him or us. It was our final test and he did not make it easy." I grimaced. "He swam out and flailed around, mimicking a drowning victim. He actually hit a gal in the class when she got too close to his waving arms and forced another student under while he attempted the rescue."

"I don't see how that explains what Arlene did," Thompson frowned.

"It's the same principle. Circumstances in the water sometimes require you to think along new lines, exactly what Arlene did today. My solution to the life guard problem was another example of it."

"You obviously passed the test," Mallory observed. "How did you manage it if he was that much bigger?"

"We were in a lake. He positioned himself in about ten feet of water. I swam out from shore, and as I approached him, I did a surface dive to the bottom. I kept him in view and pushed off with all the force I could muster, with my arm extended in front of me. I broke the surface at the perfect angle to clip him in the jaw with my fist. I didn't knock him out completely but stunned him enough to gain control so I could bring him safely back to shore."

"That's cheating," Thompson protested.

"No, it was unorthodox, and it worked. My instructor commended me on my thinking. In the water during an emergency, whatever works is right." I shivered and stood. "Gentlemen, I'm getting chilled. If you will excuse me, I think I'll go get changed."

I left them discussing the resort. I overheard enough to gather that apparently Mallory liked his cabin.

Back at the Lodge, I dried off and pulled the sundress over my head. A knock sounded on my door.

"Come in."

Janet poked her head in. "Telephone."

"Lead the way." I padded down the hallway barefoot and picked up the phone. "Hello?"

"Miss Kaye, this is Robert Mallory. We met poolside earlier?"

"Oh yes, I remember you, of course." *We're getting good at this.*

"I've been invited to dine this evening with Mr. Thompson and Mrs. Ambrose. I asked if I could make it a four-some. Would you care to join us?"

"That's pretty heady company for me," I replied, thinking fast. *What the blazes are you up to now?*

"How about we meet for a bite of lunch to discuss it?"

"We?" *Please tell me it's just us. We need to talk.*

"You and me." He chuckled when I hesitated. "Say in about fifteen minutes?"

"That would be lovely." I hung up the instrument. "Thank you, Janet. I have a lunch date."

"I saw a dreamy-looking man out at the pool earlier when I had to run to the kitchen."

"Tall, well-built, wavy brown hair, very blue eyes, expensive clothes, looks like he laughs a lot?"

"Yes. Like I said. Dreamy-looking."

"That's the one." I grinned. "He was at the pool when I had my diving lesson."

"How did you like diving?"

"I loved it, once I got the hang of it. I'm too used to holding my breath. Arlene had to tackle me underwater to get me to breathe from the tank. Mr. Mallory witnessed all that and apparently I caught his attention."

"He's in Cabin Five, and as far as I know he's by himself. If he's single—" she rolled her eyes.

"No wedding ring or even a tan line from one. That's the giveaway I always check," I laughed. "I appreciate the information. You have a terrific grapevine around here. It makes me wonder what you are saying about me!"

"Nothing bad, I promise," she returned with a smile. "You're one of the few who treats staff members like real people. I can attest that it's a nice change."

I went back to my room content with the knowledge I scored a major hit without even trying. I knew from experience that being on good terms with staff worked wonders for information. *Who knows, it may come in handy.*

I spotted Mallory seated at a table on the poolside terrace. He stood when I approached the clubhouse a few minutes later with brushed, damp hair.

"Hello again. Shall we go in or take a short walk?"

"Let's try walking. My hair needs to finish drying. The beach is that-a-way." I pointed. "Please remember my legs are shorter than yours," I stage-whispered. He tended to stride and I did not feel like running.

We strolled around the clubhouse, past one of the playground areas with swings. He pointed out Cabin Five when we passed it. I showed him the boathouse and dock. A few people played on the beach. No one paid us any attention.

"Any progress?" he asked.

"I've made some connections with a couple of staff members and come up against one oddity." I briefly relayed the conflicting stories about who wanted Vera and who wanted Arlene at the season's start. "It's a small detail, I know, and it struck me as strange."

"Constance is many things, but she's not a liar," he murmured. "For some reason, Thompson wants to put it on her although apparently he wanted Vera here."

"So you do know her," I quietly observed.

"Yes, but how—"

"At the restaurant Monday, for a brief moment, you hesitated when Arlene spoke her name. I happened to be looking at you at the time." I smiled. "Also, I was in the office when you called for your reservation. Once Mrs. Ambrose realized it was you, her whole demeanor changed. Of course, when she gushed about seeing you again, it became a certainty."

"I keep forgetting how observant you are," he wryly replied. "Yes, I dated her for a while after my wife died. She wanted to get serious. However, her family let me know I wasn't welcome."

"That explains the dinner invitation."

"It's also why I want you at the table. She has a tendency to be possessive, and I'm taking no chances. I don't want to get involved again, and she's free."

"She may think I'm a bit young for you." A thought stuck me and I snickered. "I can believe the possessive part, though. She treats Thompson like she owns him. Have you heard her call him 'Eddie' yet?"

"You're kidding?"

"Not even exaggerating. She must have been doing it for a while because he doesn't flinch, although it doesn't go with the surroundings or the image he's trying to project." I stopped and watched the breeze generate ripples on the water. "I didn't find anything about Constance Ambrose in the files. You say her family scotched the romance. Why? I mean, I find it difficult to imagine any family objecting to you."

"I think they knew that my loyalty would never be the unconditional obedience they would have demanded. Plus, I had a daughter." He frowned. "As for background information, you weren't looking under the right name. The more interesting tidbits would be under her family's name."

"Her family name? Hold a moment—" My thoughts raced like they wanted to qualify for the Indianapolis 500. "Thompson told me she owns an apartment in the city. She bought this land and built this place, plus she told me she helped design the grounds on her family's estate. All that means she must come from major money. You mentioned unconditional obedience and your daughter as conditions. I can only think of one circumstance which would combine all that." I faced him. "Are we are talking about family with a capital F? As in the syndicate?" I knew organized crime in the greater New York area had long tentacles; I also doubted he would knowingly join it.

He solemnly nodded. "Your logic is as sound as your observations. Constance thought she broke away when she married Ambrose, but apparently not. I'm not up on all the details. The money she put into this place came from Ambrose. Regardless, she is rather well connected."

"It also accounts for her imperious attitude," I mused. "I wonder if Eddie knows."

"He may not, for the same reason you didn't find anything in your files." He frowned again. "I'm not going to give you the right name."

"I promise I wasn't going to ask. Honestly, in spite of what Mr. Slater believes, I do know when to butt out. This could really complicate things."

"I know. Be my plausible diversion at dinner, and don't worry about being too young. Now, that's enough about Constance. What about Vera's accident?"

"I've seen the damaged regulator hose and the unit that won't seat properly. Arlene and I recorded the serial numbers. One tank had a cracked O ring. She saved it after she replaced it. Remember, this is brand new equipment. The whole situation isn't right."

"Do you have background information on Thompson?"

"I grabbed what I could find from the paper and library, although I haven't had time to read it yet." I sighed. "Meanwhile, I took a roll of film this morning of exteriors, and I'll get some interior shots later. Writing the article won't be difficult. I'm more concerned about the accident. I guess I should have brought my portable typewriter."

"Funny you should mention that," he said with a sly smile. "Bernie sent one with me."

"Figures. However, the resort runs well, and they certainly pamper their guests. The chef is good, not quite up to Gianni, but few are. Oh, tonight is Italian night, by the way."

"Speaking of food, I believe I mentioned lunch."

We finished our circle around the beach and entered the clubhouse. Jim, spotting me while he cleaned off a table, suggested we use the one I occupied the evening before.

"Dinner will be a lot more formal," I told my tablemate while we ate.

Mallory and I agreed to spend some time in the library nook after lunch. He confided he rarely got the chance to read for pleasure and I needed to finish slogging through my files.

I took out the file on Vera. According to her background, she had grown up around water. Suddenly I gasped.

Mallory put his book down. "What did you find?" he asked, leaning forward in his chair.

Thompson chose that moment to approach us.

I hastily closed the folder and hurriedly stashed it back into my portfolio. Forcing what I hoped was a warm smile on my face, I greeted the manager. I saw Mallory's puzzled expression but he didn't say anything.

"I think I'd better get up and do something before I fall asleep," I commented while I stood and stretched. "I was considering going for a swim in the Sound."

"We have an area roped off for swimming, complete with an anchored float," Thompson informed us, flashing his ingratiating smile. "It's a nice distance for a dip. We also have a storage box full of towels out there. After you use them, drop them in the other bin."

"I think I'll give it a try, if you gentlemen will excuse me?" I tucked my portfolio firmly under my arm.

"Don't be surprised if you end up with company out there," Mallory intoned, his glance bordering on a leer.

"I thought you were reading," I innocently said.

"There is a time for reading and a time for other things," he returned, not innocently at all.

"Well, if you do join me I'll race you back. I warn you, though, you'll be embarrassed when I win," I shot back. *Is this what you meant by a plausible diversion?*

"We could always bet on the outcome," he slyly suggested. "How about the loser buys dinner?"

"You're on," I accepted with a laugh. "Don't say you weren't warned. Meet you out on the float!"

I walked back to Lodge Two, changed, and swam out. Thompson's evaluation was accurate. The distance comprised a comfortable swim. I got there first and set out a towel while I waited for Mallory.

"What took you so long?" I queried when he climbed the ladder almost twenty minutes later.

"Thompson asked a few questions about you, which I can't answer because we just met." He gazed around the cove. "In a way, this reminds me of my brother's place."

"The one on the lake in Manville? Julie keeps telling me about it. According to what she told me Tuesday, she's up there now." I sat with my legs crossed Indian style and quizzically regarded him. "You were flirting with me! I've got to tell you it felt really strange."

He laughed. "I'm laying groundwork for the weekend. Thompson finds you intriguing, so it's just as well. Constance doesn't take kindly to other women."

"I gathered that from Arlene."

He stretched out. "You realize you're going to have to call me something besides Mr. Mallory."

"I suppose. It's going to take a while to adjust to this."

"If I'm seen to be pursuing you, it will explain why we're spending so much time together." He got serious. "Now then. What made you gasp when you were reading the files?"

"Monday night at Susan's, Arlene told us one of the cleaners thought Vera spent too much time with

Thompson. Remember?" He nodded and I continued. "Well, according to her file, Campbell was her maiden name and she used it on her application. Her full name was Vera Margaret Campbell Thompson."

"You're serious!" Startled, Mallory abruptly sat up.

"Completely. Vera Campbell married Edward Thompson three years ago."

He whistled. "No wonder you gasped. He's certainly not acting like a bereaved husband."

"I'd give a lot to know more. If they weren't living together, she may not have known he worked here when she first applied. It does open a question, though. I'd like to know why he bothered to see her." A thought presented itself. "Curious. I wonder if Constance took the applications and set up the interviews."

"This goes beyond curious. I have a friend with the police in the Glen. I think I'll give him a call."

"You might want to do that from an outside phone," I advised. I sketched the phone system setup for him. "That's why I cut you off on the phone last night," I finished. "There's the possibility the line isn't private."

"I can always take a drive," he pointed out with a knowing smile. "I saw your car in the parking lot."

"Ah-ha! It all comes out," I ribbed him with a sinister laugh. "I know you have your own car. You only want to drive my baby!"

"I concede it's a nice bonus."

"Admit it! You regret selling it to me," I mock-challenged.

"Not as long as you let me take it out once in a while. Ready to go back?" He checked his watch, which I knew was waterproof because I helped Julie pick it out for his birthday. "We have enough time to change, leave, and get back before dinner."

"I have changed clothes more times in the past twenty-four hours than I usually do in three days," I complained when we stood. "Race you back!"

His laughter followed me into the water and I won.

Resort to Murder

Knowing I would be on display at dinner, I took my time getting ready. I put my hair up in a French twist and glued it together with hair spray. I managed a full makeup job despite hating to use eyeliner. Julie sent some false eyelashes with me, which I abhor. I refused to attempt applying them, mostly because I kept imagining my eyelids stuck together.

Thankfully, my fashion consultant's impeccable taste in clothes made dressing easy. I chose a simple sleeveless shirtwaist dress with a light blue background and small floral print, adding a wide blue belt. I paired the dress with the full petticoat and donned my heeled sling-backs. I knew Mallory used my car to run his errand while I went over the rest of my files in case they held more surprises. I suspected that comparing notes would prove interesting.

"You look great," Janet complimented me when she knocked on my door to tell me my escort waited for me. "Wait until you see him! Dreamy doesn't begin to describe him."

I laughed. "Janet, I'm surprised you are still here."

"Oh, I'll get a break later," she replied, brushing off my comment.

Mallory's eyes lit up when he saw me, and I returned an approving smile. He wore tropical white slacks, a light blue shirt with a deeper blue sport coat, and a dark blue tie. The colors brought out the depth of the blue in his eyes. Our outfits coordinated perfectly by sheer chance.

"Did you two plan this?" Janet echoed my thought, gazing at us. We shook our heads. "Amazing. Enjoy Italian night!"

We started for the clubhouse and I jumped when Mallory took my arm.

"Sorry. I'm nervous. I guess I didn't realize how much."

"Steady! Remember, this is a date. We should look like a couple," he said, smiling while he teased me.

"That's easy for you to say," I crossly mumbled. "I'm not used to this. I feel very out of place in this aerie. Now I have to remember to call you Robert."

"I've been trying to get you to do that for a while. Maybe this will do the trick." He tucked my hand into the crook of his arm and patted it. "We're a little early. Let's walk around." He gazed down at me, warmth reflected in his eyes. "Lauren, I have the utmost faith in you. You look lovely and you'll be fine—if you don't faint."

"I've never fainted in my life," I irritably grumbled. I hoped changing the subject might help. "Did you get any help from your police source?"

"Some. He admits there may be something to all this. He made it plain, however, he's not pleased with the idea of amateurs poking around. Unfortunately, he can't do anything official until concrete evidence turns up."

"Did anything else show up in Thompson's background information?"

"Danny didn't give me a look at the file; he verbally condensed it. I'll fill you in fully after dinner. Incidentally, your tidbit about Vera was new to him. The police hadn't made the connection. He's going to see if he can come up with any additional information and if he does, we'll see him tomorrow out here."

"Is he uniformed?"

"No, he's administration so he looks almost normal," he responded with a low chuckle. "I've known Danny O'Brien for years. He's one of the best investigators I know and one of the best friends I've ever had."

"How come I've never heard of him?"

"He moved to Northwoods Glen about a year ago. I gave him a reference when he applied for the job with the police department." He paused, his expression serious. Eleven years of experience made me wonder if he hesitated over how much to tell me. "He's now a captain with the NGPD."

"Have you considered opening an employment agency?" I quipped lightly, thinking about how he also helped me. "You could make it a division of your business."

"I'm a business consultant, so people consult me. When a friend needs a favor, I do what I can," he said, smiling once more. "I will admit, it can be fun at times."

We strolled along the pathway which encircled the croquet field and arrived at the clubhouse. I immediately noticed a major change in the décor. The small vases now shared centerpiece honors with Chianti bottles in baskets. Each bottle held a lighted candle. Red checked tablecloths and red napkins completed the place settings. Definitely Italian.

Jim approached us, acting as host. "Welcome to Northwoods Italian Night! Mr. Mallory, I understand you and Miss Kaye will be joining Mrs. Ambrose and Mr. Thompson for dinner?"

"That's correct. Are you hosting or waiting, Jim?" Mallory inquired while the young man ushered us to the owner's table.

"A bit of both. Gerald is the waiter assigned to Mrs. Ambrose's table but he's out with Arlene, spotting for two water skiers. I'm taking the head table this evening, and working the seating around it." At that moment our dining companions walked in the door. "Excuse me." Jim strode over and escorted them to the table.

The four of us exchanged pleasantries. Mrs. Ambrose and Thompson took their usual seats. I ended up opposite Mallory with my back to the wall and a good view of the room. Jim came to the table with a pitcher of water and filled the glasses while we studied the menu cards.

The list of appetizers included breaded and fried artichoke hearts, something I knew Gianni Gianello claimed as an original creation. I stole a look at Mallory. He raised his eyebrow and nodded, ahead of me. The chef offered a choice between traditional spaghetti with meatballs and veal parmigiana with spaghetti tossed with garlic butter. Mrs. Ambrose, Mallory, and I chose the veal. Thompson opted for the spaghetti.

"Mr. Thompson, would you like to see a wine list?" Jim asked, extending it to the manager.

Thompson looked at Constance for guidance but she focused her attention solely on Mallory. Jim fidgeted, rocking back and forth a bit on his feet, very uncomfortable until Mallory extended his hand towards the waiter.

"Thank you, Jim." Mallory perused the list and addressed Thompson. "Would you mind if I chose something for the table?" he asked.

"Oh, please, Robert, that would be splendid," Mrs. Ambrose gushed before Thompson could answer. "Your choices have always been superb." She looked at Thompson. "He's an expert."

"Hardly that. I simply know what I enjoy," my dinner companion murmured. "For a start, I'd like a bottle of champagne for the table, Jim, and two orders of the artichoke hearts."

"Certainly, sir. Would you care for a different wine selection with your meal?"

"I think so, yes. Ordinarily I would request the Chianti, but I believe Miss Kaye prefers a lighter touch." He glanced up at me with a glowing smile. "Let's try a bottle of the cabernet sauvignon."

"When would you like your salads and with what dressings?" Again, Jim addressed the question directly to Mallory.

Thompson shifted uneasily in his chair but said nothing.

"I'd like to follow the European custom, if it's agreeable to everyone," he replied, glancing at us. "I think we should have the salads with the house dressing after the entrées, to clear the palate prior to dessert." Mallory gestured for the young waiter to bend down and lowered his voice. "How are you with a corkscrew?"

"A complete dud, sir," Jim earnestly whispered. "I always panic at the thought of trying to open the bottles."

"Jim," Mallory resumed his normal tone, "with your permission, I'd prefer to open the wines myself. Bring the bottle of champagne out and I'll take care of it."

"Thank you, sir." Jim headed off to the kitchen, his relief reflected in his smile.

"Jim's new to waiting," Thompson confided, "but he's doing well. He remembers everything and he's eager to learn."

"I hope I didn't offend you by taking charge," Mallory said to Thompson, who shook his head no without his usual smile.

"Not in the least," Mrs. Ambrose purred, leaning towards Mallory and putting one hand on his arm. "I seem to remember you are quite capable. Of many things."

I smothered a grin. I did not dare look at Mallory; too high a risk I would burst out laughing. Mrs. Ambrose removed a cigarette from her gold case, stuck it in her holder, turned toward Mallory, and waited for him to light it.

"My apologies, Constance. I gave up smoking about two years ago," he informed her with a smile. "I can never remember to carry a lighter now. I suppose I should, to be polite."

Thompson leaned across the table and performed the honors. I felt sorry for him. Mallory represented everything he wanted to be.

No wonder I'm the plausible diversion—we have enough to deal with!

"Robert, tell me what you have been doing lately," the resort's owner's said, her voice sultry. She blew smoke out of her nose.

I fought down the image of a lady dragon breathing fire as petty.

Laying her hand on his arm, she continued, "How is your business doing? And what about your lovely little girl?"

"Business is fine. Julie just completed her junior year of college," he told her. "She wants to teach elementary school and she's minoring in social work. I'm very proud of her."

She looked at me. "Miss Kaye? Oh, dear. Let's use first names—it's friendlier. Lauren, you're about college age yourself, aren't you?"

"Constance," I replied sweetly, again avoiding exchanging glances with my dinner partner, "I'm old enough to know when not to discuss my age."

"Robert dear, here's the champagne," she announced. Apparently deciding to play it safe by ignoring me, she shifted her gaze back to Mallory. "Are we celebrating the reunion of old friends?"

"I thought I'd celebrate meeting new ones," he said. He stood, gazing across at me, and accepted the bottle from Jim. "Let's see if I can do this without getting it all over everything. Although it looks impressive in movies, it only wastes champagne."

Mallory expertly extracted the cork slowly enough that the fizz stayed in the bottle. He poured the effervescent drink into waiting glasses and handed them to us. Remaining on his feet, he raised his.

"To friends, old and new." He took a sip, raised his glass again, and stared straight at me. His voice taking on a new tone, he added, "You look lovely, Lauren."

"Thank you, sir," I replied, trying not to blush.

A movement behind Mallory caught my eye. The outer door opened to admit a man by himself. An inch or two above my height with dark hair sprinkled with grey, he wore a slightly rumpled grey sports coat, darker grey pants, white shirt, and a dark tie. The man nodded when Jim met him and seated him at what I considered my table. The direction of my gaze cued Mallory someone entered and he swiveled slightly when he sat down. When he faced me and nodded ever-so-slightly, I surmised the newcomer was O'Brien. Cops do not blend in well.

"Old friends and new," he murmured.

"What did you say?" insolently demanded Constance.

"Nothing of consequence. I merely repeated myself."

Jim arrived with our appetizers, setting small plates in front of us and placing the double-order platter of artichoke hearts on the table. One bite told me the poor imitations only mimicked the appearance of Gianello's originals. I glanced up at Mallory and smiled. He raised his glass in response.

When I tell Gianni and Susan about this, I thought, *I can assure him his creation remains unchallenged.*

Jim brought the bottle of cabernet sauvignon and a corkscrew to the table after he collected the appetizer plates. Mallory went step by step so the young man could watch and smoothly pulled the cork.

"It's not difficult," he told the waiter. "I'm sure you'll easily pick it up."

Throughout the meal Mallory acted as host. Thompson fidgeted nervously. I noticed an occasional slight scowl on his usually smiling face.

He appears intimidated and annoyed at the same time, I thought. He responded to Mallory when necessary, which did not happen often. I carefully ducked most of the probing questions put to me. Constance generally monopolized the conversation and kept her attention on Mallory.

During a rare lull in her chatter, Thompson once more brought up my scuba lesson with Arlene.

"I'm still concerned," he explained, frowning.

"Are you asking for my opinion of her as an instructor?" I inquired.

He nodded. "We don't need any more accidents."

"You are lucky to have her. She knows what she's doing and she's sharp enough to work around difficulties." I took a sip of my wine. "Now that I've had my pool lesson, I intend to ask her if she'll take me diving in the Sound."

"I'm glad you enjoyed your experience. I agree you should follow up the pool work with an open-water dive. I was going to suggest we do that tomorrow, if you wouldn't mind the company," Mallory offered.

"I'd welcome it, and I'm sure Arlene won't object," I assured him. "Did I hear you say you know her grandparents?" *I want points for remembering the 'we are strangers' script!*

"Yes, they're friends of mine." He turned to Constance. "Are you over your fear of the water?"

"I'm doing much better. Eddie's been helping me build my confidence," she cooed, giving Thompson a big smile. "I use the pool almost daily now."

"Constance, you're a good swimmer when you forget to be scared," Thompson told her, reaching across the table to pat her hand.

"That is what I told you eight years ago," Mallory commented. "I think your mother scared you into being afraid of the water based on her own fears, and it spiraled."

"Mama always liked you," Constance murmured.

"A feeling I returned. How is she?"

"She passed away last year. She had cancer."

"I'm very sorry." His gentle baritone quietly conveyed his sympathy.

"My father hired the best specialists his money could buy, but nothing helped. He thinks he can control everything, or buy anything, yet he couldn't stop her from dying," she said, her voice bitter. "He was enraged. The cancer wouldn't obey his orders to go away. If it had been anything but Mama's suffering and death, I would have laughed in his face." Her face contorted with painful memories; she took a large gulp of wine to empty her glass and held it out to Mallory for a refill. He poured, and judging by the scowl which flickered across her face, she did not get as much as she wanted.

"Robert met your parents?" Thompson sounded amazed, yet I detected an undertone of anger.

"Now Eddie, don't be jealous. That's juvenile," she reprimanded him in blatantly patronizing tones.

Thompson bristled and silently fumed.

Constance immediately changed her mien to silky and soothing without apologizing. "It was eight years ago after all. That's a long time." She patted his hand again and he looked slightly mollified.

Mallory changed the subject by asking questions about the length of time involved in planning and constructing the resort. I made a note to tell him later he should consider changing careers. His talents in business could be supplemented by entering the diplomatic service as an ambassadorial aide at the least.

"I should make the rounds," Thompson announced a few moments later while Jim collected the entrée plates.

Constance decided to powder her nose.

Left to ourselves, I indicated the man by the window. "O'Brien?" I softly inquired.

He nodded. "I presume his presence means he has found something fairly urgent and he's leaving it up to me to figure out how to meet."

"Good luck." I looked at O'Brien and his gaze met mine. He inclined his head with the barest hint of a smile. "You'd better come up with something fast. He's staring at me."

"Relax. I told him about you and he knows who you are," he informed me.

"Company coming," I murmured, gazing over his other shoulder.

"Lauren, you're going to have to learn to gracefully accept things like this." Mallory stood when Constance rejoined us.

"I missed something!" she brazenly accused. "Now, now! We can't have secrets, Robert."

"Nothing secret, Constance. Lauren feels that the gentleman by the window has been staring at her. I was explaining that most men like gazing at pretty young women." He turned to nod at the other man. "Well, I'll be!" He went over to the other table. "Danny!"

O'Brien stood and they shook hands, quietly conversing. Thompson came back when Jim served the salads. The waiter shot me a pleading look asking for guidance.

"He only needs a gentle nudge, Jim. Go up to him, politely excuse yourself, and inform him you have served the salads," I advised. "I don't think he will mind."

Jim followed my suggestion. Mallory thanked him and excused himself to O'Brien.

"Please forgive me, I was rude." Mallory resumed his seat and picked up his fork. "That gentleman is one of my clients. He called my office and my secretary told him I was here, so he came out hoping to catch me." He smiled at Thompson. "I'm grateful you allow the general public in for dinner," he concluded. "I might have lost a valuable client otherwise!"

Conversation lagged while we focused on the salads.

I caught Mallory's eye. *Well played. Now what?* Out loud I asked, "Will you be meeting with him after dinner?"

"I'm afraid I'll have to." He reached across the table for my hand. "Danny has questions that won't wait. I'll make it up to you, Lauren."

"Oh, Robert, you'll miss the adults-only swim," Constance complained with a pout, attempting to shift his attention away from me. "I wanted to spend some time together."

"I may be able to do both if Danny brought his suit," he thoughtfully replied. "Lauren, what do you say?"

"Although I admit I was anticipating another swim, I'm not surprised you put business first," I said. "Do what you feel is best. After all, we're both here for the weekend, aren't we?" *How in blazes are you going to include me in your consultation?*

"Very true," he murmured. His fingers tightened on mine slightly before he relinquished my hand.

"Perhaps your client would like to book in for the weekend," Thompson hopefully proposed. "We have at least one cabin open."

"I'll see what I can do," Mallory told the manager. "Meanwhile, let's enjoy the rest of the meal. Jim, what's for dessert?"

"Cheesecake garnished with blueberries or ice cream parfait."

10

Our little party broke up immediately after Jim collected the cheesecake plates.

Mallory, whom I could not think of as Robert, introduced me to Danny O'Brien. The policeman, who only ordered dessert, suggested the three of us find a table on the terrace. Mallory headed to the beach side, away from people congregating poolside.

"Sorry if I've made this awkward," O'Brien apologized. "I wanted you to be aware that you are digging into something that could mean real trouble." His grey eyes focused on me. "Young lady, Mallory explained your reasons for coming out here. I want you to know I don't take kindly to amateurs poking into police matters."

"Mr. Slater sent me out to do a story on the resort," I said flatly, "and the Gianellos asked me for a favor. Mr. Mallory told me that you can't re-open the Campbell case on the basis of someone's feelings and I understand that. I also appreciate that we have turned up nothing concrete except a solid motive for Thompson wanting Vera Campbell out of his way." I kept my voice low and my tone even. "What did you find?"

"Blast it! I don't think you realize what a hornet's nest you are stirring up!" His chilly, low voice came edged with a strong, undefinable undercurrent. His broad face started to turn red.

"No, although I have a feeling I'm about to find out," I countered, sitting forward.

"Doug Ambrose's money, inherited by his widow Constance after he died in an accident, built this place. I found out Ambrose had been an accountant for a syndicate boss. I don't know which one and I don't want to know," he sputtered, running his hand through his hair in exasperation. "Frankly, it's a terrible thing for a cop to say, too, but I'm being honest. Just knowing there's a slight connection is going to make people nervous about digging into a closed case."

"Hold," Mallory commanded. "We need someplace else to discuss this. We're about to have company out here."

Constance and Thompson strolled around the corner of the building. The manager waved, so I waved back. At O'Brien's glare, I mumbled something about being polite.

"Danny, stand down." Mallory murmured it softly yet his tone implied an order. It immediately took effect.

O'Brien took in a bushel of air, letting it out in a silent whistle. "I'm fine." He clipped his words before he looked up to smile at the couple. He should have skipped it. I decided if Bernie Slater lacked the ability for intimidation, Danny O'Brien lacked the ability to fake a warm smile.

The men stood while Mallory performed introductions. Constance overshot her role of hostess by effusively greeting him. I agreed with Arlene's assessment of her, especially when I considered her actions around Mallory.

O'Brien firmly declined to stay the night. He let Thompson talk him into booking in for Friday and Saturday nights after Mallory offered to cover the cost of the cabin.

"Danny, I've been telling you for a year that you've been working too hard," Mallory told him, smiling. "This will give us a chance to work out the details of your problem, plus you can take some time to relax. If you're worried about the cost, please don't. I'll take it as a business expense."

"Mr. O'Brien, you'll enjoy it out here, I promise," Constance coaxed, putting her hand on his arm. "We're having an adult swim as our activity this evening. Since you are Robert's guest, I'd like to personally invite you to join the fun! Did you bring your bathing suit?"

"I'm afraid I didn't, Mrs. Ambrose," O'Brien tersely responded.

"Well, make sure you pack it for the weekend," she encouraged, patting his arm. She probably did not notice he wanted to pull away from her. I caught it and smiled to myself.

"We look forward to seeing you tomorrow," Thompson said. "I'll make a note of the reservation now." He offered his arm to Constance, and they started off towards the office.

"What in Hades are you trying to do to me?" O'Brien groused to Mallory once the couple left the area and we sat. "I'd like to remind you I am not one of your moneyed cronies!"

"Which is why I'm paying for the cabin," Mallory reasonably returned. "Don't even try to convince me you don't want to be at hand when this erupts, if it does. I know you better than that."

"Will one of you gentlemen please tell me what it is I seem to be missing?" I regarded each of them in turn. "Mr. M., earlier you said you'd fill me in after dinner, which would be now. What do you know about Thompson that I don't?"

"No." O'Brien firmly declared with his jaw clenched. He scowled at Mallory. "She needs to stay out of this."

"I disagree. She needs to know," Mallory responded, "otherwise—"

"Excuse me!" I forcibly interrupted the debate. "Please notice I'm already involved," I protested. I turned to O'Brien. "You undoubtedly had all the information I found about Thompson, yet you missed the connection between him and Vera Campbell. You want me out? I appreciate the concern, but no. Besides, you need me."

"No, we don't." O'Brien's scowl deepened. "You don't know what you're dealing with."

"Yes I do." I stared into his steely grey eyes. "Another tidbit for rumination: are you aware that Constance Ambrose signed a partnership agreement for the resort, complete with a survivor clause? If anything happens to her, Thompson gets this place."

"What?" both men spoke.

I related the gist of my first conversation with Carmella. "I'm sure the girl has no idea what she told me so casually is critical," I finished. "Documentation should confirm it."

"Okay, okay, I'll stipulate you might possibly be good at this," O'Brien grudgingly praised, "but you are not a professional." He sighed. "Cheese and rice! We need time and a place to talk."

"I concur." Mallory glanced at his watch. "Lauren and I also need to make an appearance at the evening swim. Suggestions?"

"I was going home but it looks like I'm heading back to my office," O'Brien sourly grumbled. "Think of me digging through more files while you paddle around a pool." He rose.

"If you need to call me, remember it's a switchboard set-up," Mallory told him while we also stood. "We'll see you tomorrow."

"Mr. O'Brien?"

He turned to face me. "Yes?" His tone stopped inches this side of a bark.

"Don't forget to bring your bathing suit."

He disdainfully snorted. "I don't own one."

"Captain, I realize you consider me an annoyance and you welcome my interference with all the joy of a cleaning woman spotting a cockroach, but consider this. Everything here kicked off with a scuba accident, and the diving equipment available shows signs of tampering. Water sports seem to be integral to whatever is going on and it wouldn't hurt to be prepared," I reasoned. "Besides, you should blend in."

His grey eyes searched my face, his gaze probing like he sought something within me. Meeting it required concentration yet I felt no hostility. After a few moments of silence, broken only by the sounds of cicadas and the gentle surf of the Sound, a genuine smile broke over his face and he nodded.

"I'll see what I can do," he said, turned, and strolled off.

Mallory took my arm, gently rested my hand on his, and led me to the clubhouse's pool side. Subdued crystal globes, hung on decorative wrought-iron poles around the terrace's periphery, illuminated our path with a soft golden hue.

Jim, our young waiter, greeted us at the clubhouse door when we stopped to admire the elegant fixtures.

"Welcome to the official start of the Adult Swim. We'll have the bar cart set up shortly near the shallow end of the pool," he informed us. "Sir, I want to thank you for the lesson about opening wine bottles. I'm hoping to get a position in a good restaurant this fall."

"Jim, it was my pleasure." Mallory smiled at the younger man. "If you have any other questions you feel I can answer, please ask."

Constance and Thompson strolled along the path to the pool deck. She wore a cute cover-up over her bathing suit, which looked far more fashionable than my tank suit.

We watched while Thompson settled her in a cushioned chaise at the pool's mid-point and arranged a small table beside her, topping it off with an ashtray. He looked around and greeted us with a friendly wave.

Mallory walked us toward them, my arm linked through his.

"Business meeting finished, Robert?" Constance sweetly inquired. Her icy glance at me contradicted her syrupy tone.

"For the moment. We'll resume tomorrow after Mr. O'Brien returns. Again, you have my apologies, Lauren." He smiled and patted my hand. "I wasn't planning a working vacation. I'll walk you to the Lodge so you can get changed."

Once out of earshot, I jerked my hand loose. "Give over. What's going on?"

"Thompson is a con artist," he promptly announced.

"Is that supposed to surprise me?"

"No. He bilks organizations and fleeces lonely women."

"How ambitious of him! Most scam artists settle for one or the other," I remarked. "Any details?"

"One of the things he claims is a degree in theology, presumably phony. About four years ago, playing on post-war confusion, he charmed his way into a church in a small Indiana town. After convincing the congregation they deserved a new building, he led the fund-raising efforts, preaching on the radio and taking pledges. In two years they raised enough money to start construction. During that time he also courted the richest woman in the congregation, winning her affections despite being fifteen years her junior."

"Could he have been genuinely in love with her?"

"According to the reports, if he wasn't he played his part beautifully, even securing approval from the skeptics. He was very attentive, and absolutely devoted to doing everything he could for her and the church. She had a new will drawn up, splitting her estate between her new husband and the church. They held the marriage ceremony on the site of the new building the day ground was broken for construction and the newlyweds departed for a Florida honeymoon. She died while they were scuba diving in a quarry down there."

"Diving again? Sounds vaguely familiar. How come he's roaming around loose rather than making license plates in a correctional facility?"

"The coroner's report states she died accidentally due to faulty equipment. Although there was some slight evidence to the contrary, it was ruled death by misadventure."

"What did he do with her money?"

"After the inquest, he returned to his flock, the perfect picture of a mournful bridegroom, and waited for the will to be read. That's when he got the bad news. Thompson didn't inherit any money from his wife. Unknown to him, she hadn't *signed* the new will, apparently planning to do it once they returned. Her old will left everything to the church. All he had to show for two years of effort was the money he had already skimmed off the fund-raising, a sizable sum but chump change compared to what he anticipated. Knowing he had fiddled the books, he resigned, claiming that without his lady love and with too many painful memories, he couldn't face the congregation. And he vanished."

"All that brings us to Vera," I mused once I digested the saga. "She wasn't rich, or she wouldn't have needed a job here."

"Danny did get some information on her background. Actually Vera *was* wealthy when they met. She had a sizable income from a trust fund set up by her grandfather, besides being the primary beneficiary of his estate. Her grandfather, who is alive and kicking, detested Thompson, accurately sizing him up as a fortune hunter, and threatened to cut Vera off from both the trust and the will if they married. Our boy wonder wooed and married her in spite of that, probably figuring it was a bluff."

"That wasn't the case?"

Mallory shook his head. "Once the old gent found out about the marriage, he carried out both threats. The happy couple stayed together for less than six months. A devout Catholic, she refused to divorce him."

"Her death yanked a major complication out of his life, it seems. Interesting. Any word on how he hooked up with Constance?"

"We have seen Eddie is ambitious and blends into society well. Constance thrives on the social butterfly routine. I'd guess she probably met him at a cocktail party or a bar. She tends to collect men." He shrugged. "He may not be aware of her family connections."

I laughed. "The man is totally bereft of scruples but inept. He should have done his homework better. If he scams her or arranges a fatal accident, he could end up in a proverbial cornerstone. O'Brien doesn't seem to be aware of how direct that particular connection is, either. From his comments, he thinks the tie was strictly through Doug Ambrose."

"I concur and I'll brief Danny if it comes up. Meanwhile, don't underestimate Thompson," he warned. "He's dangerous and he's free to marry again."

"Don't worry. I'm poor so I'm safe. Besides, he's obviously going after Constance, and she already signed on the dotted line. He'll get her and the resort. She told me this place was originally his idea, although she put up the money."

"I admit he has the resort running well." He frowned. "You are going to have to tread with caution. Constance has an uncanny ability to spot potential rivals. If she is determined to have him, you could become a threat."

"I see that. However, according to your reasoning, you are in more danger from Eddie than I am from her. Constance is attracted to you, plus you represent everything he strives for: gentility, class, poise, and money. Thompson is already wary of you, so you might want to watch your own back."

"Oh, I'm very aware of it. It was the primary reason I asked you to be my dinner partner tonight. I'm hoping they both see I'm not interested in her." Mallory sighed. "Danny's right. We three need to talk." He stopped in front of Lodge Two. "How fast can you change?"

"Give me about fifteen minutes."

"That long?" he teasingly asked. "You're usually a quick-change artist."

"I have to take down my hair and braid it again so I can go swimming. I hate bathing caps, which never work anyway."

He chuckled. "I'll be back to get you."

I bit back my verbal reply; the sour expression on my face said it for me.

"Humor me?" he waited until I nodded agreement before he strolled off.

Janet greeted me. "How did dinner go?"

"We enjoyed it. The food was good and we were lucky enough to have Jim as a waiter. He was more than happy to let Mr. Mallory open the champagne and wine. I'll bet he wrote some notes once he got back to the kitchen."

She chuckled. "He's a good kid. I think he's working up his courage to ask Carmella out."

"That might work out well for both of them," I said. "Janet, please don't take this wrong, but my curiosity is getting the better of me and I have to ask. You seem to be here all the time. Do you live here in the lobby?"

"Not quite," she snickered. "In fact, I just got here. One of the rotating concierges is sick and I split the extra shifts with Dorothy Schneider. She checked you in yesterday," she reminded me. "She will relieve me in about an hour so I can have another training session at the switchboard operation."

"Am I the only one staying in the Lodge?"

"You were last night. Four women checked in today, and we have a few more bookings for the weekend, but we're nowhere near full. Are you going to the adult swim?"

"Yes. I have to change. Mr. Mallory will be coming to collect me."

"Lucky you!"

Back in my room, I kicked off my shoes, hung up my dress and petticoat, and quickly donned my tank suit. I tackled the fun part next. My straight, very fine hair required threats and a detailed diagram to do anything other than hang there. The process took longer due to the hair spray I used to keep the French twist in place. Janet knocked on my door ten seconds after I finished coaxing my lank locks into a symmetrical tangle resembling a braid.

"He's here already?" I asked, glancing at my travel clock. "I told him fifteen minutes."

"No, you have a telephone call." She retreated to her desk.

I put on my cover-up, a plain blue, man-tailored shirt bought for this purpose. Julie argued for something more feminine in both a suit and cover-up, while I held out for the tank and shirt. I wanted a pocket. I grabbed a towel, slipped my feet into my zories, and locked my door on the way out. I put the key in the shirt pocket. My slippers sounded like hands slapping a face, sort of a flip-flop noise, with each step.

"Hello?"

"O'Brien." Brusque with no amenities, his brevity fit him.

"What can I do for you, Mr. O'Brien?"

"Robert Mallory isn't answering his phone, so I thought I'd leave a message with—"

"Hold the wire, please?" I interrupted. "He's walking in now." I held out the handset. "Mr. O'Brien."

I stepped back and listened to a series of grunts, none of which proved remotely informative. I tried to look nonchalant, but Mallory knew me too well to fall for it.

"Thanks, Danny. I'll see you tomorrow." Mallory hung up. "Ready?"

"All set."

"Enjoy your swim!" Janet called after us.

"Now what?" I asked once we exited the building.

Mallory strode off without a word, his long legs rapidly putting distance between us.

"Excuse me!" I called to him. "I am not wearing sneakers!"

"Sorry." He slowed his pace. I made no attempt to catch up to him.

He kept going until he realized I had not followed him, and retraced his steps. We could see the soft, haloed clubhouse lights beyond the deepening dusk surrounding us. Crickets serenaded us with their chirping songs, slowly replacing the cicadas in the tranquil evening. A few lightning bugs blinked around us.

"I'm not moving until I get some answers." My voice reflected my determination.

"Lauren, even Danny is not sure if what he told me is important. Once we make an appearance at this party, let's swim out to the float for a bit. Bear with me, please?" he cajoled.

"I'm sorry." I took in a gallon of air and exhaled in a silent whistle. "No, I take that back. I'm not a bit sorry. I feel I have to be on guard and I'd like a hint of what directions to watch." I slowly walked toward the lights which spread their glow across the terrace like a soft golden blanket. "Contrary to Mr. Slater's opinion, I do not have eyes in the back of my head."

"I understand, and again, I'm sorry." He opened the terrace gate, took my arm and murmured, "Here we go. Smile?"

"I will if you will," I muttered.

11

We entered the terrace near the bar. I noticed Constance rose from her chaise to greet certain members; she memorized the trail from her domain to the bar so well she could probably navigate it with her eyes closed. I dropped my shirt on a chair with my towel and, wasting no time socializing, made my way to the deep end. I used a shallow racing dive, cleaved the smooth surface, and entered the cool, welcoming water. It washed over me and enveloped me like a friendly hug. I came up directly opposite Constance, lazily floated on my back, and gazed at the scene.

Constance sat on her chaise surrounded by people, like Cleopatra sailing up the Nile with an entourage. She gave off the air of holding court. I discovered "adults-only swim" really meant adults only lounging by the swimming pool with the bar cart parked at one end. Twenty-five people, give or take a couple, milled around the pool but despite the term 'swim' in the activity's official title, only one person actually took advantage of the water: me. After Constance insisted on introducing Mallory to anyone handy, he circulated politely for a few minutes and dove in to join me.

"I thought I'd wait for Constance to miss a step and fall in. If she did, it might answer the 'can she swim' question," I ventured.

He chuckled. "She can. She lacks confidence in the water, so she doesn't enjoy it. Do you want anything to drink?"

"Maybe later." I pushed off the side and we swam a few lengths, ending up in the corner furthest from the bar. "I guess I'm too naïve or plebeian to fit into society," I said while we held on to the side.

"Oh?"

"I thought an adult-only swim would mean no kids around with adults swimming. I didn't think you and I would be the only ones actually in the water. Silly me."

His laughter drew Constance's attention.

"Robert!" she trilled, "you should be enjoying yourself up here with the rest of us, not lounging down there in the water!"

"That doesn't exactly make sense," I muttered.

"She's drinking and she's never been good at it," he murmured to me. "Constance, I am enjoying myself, I promise," he called to her. "You told me this is a swimming party. Well, we're swimming."

"Come out and join us," she petulantly persisted. "I'll get you a drink."

"We should mingle," he whispered.

"You already did."

"I said *we* should mingle," he chuckled again. In contrast to Thompson's annoying cackle, Mallory's sounded friendly and warm. "Emphasis on 'we.' Please, don't make me go back up there alone!"

"I think this is where I came in," I commented, recalling the circumstances of our latest dinner date. "All right, if you insist but I doubt if I'm going to be much help."

We used a side-stroke to the steps. Climbing out, Mallory handed me a towel, and I wrapped it around my waist. Constance abandoned her chaise to join us.

"You need a drink." She stood close enough to him that he took care not to knock her over while he toweled off. "Just tell the boy what you want."

"Give me a moment, Constance." Tossing the towel over his shoulder, he offered me his hand but she tugged at his arm to drag him off to her chaise. Thompson, on his feet, watched them, a frown on his usually smiling face.

"Robert, would you like something from the bar?" I considerately offered, suppressing a snicker. "I'd be happy to get it for you."

"I'll have whatever you're having," he replied with a wink over his shoulder.

Three sarcastic retorts flashed through my mind; I settled for smiling. Mallory knew my tastes. I approached the bar a few feet away. Jim stood next to it, watching the activity and talking to the man mixing drinks.

I perused the selection of bottles, mixers, and the colorful metal glasses arrayed on the cart.

"What can I get for you?" asked the bartender, whose name tag read *George*.

"I would like two glasses of club soda on the rocks with a twist of lime," I requested, keeping my voice down. "Charge them to Mr. Mallory's tab, Cabin Five."

"No problem. Would you prefer metal or plastic glasses?"

"Oh, I didn't see plastic ones. Those would be great."

"You don't drink?" Jim asked while George got busy.

"Not much. When I lived on college campus, I learned two important lessons about the social scene. The first was an elementary observation: I found it was more fun to watch other people get drunk than it was to be drunk. The second was more in the line of camouflage. I discovered if you're at a party where everyone else is drinking alcohol and you don't have something that looks like a drink, you get pestered. I have two stand-in beverages which mimic the appearance of standard drinks. This one looks like a gin and tonic."

George handed me two clear glasses. "That's clever! Much less obvious than a Shirley Temple. What's the other stand-in?"

"Ginger ale with an orange slice and a cherry. It looks like a whiskey sour made with ginger ale instead of syrup. I would have asked for that except I didn't see any ginger ale." I smiled at George's nod. "Keep it mum, please?" They both nodded, and I thanked them.

Carrying the two drinks, I wormed my way through other people to the resort owner's court. Luckily, the dry concrete made dodging relatively easy.

Constance, once more on her reclining throne, entertained Mallory on one side while her Eddie danced attendance on the other. I noticed Thompson's efforts to distract his partner's attention away from his presumed rival escalated with her refusal to focus on him.

I stopped to consider my seating options. I concluded I did not have enough room for a chair on the other side of Mallory. Sensing my dilemma, he rolled his eyes with a tiny, helpless shrug. I handed him both drinks, undid my towel, folded it a couple of times, and sat down on the concrete.

"For a moment I thought you were going to dive back in," he murmured, leaning over to hand me my drink.

"I'd be lying if I told you it didn't cross my mind." I raised my glass to salute him. "Enjoy."

He took a sip. "Terrific! Thank you. Very refreshing after a swim."

"Robert, since when do you drink gin and tonic?" the queen pompously inquired.

"Constance, it has been eight years. Some things change." Mischief shone in his blue eyes and he smiled at me. "Are you comfortable sitting down there?"

"It'll do for a while. I'm not planning to be here all night, you know," I said with a shrug. "Besides, I'm young," I impudently grinned up at him.

I heard Constance inhale sharply and her tone turned acidly condescending. "You certainly are."

Mallory choked on a swig of his drink trying to squelch his laughter.

"Looks like I'm not the one in an uncomfortable seat," I murmured, pleased with the way the exchange turned out.

"Watch it," he leered. "I have ice cubes and I'm lecherous enough to know where to drop them."

After giving consideration to our relative positions, I rotated slightly to decrease the possibilities, laughing at his mock scowl. "I may be young, but I'm not stupid," I loftily informed him.

"For two people who just met," Constance observed, haughtily and sulking, "your bickering is—" She left her thought unfinished when Thompson whispered in her ear. "Oh, Eddie, that's so sweet of you," she simpered. She waved a hand with a magisterial gesture, dismissing us. "You two can go play if you want to."

Mallory drained his drink, stood, and reached to assist me. My foot caught my towel. Like a toy top with its speed slowly winding down, I teetered. Before I hit the concrete, he caught me in his capable arms, lifted me, took two steps forward, and jumped.

We hit the water with an immense splash, sending spray into the air and a small tidal wave rippling across the water. He grinned when we surfaced, one arm around my waist, his deep electric-blue eyes dancing with mirth. My laughter joined his; we leisurely treaded water side by side while we surveyed the resulting confusion. The splash showered the deck around Constance, soaking everything.

"That wasn't necessary, you know." I grinned and slipped my arm around his neck. We swiveled to better appreciate the sight. Sorting wet from dry looked like a hopelessly futile task.

"That depends upon how you look at it," he replied. "I thought they could use a shower."

"Have you finished wreaking havoc? Please understand I would never dream of trying to dissuade you," I assured him. "I'm only asking for a hint."

"Since you ask, not quite. I have an idea." He shifted his hold on me so both hands rested on my waist, his eyes gleaming with mischief. "Do you remember how to dive off my shoulders?"

I placed my hands on his arms. "Some things you never forget. Bear in mind I'm taller and heavier now." I smiled at the memory. When we were kids, Mallory took Julie and me to a local pool and taught us how to swim. Once we started diving, he taught us how to stand on his shoulders underwater; once balanced he stood while we dove.

"Not by much. Trust me, it will work."

We moved to deeper water, and he turned me so my back rested against his chest, both facing the steps.

He whispered in my ear, "Ready?"

I nodded. He dropped to a kneeling position and I put my feet on his shoulders. Mallory waited until he felt me balance; he tapped my ankles to warn me before he rose. I executed a perfect dive and swam the length of the pool underwater. He followed and hugged me when I surfaced. Everyone applauded.

"Impressive!" he complimented me while we climbed out.

"Yes, and a marked improvement over how you went in," Thompson tartly stated, holding towels out for us when we rejoined them. "We're all wet."

"It's only water," Mallory nonchalantly observed. "Consider it refreshing. You ought to try it. Better yet, take Constance in with you."

"Not your way," Constance stated sourly from her chaise. "Was it necessary to soak us?"

"Believe it or not, I asked him the same thing," I informed her, drying off.

"What was his answer?"

"I said it all depended upon how you look at it. We were the only two people in the pool at a swimming party. I thought the rest of you looked far too dry, so we added water." Mallory's smile broadened. "Fortunately, Lauren is an excellent swimmer."

"She dives well, too," Constance waspishly contributed. "I remember you tried to teach me that diving trick." Her face contorted into a scowl while she tried to bore a hole through me with a glare.

Mallory held out a hand to her. "It's never too late. Let's try it."

Her emotional switch flipped. Her face cleared and she beamed at him.

"You're on! I'm just high enough to be stupid enough to agree." She let him pull her to her feet. "No repeat of the entry. I want to go in on my own."

"Sorry, that's not an option. I'm not giving you the chance to chicken out."

Mallory scooped her up. She giggled while he carried her to the steps and into the water. The two of them swam towards deeper water. The spectators fell silent; most of them watched the two swimmers. The only noise came from crickets. I kept my eyes on Thompson, whose mouth hung slightly open in surprise.

"I can't believe she's doing this," he grumbled. "He just asked, and she agreed." Jealousy colored his voice. "She really trusts him."

"Well, he is an old friend of hers. I think they dated for a while before she got married."

"That's what she told me. He seems to be interested in you now." Thompson's tone approached accusation. "She's spoiled and has a bad temper."

"I've noticed."

"You don't want to make her jealous."

"She shouldn't be. He and I simply enjoy each other's company. After all, we only met this morning when I had my diving lesson," I said. I surveyed the area and spotted someone else joining the party.

Arlene stood just past the pool deck. Catching my eye, she nodded. I moved closer to the middle, staying back from the edge so I wouldn't distract Constance. Thompson followed me, sticking to my side like a corn plaster. I heard Mallory give Constance instructions while he turned her around. He glanced around and caught sight of us two lifeguards standing ready if any problems occurred.

"If this works you need to make a big fuss over her," I murmured to Thompson.

"Of course!" He crossed his fingers. Thankfully, he did not chuckle.

"Are you ready?" Mallory asked, his baritone carrying in the warm, windless evening.

Constance, taking a breath deep enough to inflate a party balloon, nodded. Mallory submerged, lifted her feet on his shoulders, and slowly rose.

She did not dive but she did jump.

"*You did it!*" Thompson yelled, applauding with the rest of the crowd. She gestured for him to join her. He did a shallow entry dive, surfacing next to her, and gave her a big hug. She laughed, wrapped her arms around his neck, and kissed him.

"Everybody into the pool!" Constance commanded, waving her arm like a semaphore. "This is a swimming party!"

The rest of the guests treated her words like royal decree. Mallory, however, demonstrated an enviable crawl to the side and pulled himself out. We stood observing the now-crowded pool while Arlene joined us.

"Wow," she said. "That was amazing. She's generally afraid to do anything but cling to the side of the pool."

"When did you come up?" I asked.

"I was down at the boathouse and heard a commotion, so I ran up the path to see what was going on."

"You missed my shining moment. It was the best dive I've ever done," I told her. "Oh well."

"Arlene, are we allowed to use the float at night?" Mallory asked.

"Sure. The lights are on along the beach and you can see what you're doing."

"Join us," I offered.

She regarded at the people in the pool. "I think I should stay here. Some of them look pretty drunk." She smiled. "I'm sorry I missed your dive. You'll have to show it to me tomorrow. Normally, I don't allow horseplay in the water, so I'll make an exception."

"Oh! I'm sorry," I apologized. "I forgot about that. If it helps, we were the only two people in the pool at the time. Plus it did get her into the water."

"We're going to swim out to the float. See you later!" Mallory called Constance, who happily paddled around, playing with Thompson. She waved and blew him a kiss.

We strolled to the boathouse. I decided to check the door; the knob easily turned.

"It's not locked," I told Mallory. I headed back to the pool to let Arlene know and ran into her heading toward me.

"The door!" we told each other.

She followed me back to where Mallory waited.

"We should check to make sure everything is secure," he suggested. "I would also like to see the diving equipment and reserve a time for us tomorrow with you as our guide. I think Lauren should do an open-water dive."

"Of course." She took us through, unlocked her inner office, and gasped.

12

No longer the neat office I visited, the scene in front of us looked like a cyclone went through it. Her chair lay overturned with papers strewn all over the floor and—

"Oh, *no!*" Arlene cried out.

The five remaining scuba regulators lay in a tangled heap on the floor.

"When was the last time you were in the boathouse?" Mallory asked.

"I was in the boathouse this afternoon, but I didn't come in here. I locked the main door before I took the Rosens waterskiing. I asked Gerald, one of the waiters, to spot for me."

"Jim told us Gerald was with you. What time were you here?" Mallory questioned.

"Steven and Doris asked for a late time, so we met here at six-thirty. I fitted the equipment, checked it out, and locked up before we left."

I set her chair upright. "What time did you hit the water and how long were you gone?"

"We were out from six forty-five to just past seven-thirty. I brought the skis into the boathouse, locked it, secured and covered the boat, and went to grab something to eat." Arlene grimaced. "I was starving, and figured the rest could wait. I came back after eating and was cleaning up when I heard the commotion at the pool. I didn't come into my office."

"When were you in here last?" I asked, kneeling and gathering more sheets.

"Mid-afternoon."

"Where do staff members eat?" Mallory asked.

"There's a small dining and break area in the staff dorm where we have our meals. Since our hours vary so much, the main dining area isn't always open. Also, if we eat in the break room, we don't have to pay for it."

I sorted some of the loose pages. "Arlene, where is the sheet with the serial numbers?"

"I have individual sheets listing each type of equipment with spaces for names and dates. I put the serial numbers on the back of the scuba sheet."

"It's not here." I grabbed more papers off the floor and rifled through them. "The other sheets, for water skiing, rowboats, and canoes are. No diving sheet."

Mallory examined the regulators. "Which ones showed tampering?"

"The ones with the chalk marks," Arlene said.

"Chalk marks?" he echoed, carefully examining each one. "I don't see any."

"Blast and bother!" I spat out, fuming. "Someone's onto the fact we're onto them."

"Try that again and make sense," Mallory requested.

"Someone knows that we know that something is going on," I replied, peeved. "Otherwise, why bother to do all this?" I gestured at the room.

"What's the serial number of the faulty regulator?" he asked, confident I would supply the answer.

"The leaky hose is on serial number 3721-2867-4538. The one that won't seat properly is serial number 4217-1840-2332."

"You remember that?" Arlene asked, amazed.

"Lauren's memory is phenomenal and works in some very strange ways," Mallory told her, "especially if something was spoken. Did she read them aloud?"

"Yes. I wrote down what she called out."

"You've heard of people with photographic memories for what they have read? Lauren has a memory for spoken words." Mallory scrutinized the regulator in his hand. "Ends in 4538?"

I nodded.

"Let's leave the mess," he suggested. "When we go out tomorrow, we'll double-check the numbers."

"Mr. Mallory?" Arlene's voice sounded anguished, ready to cry. "Should I report this?"

"I think you should notify Thompson you found your office vandalized and assure him that nothing is missing, but do it in the morning as if you found this when you opened up."

"Mr. M., you and I should be on the float if anyone comes searching for us, and I don't think Arlene should be here alone at night," I said, tossing the pages I held and watching them scatter.

He nodded and gently put his hand on Arlene's shoulder. "Why don't you head back to the pool?"

"I can't tell you how glad I am you're here," she said. She escorted us out and locked both boathouse doors. "This is too much for me." With a wan smile, she headed back to the pool.

"That's one worried girl," I remarked.

"She has reason to be," he quietly said.

Mallory and I enjoyed the swim out to the float.

"This is getting more and more bizarre," I said.

We stretched out on a couple of towels. The few ripples on the water lapped softly against the float, creating a gentle, rhythmic rocking sensation.

"We could be dealing with more than one threat."

"More than one threat coming from more than one direction," I grumbled. "It would be helpful, not to mention nice, if we could figure out who was planning to do what to whom. Right now, though, I'm a bit confused about Thompson."

"Something specific?"

"Several. First, when you took Constance into the water, he wondered how you managed to get her to do it. I marked that down to jealousy. Second, he was standing next to me when Constance did her jump. He literally held his breath with crossed fingers, and yelled 'you did it' after she jumped. Third, he kept getting her drinks even after she started getting tipsy."

"It does seem contradictory," he agreed. "I'm hoping he gets her drinks watered. I used to do that once in a while. I've noticed she's drinking more now."

"I admit most of this is matter for speculation. We do have a few facts. Authorities ruled Vera's death a simple drowning accident and death by misadventure."

"His first wife's death was also ruled misadventure, although it was apparently caused by faulty equipment."

"What Arlene found makes me wonder if the equipment in Florida had help becoming faulty, yet there wasn't enough evidence to change either that verdict or Vera's." I shook my head. "Sticking to what's going on now, we have uncovered more damaged equipment. I think we should determine if any of this is related to Vera's so-called accident."

Mallory nodded. "I concur. The two diving deaths do seem to form a pattern, especially now with the added complication of vandalism. We know someone broke into the boathouse and found the sheet with the serial numbers of the bad regulators, therefore whoever did the tampering must realize we are not convinced all this is accidental or coincidence."

"Yes, but who is the target? Constance doesn't dive and I doubt she could tamper with the equipment." I scowled my frustration and sat up. "All this could be smoke and shadows. Nothing makes sense as a whole picture."

"There's the possibility that whoever tampered with the diving gear wanted to kill Vera and is now done." Mallory turned on his side to face me.

"I considered that and tossed it out."

"Why did you reject it?"

"If that's the case and it's over, why didn't the bad guy simply steal the remaining damaged regulators and pass it off as a straight theft? They were even marked. Why break in and go through all the effort to throw papers around, steal the sheet with the recorded numbers, and leave the regulators themselves?"

"I admit it's puzzling. How many keys are there to the boathouse?"

I related Arlene's information. "No help there."

"Three extra keys and over five hours? Danny is not going to like this, especially since we don't have any new solid evidence to reopen the Campbell case."

"Unless—" I frowned in concentration. "We could be missing something major. Speaking of Mr. O'Brien. Are you going to tell me what he said over the phone or do I have to wait for him to show up tomorrow and ask him directly?"

"Lauren, I'm trying to decide what to do about it. Until I do you'll have to be patient." His voice, although calm, held a steeled intonation which he used whenever pressing him further would not change his mind.

"Danny lobbed a ball into my court, and I'm not sure how to handle it. He got a tip about some confidential information and I'm trying to figure out how to use it, or even if we should."

"Let's hope the switchboard operator didn't listen on her line."

"I don't think so. I gave it a slow count of ten after he disconnected to listen for any additional clicks."

"May I change the subject?"

"Please do."

"May I ask how you met Constance? She's being overly conspicuous about her interest in you, and I'm curious."

"When Caroline died, I bought the house on Long Island but it took me a couple of months to realize I couldn't simply bury myself in work and raising Julie." He chuckled. "I never realized what fun meeting neighbors could be."

"Let's leave the apple tree out of this, please? I remember my mom told me to not pester anyone with questions about why Julie didn't have a mother." I grimaced. "It wasn't easy. You know I like asking questions."

"Do I ever," he chuckled. "You and Julie became thicker than honey on a cold morning. Mrs. Fiddler once told me that if I had to look for Julie, I should start at your house."

"Mom used to say the same thing to Dad," I told him. "Go on."

"Two years after the move, I also realized the war with Germany would engulf this country. I went into the Army and luckily ended up stationed in New York City. I knew Mrs. Fiddler was capable of taking care of Julie during any absences that arose although I managed to get home most weekends. Occasionally I had to stay in town." He smiled at me. "You know I keep a permanent suite at the hotel."

"Julie described it to me. It sounds sumptuous."

"It has all the comforts of home and more, considering room service. The next time I take you girls to a show, we'll stay overnight." His smile faded. "The hotel's bar is a well-known watering hole. Constance wandered in one Friday evening, evidently between regular escorts. I bought her a couple of drinks, and we talked. The next evening I took her to dinner. She was vivacious and charming while I was lonely and feeling sorry for myself. We dated steadily for about three months before her father called me for a one-on-one meeting. Since I had already met her parents multiple times, I suspected I was in for a serious talk."

"And?"

"Although he and his wife liked and respected me personally, he made it clear he had reservations about allowing me to continue to see Constance. According to him, she was pushing for his approval to marry me."

"Did Julie ever meet Constance?"

"No. I wasn't going to bring Julie into the relationship until I could be absolutely certain it was permanent." He sat up, put his arms around his knees, and stared straight ahead with his face grimly set. I heard his voice harden. "I had a few nagging doubts of my own before her father intervened."

"Does Constance know her father stepped in?"

"I can't say for sure. From my viewpoint his timing was excellent. I received orders to go overseas for a month, so the relationship might have cooled on its own. Constance cannot bear to be alone. When I got back, I discovered she was dating Doug Ambrose. She called me once or twice to try to get together again but I was genuinely tied up. Shortly afterward, she married Doug.

He died three years ago in a car accident, according to Danny. Thinking back on the entire romance, if you want to call it that, I'm glad it didn't work."

"Thank you for filling in a few gaps."

"Lauren, you know you can ask me anything at any time." His gaze shifted to me. His expression softened and he smiled. "If it's something I don't want to discuss, I'll let you know."

"I didn't want to pry, yet with her making eyes at you while she groped her Eddie, it seemed to be the question to ask."

"Groped? Are you serious?"

"You weren't watching her in the pool before we left. She had her hands all over him yet I also noticed she occasionally glanced at you to see if you were watching. I would have thought she'd be more discreet yet she's throwing it in Thompson's face."

"I didn't notice." He frowned. "If she is trying to play us off against each other, you could be right about my position being a tad precarious. You and Danny are two of a kind," he concluded with a laugh.

"I'm not sure why that amuses you."

"Take it as a definite compliment." He caught the expression of skepticism on my face. "Believe me, I meant it that way. I'm not sure—"

"Yooohooo! Robert!" Above the rustling of small waves hitting the shore, Constance's voice drifted across to us, cutting off his thought.

"Do people really say yooohooo?" I mumbled. We looked toward the beach.

Thompson walked to the water's edge with Constance in tow.

"Ready or not, here we come!" Thompson called out with a wave of his hand. He stumbled and fell onto the sand.

"Do people really say *that*?" Mallory echoed. We watched them flounder into the low surf.

"Is it too late to swim back?" I murmured. "We could pass them on the way."

"I think we're stuck for now."

I kept an eye on the pair swimming out ready to intervene if necessary, a habit I acquired from my lifeguard training. I concluded drinks continued to flow following our departure from the party. They reached the float and Mallory extended his hand to help Constance. Thompson's foot slipped at the top of the ladder and he fell back into the water.

"Whoops! I'm okay," he giggled. "Be right there." He giggled again.

"My second triumph of the night," Constance announced, leaning against Mallory and draping her arms around his neck. "Aren't you going to congratulate me?"

She swayed, her eyes rolled up, and she limply slid to the deck before Mallory could catch her.

We barely exchanged glances when I heard an odd gurgle from the water. I peered over the edge of the float and looked back at Mallory. "Trouble." I slipped into the water, did a surface dive, and hauled Thompson to the surface.

"He's out cold but he's breathing," I called up to Mallory. "Let me swim him to shore. Turn her on her side in case she retches. Once I get him on the beach, I'll come back."

"You're the lifeguard."

"Good thing, too."

I swam Constance and Thompson safely to the beach and flopped onto the smooth, still-warm sand, and took a moment to catch my breath.

"I can't say this will rank as my favorite way to spend an evening." I shivered in the slight breeze playing over the water.

"If I had a coin I'd toss you for which of us stays while the other goes for help." Mallory knelt by Constance's side. "She seems to be okay for the moment. We need to get them to their cabins."

"Agreed, and we can't do that alone." I crawled over to check Thompson. "He's breathing regularly and his pulse is strong. Let's prop him up slightly so he's not flat on his back. Keep Constance on her side." I stood. "I'll run up to the clubhouse—it'll help me warm up. Janet told me the main switchboard is there."

I found the small office in a corner of the building and popped my head in the doorway. Janet, seated at the elbow of an older woman in front of a switchboard, glanced up in surprise.

"Sorry to interrupt! Mr. Mallory and I need some help at the beach." I briefly outlined the situation.

"Do you want me to call a doctor?" Mildred (according to her name tag) asked, pulling up one of the board's wires.

"I think we should get them to bed before we make that decision," I replied. "They were both drinking pretty heavily and decided to swim out to the float. If you'll pardon me for being blunt, it was Grade-A stupid of them. Maybe we should see if we can handle this quietly, without alarming the guests."

The operator nodded. "Let me know. I have a list of local physicians in case we have to call one."

Janet spoke up. "Mrs. Abernathy, let me go get Jim. He left here a few minutes ago and he should still be up. Between the four of us, we should be able to get them to their cabins." She left at a trot.

"We'll need keys to the cabins. Mrs. Abernathy, can you call Carmella?"

She nodded. "That shouldn't be a problem. I'll have her meet you at the cabins."

I returned to the beach and found Mallory talking to a very groggy Edward Thompson.

"I don't understand," Thompson mumbled. He gingerly put his hands to his temples, holding his head like it might fall off if he let go. "I just don't understand." He giggled and slumped back to the sand.

"Help is coming." I murmured. I bent over Constance. Her pulse felt normal and I counted slow, regular breaths.

Jim ran onto the beach.

"Over here!" I hailed him and waved.

"Janet should be right behind me," he said. "What can I do to help?"

"Someone needs to stay with Edward while you and I carry Mrs. Ambrose to her cabin," Mallory explained to him.

"Sorry to be late!" Janet announced, running up a bit breathless. "I stopped by the switchboard to let Mrs. Abernathy know I found Jim. Carmella will meet us at the cabins."

"Lauren, I'd like you to come with us," Mallory suggested, "if Janet will stay here with Edward."

"That's fine," she agreed.

"He's not making much sense, but he is more or less conscious," Mallory told her. "Jim and I will be back as soon as we get Constance into bed."

13

Mallory and Jim took turns carrying Constance to the large owner's cabin, located near the front entrance. Carmella waited for us, pacing between it and the slightly smaller manager's cabin.

"I unlocked both cabins," she explained, opening the door to Constance's cabin. "I didn't know which one you'd need first."

"We appreciate that," I said. "Um, Robert, why don't you and Jim bring Thompson to his place? Carmella and I can manage here." *I need to get more comfortable calling him Robert.*

Between us we got Constance into a nightgown. Once we settled her in bed, I checked the basics: pulse, breathing, pupillary reaction. Something about her condition bothered me. Intoxication explained only part of it; she also looked drugged.

"Carmella, see if the guys have gotten Mr. Thompson to bed."

"We have," Jim's voice issued from the main room. "Mr. Mallory sent me to see if you two needed any help."

"How's Mr. Thompson?" Carmella asked once we moved out of the bedroom.

"He's awake and acting strange," Jim admitted, "sort of goofy and silly."

"Lauren, may I see you outside for a moment?" Mallory called from the porch. "Jim and Carmella can stay inside."

We chose a spot between the two cabins.

"I'm worried. Frankly, I don't think they are simply drunk," I reported. "Constance is still out cold, and her pupils are sluggish to react."

"Thompson is high, and it's not just alcohol. He insists he only had two drinks." Mallory glanced back at the owner's cabin. "Does she need a doctor? She hates them."

"Did she retch when you were on the float?"

"Yes, she did. I got her to the side, so it went into the water. It was as close to consciousness as she came."

"In that case, my guess is she can safely sleep off the effects. We need to check both bathrooms for pills."

"What are we looking for?"

"Uppers. Downers. Anything that could have been given in alcohol."

"Good idea.Can we send the others back to bed?"

"What time is it?"

Mallory checked his watch. "It's not quite eleven-thirty."

"We can't leave our two charges alone, and I think we could use some official help."

"I concur. Danny?"

I nodded.

"Let's try this," he said, thinking aloud. "I'll go to the switchboard and call Danny. I want to ask him to get background information on Janet, Jim, and Carmella."

"Background information?"

"I want to make sure we know who the players are in this mess. We also need last names."

"Mrs. Abernathy can provide their last names. I don't think we should broadcast what actually happened. We can fill Mr. O'Brien in on details privately tomorrow."

"I don't think we need him tonight, do you?" Mallory asked.

"Not unless something else goes wrong. Mr. O'Brien needs to bring all that with him when he gets here. We can let the trio go when you get back and proceed to check for drugs."

"You realize all this could have been accidental."

"What are the chances?" I asked. I sounded cynical, even to me.

"Slim to none." He sighed sadly and put his hands on my shoulders. "Are you okay?"

"I'll be fine. Go. It's going to be a long night."

Mallory headed off to the clubhouse. I shivered. It dawned on me that he and I still wore our suits and I figured clothes would be a big help.

"Miss Kaye?" Carmella called softly from the doorway of the owner's cabin. "I think she's waking up."

I entered the cabin, taking time to notice Constance enjoyed a lovely home-away-from-home. The main area sported a better quality of rustic furniture than my room; the kitchenette looked much nicer than the one in my studio apartment. Decent artwork, mostly scenic, graced the walls. A display of photos decorated the top of a roll-top desk, mostly family. One was an old-fashioned black and white wedding portrait in a silver frame. Another frame held a picture of her with Thompson, a nightclub shot judging by the formal clothes and champagne glasses.

Carmella stayed in the doorway of the bedroom with Jim behind her.

"While I do this, Jim, would you check on Mr. Thompson?" I sat on the edge of the double bed. Although unconscious, Constance moaned when I pinched her arm. "You're right. She is coming out of it." I blessed the first aid course I took with my lifeguard certification.

"Miss Kaye, I know Constance likes to drink, but this is awful! Will she be okay?"

"I'm not a doctor, but I think so. Carmella, would you stay with her a little longer? I want to run back to my room and change. I'm chilly. If Mr. Mallory returns before I do, would you tell him where I've gone?"

"No problem. Are you going to stay with her for the night?"

"Yes. I think someone should, don't you?"

She nodded. "She was drugged, wasn't she?"

"Hard to say." I shivered again, not only from the temperature.

"Is Janet in Mr. Thompson's cabin?" Carmella hesitantly asked.

"Uh-huh. Mr. Mallory left to take care of something, and once he gets back you three can get some sleep."

"Miss Kaye," she began.

I held up my hand. "Carmella, call me Lauren, please?"

"Lauren," she flashed a brief shy smile, "you should know that Janet has a big crush on Mr. Thompson."

"Does she? Interesting. I'll be back as quickly as I can. Thanks for helping out."

I walked along the pathway to Lodge Two and ran into Mallory on his way back.

"Carmella will stay with Constance while I change," I told him. He had changed and now wore the casual slacks and shirt from earlier in the day.

"I'll tell you about Danny's explosion when you get back."

I took off my zories. Barefoot, I ran the rest of the way to the Lodge and nodded to the concierge at the desk. Halfway down the hall I remembered I did not have my key. In fact, I could not remember where I saw it last. *Bother! I'll deal with that later.* I returned to the desk.

"Hello, I'm your somewhat cold guest," I greeted her. "You're Dorothy. You showed me to my room yesterday."

"I remember. You do look chilled," she agreed with a smile.

"It's been a hectic evening, and I confess I have lost track of my key. I need to get some clothes on and I'm throwing myself on your mercy."

"You're not the first and you won't be the last," she kindly assured me, handing me a key. "Here you are. Room eight."

I tossed, "Thank you," over my shoulder while I sprinted to the end of the hall.

I stripped out of my suit, toweled off, and put on the sundress and sandals from earlier in the day. Undoing the braid and giving my hair a quick brush, I knew it would once more dry on its own. Grabbing my sweater, I locked my door. Heading back down the hall, my key hit the counter at the same moment the phone rang.

"She's right here." Dorothy handed me the instrument. "It's for you."

"What a surprise." With a resigned sigh, I took the handset. "Hello?"

"Lauren, what the devil is going on there?" An irate and familiar voice boomed my ear.

"Oh, hello! How did you get the idea something might be up?"

"I got a call from Danny O'Brien. He wanted to know if I think you are a nitwit," Slater expounded.

"What did you tell him?" I felt this would not be a good time to ask how they knew each other.

"I said if you were acting oddly enough for him to ask me, he needed to decide for himself because I wasn't going to say a word." My boss took a deep breath. "You haven't answered my question."

"I don't have time. Robert Mallory is waiting for me," I informed him while I did some very fast thinking. "Good b—."

"*Wait just a blasted minute!*" he yelled, cutting me off.

"Ouch! We have our hands full. I promise we'll call you as soon as we can."

"Lauren, if you don't—"

"I know. If I don't show up Monday I'm fired." I hung up and looked at Dorothy. "My boss thinks he owns me."

"Some bosses are like that," she said with a knowing smile.

I finished warming up by running back to Constance's place and joined Mallory, Carmella, and Jim gathered between the two cabins.

"Where's Janet?" I asked, surveying the group.

"Lauren, you're not overly predictable, but I'm pleased to say I called that one." Mallory chuckled. "She's in the cabin with Thompson. I'm considering letting her stay there."

"It would keep her off the switchboard, but I think you'd be a better choice," I said. "I had a phone call or I would have been here sooner. Mr. Slater wanted to know what was up."

"Did Danny call him?"

"Oh, yes. Mr. O'Brien had called to ask a question. Mr. Slater sort of imploded all over me."

"That's what Danny did to me." Mallory nodded to the two kids. "By the way, they have figured out we've known each other longer than sixteen hours."

"I gathered. For the record, it's been about eleven years." I responded. "How's Constance?"

"I'd like you to check on her."

"Carmella, would you come with me? There are a couple of questions I'd like to ask you."

"Sure."

I found Constance sleeping fairly normally for someone who consumed an unknown combination of drugs and alcohol. We left the bedroom and sat in the living room.

"Did her family send you here to keep an eye on her?" I asked.

"You guessed?"

"Call it a reasoned-out hunch." I regarded the pretty girl fidgeting nervously on the settee next to me. "Is this normal? To have someone on hand all the time?"

"Constance has—problems. She's my cousin—my mother is her father's youngest sister— although we've never been close. My uncle thought it would be a good idea if someone from the family was around. I did need the job, so it all worked out." Carmella sighed. "It gets complicated remembering to not act as family."

"I can imagine. You were concerned about drugs. Does she take any?"

"She's supposed to take some kind of tranquilizers, at least that's what I understood from Uncle Vincenzo. Her doctors have warned her not to mix the medication with alcohol, but she does it anyway."

"So tonight could have been an accident."

"It happened once before, unfortunately, but this time it's much worse." Carmella shuddered.

"Where does Janet fit in?"

"That's simple," she grimaced. "Janet wants Mr. Thompson. I think he gives her enough encouragement to convince her that he wants her, too."

"Swell. Does Constance know?" I guessed no, although I waited for her answer.

"I doubt it. Janet still has her job."

"Constance is that possessive?" *No surprise if she is.*

"I remember going to a family party when I was a kid. Constance showed up with Mr. Mallory, and another woman started flirting with him. Mr. Mallory didn't go along with it, he's too much of a gentleman for that, but Constance was livid. I overheard them in the ladies' lounge at the hotel. Constance gave her a good dressing-down. That woman has never been invited to another family affair. If Constance knew about Janet and Mr. Thompson, Janet would be out on her rear, fast. Constance has a bad temper, she's vindictive, and she generally gets her own way." Carmella shyly smiled. "I think you should know that of all the men I've seen with Constance, Mr. Mallory was my favorite. I recognized him right away."

"What about her husband?"

"Doug Ambrose was nice, very patient, and I think he loved her deeply. But she married him on her father's orders. She resented it and treated him badly. He worked for the family business, as some sort of accountant, I think. Uncle arranged the marriage so she'd have someone to keep an eye on her. Doug died in a car crash three years ago."

"One more thing," I said, filing that tidbit away for future thought. "Does Constance know you're the family eyes placed here by her father?"

Carmella hesitated, biting her lip. "Lauren, do you know what family we're discussing?"

"Only in a general sense. I could easily find out, although I don't plan to investigate it. My guess is you got this job because Constance wouldn't suspect you."

"Mr. Mallory mentioned that you are good at these things." She grinned; it lit up her face so she actually looked like a college kid. "Yes, my uncle called my mother to arrange it, and when Constance saw my application she told Mr. Thompson to hire me."

"All secrets and hidden agreements are now safely tucked away, right?" I smiled and she nodded. "Good. I'm changing the subject. Has Jim asked you out yet?"

"Jim?" She fidgeted some more and blushed beet-red, the gaze of her large brown eyes dropping from my face to the floor. "Uh, no—"

"Well, when this is over, if he does ask, say yes." I chuckled. "He's nice.Now, get some sleep. We'll take it from here."

I walked out with her and reported my conclusions about Constance. Mallory extracted Janet from Thompson's cabin, and we sent the three of them back to the staff's quarters. Jim and Carmella took off together. Janet told us she would detour for a word with Mrs. Abernathy first.

"There's something I want. I'll be right back," Mallory told me. He strode toward the terrace, returning with a couple of folding chairs and my cover-up shirt. He set the chairs on the grass between the cabins. "Better," he commented while we made ourselves more comfortable. "I was getting tired of standing. Have you got anything else I should know about this?"

I gave him a summary of my conversations with Slater and Carmella.

"Is that the confidential information O'Brien dug up? Constance has some major psychological problems and her family sent someone to keep an eye on her?" I asked.

"In broad terms, yes. You've got the gist, although there are a few specifics."

"How's Edward doing?"

"He's sleeping now. I think someone hit him with a form of amphetamine, and his system went a bit haywire between that and the alcohol."

"Speed?" I whistled. "That would explain the goofy, giggling behavior. Very dangerous with alcohol. What did you find in his bathroom cabinet?"

"If this venture doesn't work, he could open a drug counter. It's full of vitamins, aspirin, and cough syrup. I didn't see any amphetamines or tranquilizers. In fact, there are no prescriptions of any sort. What did you find in hers?"

"Several prescription bottles for things I can't pronounce. According to Carmella, they are probably some form of tranquilizer. Did O'Brien get a diagnosis?"

"He's working on it."

"When will he get here?"

"Undoubtedly sooner than we want to get up. He told me he'll find me." Mallory gazed down at me as we stood. "Will you be able to manage Constance?"

"If the telephone in Thompson's cabin rings, don't bother to answer it. Just show up!"

14

I dreamt someone mistook my head for a maraca.

"Hey, sleepyhead, time to wake up!" Mallory shook my shoulder. My head wobbled accordingly, which explained the sensation in my dream.

"Why?" I crossly returned. I sat up and stretched; it proved to be a mistake. Sleeping on the short settee in Constance's living room left me feeling like a pretzel.

"Thompson is up and demanding to see Constance. I thought I'd wake you first."

"She would appreciate being awakened by you more than by me," I mumbled. "What time is it?"

"Almost seven-thirty." He glanced at the doorway. "Tell you what: let's both go." He stretched out his hand.

I grabbed it and he pulled me to my feet. Fatigue combined with my normal klutziness, resulting in a repeat of the poolside incident without the water and splash. I stumbled, and he steadied me. I sighed, resting my head on his chest, thankful he only snickered.

"How cozy." Constance leaned against the door frame of her bedroom, her voice oozing feigned saccharine. "Robert, I was under the impression you have your own cabin. Why do you need mine for your romantic pursuits?"

"Constance, how much do you remember of what happened last night?" Mallory asked, letting go of me once he was certain I would stay upright.

"We were at the adult swim. I jumped off your shoulders, and—" She frowned, searching her memory. "I think Eddie and I swam out to the float."

"You did. After you climbed the ladder, you passed out," Mallory said.

He guided her to the settee and placed her with her back to the room. I perched on the chair in front of the desk, out of her sight.

Mallory continued, "We brought you back here, and Lauren stayed with you."

"That was nice of her." Constance reluctantly admitted. "What happened to Eddie?"

"He's in his cabin. He had a rough night, too, but he's fine. I told him to wait until you were up before he came in."

"How bad was I? Did you call a doctor?" she asked, her voice suddenly fearful. "Robert, you didn't, did you?" she begged, reaching for his hand. "Please? Tell me you didn't call a doctor."

"We thought about it, but you both seemed to be okay. We decided to let you sleep it off, periodically checking on you." Mallory smiled at her.

"Thank God. I *hate* doctors." Her shoulders slumped. "I got sick, didn't I?"

He nodded. "You retched out on the float and that may have saved your life. You shouldn't mix your medication with alcohol."

"Robert, I'm sorry. It was my own doing and I was snapping at you." Constance frowned again. "I don't think I took my medicine yesterday. If I'm going to be drinking, I usually don't. I can't always remember what happens, but I haven't been that bad in a long time."

"Do you remember anything about what you did at the pool? Lauren and I left while you were in the water."

"We got out shortly after you left and we went to get a round of drinks. I spilled mine, so Eddie gave me his and he went back into the water. I got him another one while he swam for a few more minutes."

Startled, I snapped wide awake in a split second. *What in blazes? We'll have to go over that again. For crying out loud, it can't be that simple! It would explain a few things, yet it opens more questions than it answers.*

Mallory's eyes never left her face and although his expression did not change, his shoulders tensed. I knew him almost as well as he knew me, and I figured he also caught the implications.

"Can you get dressed? You should have something to eat," he encouraged.

"I'm all right now." She got up and gazed down at him. "Thank you for not hating me."Without waiting for a reply, she returned to her bedroom and shut the door.

"Let's go," he murmured, firmly taking my arm. "You need tea and I need coffee."

We headed up the pathway to the clubhouse. Jim greeted us at the door.

"Morning. Your usual table, Miss Kaye? I'll have your tea out soon."

"Jim, after last night, make it Lauren," I told him. "Mr. Mallory prefers coffee."

"Coming up."

"He's very good at his job," I said while we seated ourselves. "He told me he's going to look for a job after the summer season. Do you have the same notion I have?"

"Probably. It wouldn't be the first time we have thought alike." He gazed out the window. "Uh-oh. Danny is charging up the pathway. We're going to need a bigger table."

161

I followed his gaze. Mallory used the term *charging* and it accurately described O'Brien's gait. He resembled Teddy Roosevelt going up San Juan Hill. We requested a larger table. O'Brien walked in while Jim moved us to a table for four.

"Coffee, sir?" Jim asked the newcomer.

"Please." O'Brien waited until Jim vanished into the kitchen before starting in on us. "What in Hades were you two up to last night?" His low voice held plenty of force.

"Not yet, not here," Mallory murmured.

"Good morning, Mrs. Abernathy!" I called out when the operator exited her office and waved. "I want to thank you for your assistance last night."

"I'm glad it all worked out," she replied with a yawn, coming to the table. "Pardon me. I just got off duty, and I'm heading for my room." She wished us a good day and left.

"I know that voice," O'Brien said. "She's the switchboard operator."

I nodded. "She was a big help last night. She kept track of everything going on, including who was where, and managed to find people when they were needed."

Jim brought out a tray with a big coffee carafe, a smaller one with a tea tag hanging out of it, a small pitcher of milk, and three mugs.

"The buffet is open," he announced. "Plates are at the beginning of the line. If you would rather have something cooked to order, I have been instructed to arrange it." He nodded to the owner's table.

Thompson put his newspaper down and joined us. "I don't know how to thank you for what you did last night," he said earnestly, shaking hands with Mallory and me. "I'm not exactly sure what happened, but I'm fairly certain I wouldn't be here if you hadn't been out on the float." He turned to me. "I understand you got me out of the water after I lost consciousness."

"I told you I'm a lifeguard. Pulling you out of the water seemed the thing to do."

"Thank God." He shuddered. "Thank *you*. And thank you, Robert, for staying with me all night. I'm still a bit shaky." He chuckled; I wished he would skip it.It really grated this early in the morning.

"Get something to eat," Mallory told him. "It'll help."

"If you want something and don't see it on the buffet, just ask. Jim has orders to cater to you both." He headed back to his table, stopped, turned around, and returned. Pulling out the empty chair so he could sit, he smiled at me. "There is one other thing. Lauren, we're going to have an empty cabin for the next two nights. I'd like to move you into it, no extra charge, to thank you."

"Out of curiosity, which cabin is it?" Mallory inquired.

"Number Four. It's down by the water near the boathouse, right behind yours."

"Let me think about it," I told the manager. "I appreciate the offer."

"Where will I be?" asked O'Brien.

"Number Ten. It's directly opposite Number Five on the other side of the clubhouse."

Thompson smiled and stood. Returning the chair to its place, he retired back to his table. Thankfully, he refrained from chuckling again. The more I heard it, the more irritating it got.

"Well, whatever happened seems to have made you a heroine," O'Brien said wryly to me. "I wish I knew what it was."

"Let's check the buffet," suggested Mallory. "After a night like that, we need nice, normal things like bacon and eggs."

"If you're not going to tell me what happened, the least you could do is quit referring to it," groused O'Brien.

Mallory chuckled, a much nicer sound than Thompson's irksome cackle.

Constance entered while we perused the buffet. Spotting Mallory, she advanced and draped herself around him, forcing him to put his arms around her. He started to lose his grip on his plate and I made a quick grab for it. O'Brien snorted.

"Robert," she purred, blithely ignoring the rest of the world, "I want to thank you again for what you did for me last night. You saved my life," she theatrically affirmed.

Standing in line with the resort's owner draped around his neck, Mallory's expression mingled embarrassment and annoyance while he unsuccessfully tried to extricate himself. O'Brien stood back and gestured for me to make a move. I handed the two plates to Jim and crooked my head toward our table; he nodded. I managed to slip between the buffet and Mallory, weaseling my way around his living scarf.

"Constance," I said sweetly, taking Mallory's arm and forcing her to let go, "it's good to see you up and around. Robert," I continued in the same breath while I snuggled a bit closer, "Jim has taken our plates to the table. We should eat before it gets cold."

"We'll see you later," he told Constance.

I dropped my grip on his arm and he slipped it around my waist as we walked to our table. O'Brien followed us, snickering.

Once seated, I regarded Mallory. "Bother! I'll be blasted if I'm going back to the line," I told him. He rolled his eyes in response. I signaled our waiter.

"Jim," I asked when he stopped at the table, "would you please pick out some well-done bacon for me, and bring a couple of pieces of rye toast?"

"Sure thing! Mr. Mallory, is there anything else you want?"

"I'll have some of her toast," he said. "Danny, did you get syrup for your pancakes?"

"No, there was someone in the way so I couldn't reach it," O'Brien sardonically observed.

"I'll be right back," Jim told us, barely managing to repress a smile.

I ate automatically; the hot tea proved exactly what I needed. While we lingered over third cups of caffeine, I asked my tablemates if I should stay in the Lodge or move to the offered cabin.

Mallory said, "Move." at the same time O'Brien said, "Stay."

"You two are so helpful it's painful," I said. I gazed at O'Brien. "Something we don't know yet?"

He nodded. "Tell Thompson you're mulling it over. I want to meet Arlene and anyone else who got involved in whatever it was that happened last night that I don't know about yet."

"Lauren and I are going diving this morning," Mallory told him. "Arlene will be down at the boathouse."

"At the moment, however, she's coming in the door," I murmured, "and heading our way. Remember, we told her to report the problem in the morning."

O'Brien sourly muttered, "There you go again," but refrained from making any further comments when Arlene stopped at our table.

"Mr. Mallory, you reserved scuba gear for this morning," she began, "and I wanted to see what time you wanted to dive." She pulled out the chair Thompson used. "We weren't the last ones in the boathouse last night," she informed us, lowering her voice. "Someone put everything back. If I go by what I found this morning, I have nothing to report."

"I thought we'd book the dive time starting around eleven?" Mallory replied, his face reflecting the difficulty of trying to think along two lines simultaneously.

"Sounds good," she agreed in normal tones. "Should I report it?" she continued, again lowering her voice.

"No. It would let someone know we know the place had been tossed," I softly commented. I looked at the two men. "Agreed?"

"Why not," said O'Brien. "I'll go along with you—at least until you tell me what you're talking about."

"I'll see you at the boathouse around ten forty-five," Arlene confirmed, rising. "Thank you!"

The three of us departed the clubhouse. O'Brien headed for the office to check in and get settled. Mallory and I strolled down to the boathouse to gauge the new situation.

Once more neat and tidy, Arlene's office looked normal. She sat at her desk, totally dejected.

"I don't understand any of this," she moaned. "Vera died, yes, and I don't believe it was an accident, but the rest of this! It's so scary. By the way, the second tampered regulator should be okay to use. I changed the O-ring."

"I'm afraid you landed in the middle of this confused tangle. If it's any help, I don't think calling Lauren in made it worse," Mallory consoled her with evident sympathy.

"Whoever it was—no, hold a moment. I'm getting tired of saying 'someone' or 'whoever it was,'" I announced. "In all the old mystery movies, the guilty party was always assumed to be the butler. I'm going to call our bad guy the butler. What do you think?"

"It's fine with me," he agreed. "You are saying the butler vandalized the boathouse?"

"And possibly arranged Vera's death and drugged some drinks."

"He's been a busy boy," Mallory commented.

"Yes, even if he's a she," I sourly stated.

A knock sounded on the outer door and O'Brien came through to the inner office. Mallory officially introduced him to Arlene.

"What in Hades is going on?" the policeman demanded without preamble. He glanced around the small office. "This place doesn't look as if it has been vandalized."

"It was," Mallory informed his friend while Arlene and I nodded our confirmation. "Papers all over the place, regulators in a heap on the floor, overturned chair—"

"Yet it was all back in place this morning?"

Arlene nodded again.

"Tell me what happened yesterday." O'Brien commanded Arlene. He perched on a corner of her desk.

She recapped her movements with the water skiers and recounted how we found the place a mess during the adult swim.

"How many members were at the resort, staying over?"

"Besides Mr. Mallory and Lauren, there were the Tyler family of five, the Rosens, the Williams, Mrs. Watson, Mrs. McKenzie, and Mrs. Stevenson." At his puzzled look, she explained, "We usually get some women guests during the week who are joined by their husbands on the weekend. There were also some members at the pool party who didn't stay the night."

"If we make the assumption that the guests are not involved, how many people were running around last night?"

"Besides us, Thompson, and Constance Ambrose, there were three. Carmella, Janet, and Jim were involved," I supplied.

"When did you go back to your room?" O'Brien asked Arlene.

"I went back to the pool to make sure the gates were closed at eleven and helped put the bar cart away. I left Gerald, George, and Jim to finish cleaning up, and I headed for bed. I was out a minute after my head hit the pillow."

"What about keys?"

While I listened to Arlene explain where the keys were it occurred to me I still missed mine. I grabbed the over-shirt I wore to the adult swim and checked the pocket. No key.

"Excuse me for interrupting. Mr. Mallory? Did you take a key out of the shirt pocket when you brought it to Constance's cabin?"

"No. Why?"

"When we left the women's lodge last night for the adult swim, I put my key in the pocket of my shirt. It's not there now."

"How did you get into your room to change after we got Constance in bed?" Mallory inquired.

"Dorothy, the night concierge, let me have a spare which I returned to the desk."

"You're saying the key to your room is missing?" O'Brien demanded.

"Yes. I left the cover-up at the pool when we went down to the boathouse, and from there we went straight out to the float. After I towed Constance and Thompson back to the beach, I went for help—"

"Hold," O'Brien interrupted. "I'll get all that later. Where was the shirt?"

"Poolside," Mallory supplied. "I found it when I went for chairs so we could sit outside and still be able to hear our patients. I brought the shirt to the cabins with the chairs."

O'Brien rubbed his face with his hands and sighed. "Arlene, is there anything else you can tell me about the break-in here?"

"No, I don't think so."

"If something occurs to you, let me know. Who are Janet, Jim, and Carmella?"

"Jim's the waiter we had this morning, Carmella is one of the housekeepers, and Janet is a concierge at Lodge Two. Janet is also training on the switchboard," I offered.

"Those are the people you asked for background on," he stated, turning to Mallory for confirmation. "Okay, you two," he continued, looking at me and Mallory, "let's talk in Robert's cabin." He made it an order.

"We'll be back in an hour or so," Mallory told Arlene.

Cabin Five sat next to the boathouse. Once settled in the living area—nice yet nowhere near the nice of Constance's place—the policeman leaned back in his chair.

"All right, let's have it. What in blazing Hades was going on last night? I mean the rest of it."

Mallory and I recounted the sequence of events.

"Congratulations. This quagmire is about as clear as mud," O'Brien said once we finished. He ran his hand through his hair and looked at me. "You say you had a talk with Carmella."

I relayed it.

"A word for word report? Do you do that often?" O'Brien skeptically inquired.

"It's the way my memory works," I explained, which Mallory seconded. "You now have what we know. What have you got for us?"

"You already know the background on Thompson?"

"Mr. Mallory briefed me on what you told him."

"We're still trying to ascertain his real name, but I'd wager Edward Thompson isn't it. I haven't found anything on Janet Benedict, but Carmella Viscotti is exactly who she claims to be. So is Jim Pomeroy." O'Brien paused. "Now, about your key."

"It could be anywhere around the pool if it fell out of my pocket," I offered.

"Or in someone's pocket," O'Brien suggested.

"There's a concierge on duty at all times," I pointed out. "If the butler has it, it would have to be a 'she' in order to use it."

"Butler?"

"Lauren decided she is going to refer to the perpetrator as the butler," Mallory explained with a grin.

"As in, 'the butler did it' I suppose," he mumbled. "Well, why not. It makes more sense than anything else around here."

"Did you get the autopsy report on Vera Campbell?" I asked.

O'Brien groaned.

"I warned you she's thorough," Mallory commented.

"I read it last night. The report states death by drowning misadventure. Apparently her face was contorted and some of her long muscles were contracted, which the coroner put down to anoxia. The fact that the body was in the water didn't help much." O'Brien ran his fingers through his hair again while he regarded me. "You knew all that, right?"

I nodded. "Most of it. I had hoped for something more enlightening."

"It's an imperfect world," he responded, his tone not entirely sarcastic.

Mallory consulted his watch. "We need to think about getting ready for our dive."

"You can't honestly tell me that with all this going on, you are still going to take her *diving!*" O'Brien erupted. His vehemence startled me, especially since his concern focused on me. "With possible faulty equipment?"

"As long as we don't use the regulator with serial number 3721-2867-4538, we should be fine. Arlene will be with us too," I assured him. "Besides, we have to keep up appearances."

"We've made it known we're going diving, so we should follow through." Mallory added. "There's another set of gear. Want to come with us?" A glint of mischief shone in his deep blue eyes.

"Not on your life! I'll get a beach chair and take a nap or something. I'm not here officially, although I have to keep reminding myself of that. I'll have to go back to the station at some point, too. If you can't find me, call there. I started some inquiries and I'm waiting to get the answers."

I left the two men after I insisted I could walk to my room and back all by myself in order to change. Janet, on-duty again, laughed when I stopped and asked for a key. She repeated what Dorothy had told me: my predicament would not be the last.

"You never know, it could show up at the office or back here," she added. "That was quite a night."

"No kidding. That's the sort of excitement I can do without."

"Mr. Thompson told me you pulled him out of the water."

"Honestly, it seemed to be the thing to do at the time," I said. "Thanks for your help—sorry we interrupted your switchboard training."

"There will be other nights," she replied with a smile. "It's my third position here."

"Third?"

"Yes. I started as one of the housekeeping girls, but Mr. Thompson felt I was capable of being a concierge."

"You're lucky. Not every job will let you promote up that way." I glanced at the clock on the wall behind her. "Yikes! I have to get changed. I'm going on my first open water scuba dive!"

I made it fast. I walked down to the lobby and heard the phone ring. I stayed put while Janet answered. She waved me off—thankfully not for me. I nodded, left the key on the counter for her, and headed back to Cabin Five, pondering a few more things.

15

Mallory and I geared up with explanations about the buddy system, buddy breathing, safety vests, hand signals, and reserve rods buzzing in our minds. Carrying our fins, we made our way to the beach with Arlene.

"Let's keep it simple," she recommended while we waded into the water. "Let's stay within the roped-off swimming area at first so you can get the feel for it. After ten minutes or so, we'll move out to more interesting scenery. We won't be going below thirty feet so we don't need to worry about decompression."

"How long does one tank last?" Mallory asked.

"It varies from person to person, and of course, water conditions affect it. In these waters, which are cool, generally between a half-hour to forty-five minutes," Arlene replied. "The longest I've ever stayed down on one tank was an hour, and that was in the Caribbean."

Diving in the Sound proved much different from my pool experience. The sandy, even bottom under the float gave way to a more rocky landscape once we ventured outside the roped off area, nothing dramatic but certainly more interesting. In our briefing, Arlene warned us the cloudy water and limited visibility blurred everything.

Losing all track of time with the sound of my air bubbles in a steady rhythm, I enjoyed the sensation of being suspended in the water. Arlene emphasized maintaining contact with our diving partners at all times; I constantly swiveled my head, keeping her and Mallory in my field of vision. Going along nicely, I gradually noticed I needed more effort to inhale.

Okay, more difficult to draw a breath, this is exactly how Arlene described the tank going dry... harder to breathe. I reached back and pulled the rod as instructed. It moved. I inhaled. Except I did not get more air. I moved the rod back to its original position and tried again. Nothing. My tank was empty.

I stared up at the wavy, mirrored surface. It suddenly seemed a long way away. I waved to my diving buddies and used the hand signal for 'out of air' by miming slashing my throat.

Arlene swam over to me, checked my reserve valve, and took my mouthpiece. After trying to take a breath, she handed me her mouthpiece. I took two breaths, and handed it back. Mallory joined us and she signaled to surface. Arlene stayed with me, angling back to shore while we ascended and I took one additional breath off her tank. The three of us broke the surface by the float.

"You were buddy breathing. What's wrong?" Mallory demanded.

Arlene indicated my mouthpiece. "Her tank is dry," she announced. "The reserve didn't work. You didn't panic, Lauren, and I'm proud of you!"

"Thanks. It looks like we found some more tampering." I grabbed the ladder and started climbing; hard work with the gear. "If you can, I'd like you to check this before we get it back to the boathouse." I removed the backpack with her help.

"The screw that holds the rod to the inner mechanism has been loosened," Arlene announced after her examination. "Pulling on it moves the rod but nothing happens on the inside."

"Swell." I sat down on a towel. "I don't know if I'm reading too much into this, but has it occurred to you Vera may have had this problem? If she did, her death wasn't by misadventure."

"Good point," Mallory admitted. "All we know is that she ran out of air."

"Blast and bother! Even if we assume it was not an accident, we'd have a hard time determining if my dry tank today was a continuation of Vera's mishap or a deliberate attempt on one of us. We don't know when the damage occurred. It could have happened weeks ago or last night." I scowled in dismay. "Our butler doesn't care who gets hurt, and that frightens me."

"Well, I'm closing the diving for the time being," Arlene declared. "I refuse to take any more risks."

"I think you should take all the equipment to a dive shop and have it checked professionally," Mallory told her. "Where's the nearest one?"

"I can take it to the Glen's fire station. One of the guys there is a dive pro with Navy experience."

"I'll help you load it up," he offered. "First, though, do we want to use this new incident?"

"Meaning?" I asked.

"Do we want to say anything about it or do we want to let it slide rather than draw attention to it?" Mallory regarded me. "Right now, it's up to us."

"You mean dramatize it a bit?" I gave the notion some thought. "Hold a moment. Wasn't Thompson talking about taking Constance diving?"

"Yes," Arlene acknowledged, "and I may have to make that an exception to closing down diving, but I'll be going down with them, like I did with you two. Mr. Thompson wants to take her by himself, but I can't allow that."

"I concur. He shouldn't take her down alone. If she insists on diving, we can make up a diving party," Mallory suggested.

"Since that's the case, let's keep this quiet other than telling Mr. O'Brien," I proposed. "He needs to know."

"Who exactly is Mr. O'Brien?" Arlene asked Mallory. "I know he's your friend, but don't you think it's time to call the police?"

"Arlene, Danny O'Brien *is* the police. He's the captain of the Northwoods Glen PD," Mallory explained. "I called him in unofficially because I was getting concerned about these events. He and I go back a few years."

"Speaking of Mr. O'Brien," I nodded towards shore, "here he comes."

The three of us watched while the policeman swam across. His eccentric, splashing stroke looked like a blend of flailing arms and dog paddle.

"Remind me to give him a few lessons," I murmured to Mallory.

"I'll help," offered Arlene.

"Not a word, you two," Mallory cautioned us. "He's in the water and trying!"

Arlene and I stifled giggles. Mallory stood to greet the swimmer when he reached the float.

"Blast it, that's further than it looks," O'Brien complained, slightly out of breath.

"Distances over water can be deceiving," Arlene commented, careful not to catch my eye.

O'Brien flopped down on the deck. I fought down the urge to tease him about the calypso-loud print of his bathing trunks. He took the towel Mallory offered.

"I swam out because you three didn't come straight to the beach. Why did you stop here? Is something wrong?" O'Brien regarded each of us in turn, and stopped with his gaze on me. "What happened?" he demanded.

"Why must it have been me?"

"Call it a hunch," he said. "What happened?"

"I found out what it's like to try to breathe from a dry tank." I shuddered.

Arlene explained my experience and her subsequent discovery.

"Deliberately loosened?" he asked in surprise. "I'm not a diver. What is the rod supposed to do?"

"When the reserve rod is up, it functions like a warning that the air supply is running out. The diver feels the tank going dry and pulls the rod down, freeing up a small extra supply of air, enough to get safely to surface."

"Like a five-minute warning?"

"Exactly. Pulling the rod warns the diver a reserve supply of air is now in use." Arlene frowned. "That rod assembly is designed to function through years of use. This equipment is new, too. If anything, it should have been a bit tight or stiff."

"I guess now we have to determine if this is something deliberately aimed at, well, someone specific. One of you?" O'Brien once more stared at each of us in turn.

"We were discussing it when you swam out," Mallory told him. "If Vera's tank went dry and nothing happened when she pulled the reserve, what occurred today could be part of the same plot."

"Thompson has been talking about taking Constance Ambrose down for a dive," I said. "I'm having a problem with the idea that the butler doesn't seem to be concerned about who gets the faulty equipment."

"The butler? Oh, right, your term for the bad guy." He frowned at Arlene. "You found other damage."

"A regulator hose with a hole in it, and a cracked O-ring," Arlene summarized. "I replaced the O-ring."

"And now this. What would have happened if this tank had been used with the tampered regulator?" the policeman asked.

"Pretty much what happened today. An experienced diver would have been able to get to the surface. Lauren could have managed on her own. We weren't deep and she's a skin diver. We did some buddy breathing anyway." She smiled at the blank look on his face. "We shared the air in my tank by taking turns with my regulator."

"Vera Campbell was experienced, we agree on that. If she ran out of air, why did she die?" I asked.

"Could she have panicked?" Mallory asked.

"Not likely," Arlene replied with a deep sigh. "To tell you the truth, I think this is what has been bothering me all along. She was a water safety instructor and an experienced diver. If her tank went dry, all she needed to do was doff it and surface."

"Doff?" O'Brien questioned.

"Take it off. Basically, release the harness and drop the tank underwater. Also, if she had pulled the cord on her safety vest, it would have popped her to the surface in a few seconds. Running out of air should not have been a problem at thirty, thirty-five, or even forty feet."

"You lost me. Can you go over the rest of what you're wearing so I can understand this?" O'Brien actually made it a request.

"Sure." She used my gear, now scattered on the float, as props and she went over each piece of equipment with a brief explanation of its function.

"What about the O-ring you replaced? What would have happened if it had been used?" O'Brien questioned.

"The regulator is seated on the tank. The O-ring makes the seal airtight. A cracked or worn O-ring lets air out, and the tank bleeds. You very quickly lose a lot of air." She frowned again. "However, *none* of this would be fatal to someone at home in the water. Ascending from thirty feet isn't difficult, and I doubt Vera dove that deep. Lauren handled it on her first dive without panicking. She had already started up when I got to her."

O'Brien considered the information in silence for a few moments.

"I know they did an autopsy," Arlene said. "Did they find anything?"

"The case didn't get to me because they found the tank dry. I'll have to check to see if the reserve valve was faulty on the tank we have, but the misadventure ruling satisfied everyone. The case was closed." He sighed, and it sounded like it came from his toes. "I told these two," nodding at Mallory and me, "that I read the coroner's report last night. The incidents this weekend may get the case re-opened. However, before you report any of it, I said *may*." He emphasized his point with a glare at me. "We need more than what I've heard so far."

"Understood." I stretched my legs out. "What would it take to open this up again?"

"Since you ask, it would have to be something concrete. Last night's circus could have been accidents. Granting that this equipment has been deliberately tampered with, and it certainly looks that way, your butler has been a very busy boy. That doesn't make it murder," he concluded.

"Unless the autopsy included a toxicology screen which came out a little funny," I pondered.

"According to what I read, one wasn't done," he admitted. "I don't want to jump the gun here. I took steps last night to see if there *is* any evidence we overlooked. Until I get the reports back, this is all speculation."

"Understood," I repeated, and smiled at the surprise on his face. "The plan now is to keep this between the four of us, right? While we stay alert for anything else going on?"

"Yes. If anything changes, I'll let you know," replied O'Brien.

"Circumspect vigilance," I pronounced. "I wish I did have eyes in the back of my head."

Mallory checked the time. "We'd better get back. Arlene, can we get the equipment to your car with a decent excuse? We don't want to ring any alarm bells."

"I can say that I want to fill the tanks at the fire station. The regulators can go in a box, and we can load the equipment on the cart I use to haul it around the resort. I'll leave immediately. If I use my mid-day break, no one should complain." She hefted my backpack. "It'll be easier to tote if you wear it."

"Just out of curiosity, what's the evening activity for tonight?" I asked while we prepared for the swim back to shore.

"Buffet and dancing. The staff will set up a dinner buffet inside and a record player on the terrace." Arlene smiled. "Dinner starts at six with the dance following at eight. According to what I heard, this is scheduled once a month and the first one in May was well attended. Our weekday widows are joined by their husbands, some of our day members come in, and we staff are encouraged to participate."

O'Brien groaned.

"What's the matter, Danny? Don't you dance?" Mallory ribbed with a grin.

"It's been known to happen," he grudgingly acknowledged. "I'm just not looking forward to the swim back to the beach."

"It's good for you," Mallory encouraged. "What are you complaining about? We have the gear!"

Janet greeted me from her desk as I entered the Lodge. "How was your dive?"

"Terrific! I could really get used to doing that," I told her honestly, skipping the complication. "There's a freedom to it that you don't get any other way."

"I'm glad you enjoyed it," she smiled. "Oh, I have some good news for you: your key turned up."

"Where was it?"

"Jim spotted it on the terrace and brought it to me," she explained, handing it to me.

"It must have fallen out of my pocket with all the running around we did. I'll have to thank him. I've got to change. Again. I'm meeting Robert Mallory for lunch."

"You two are getting cozy," she observed. "If he dances, get him to take you to the dance after dinner."

"I think he's planning on it. Truthfully, I'm the one on shaky ground when it comes to dancing. He seems to be good at anything he tries, so I'm guessing he'll be tops on the dance floor." I grimaced. "I hope I can stay off his toes."

Janet laughed. "I'm with you," she admitted. "I've checked, and I do have a right foot, but it always seems to act like a second left one."

16

A few minutes later, I walked to the clubhouse in the blouse and slacks I wore the first day, adding a scarf tied around my neck. I thought the scarf looked silly, but Julie overruled me in the store. Janet complimented me on it, so once again I mentally bowed to Julie's taste, whose experience with the upper crust of society and fashion surpassed mine.

Jim greeted me with a message from Mallory.

"He's going to be late," Jim relayed. "He apologized, and instructed me to see you were comfortable."

I laughed. "He's a true gentleman."

"He also mentioned he has an idea he wants to discuss with me," the young waiter informed me, "about a job after the summer season."

I nodded. "I am going to let him bring it up. If it's what I'm guessing it is, you couldn't do better. On another subject, did you manage to get some sleep in what was left of last night?"

"A little. I hope we don't have to go through anything like that again," he confided. "What can I get you to drink? The chef made fresh lemonade a little while ago."

"That sounds terrific."

Mallory joined me while I sipped it.

"I decided to call Julie," he told me. "She said to tell you hello, and asked me how the wardrobe was holding up. I told her you presented a perfect picture!"

I crossed my eyes, causing him to chuckle. "She's enjoying her time at the lake?"

"She always does. You'll have to come with us sometime. I also told her we went scuba diving and now she wants to learn. Maybe I can rent some equipment locally up there. There used to be an old road crossing the area before the small dam flooded the lake."

"What can I get you for lunch?" Jim asked upon returning.

"Something light," I requested, thinking of the buffet supper and dance later.

"We have tuna salad sandwiches," he suggested.

"Would it be possible to have the salad on a bed of lettuce, rather than on bread?" Mallory, ahead of me as usual, smiled. "I'd like some lemonade, as well."

"Did you see Arlene and the equipment off to the fire station?" I asked once Jim left us.

"Yes. We tucked the regulators into an innocuous-looking duffle bag. I'm worried that there's more going on here than we realize."

"Jim's heading our way," I cautioned. "Am I right in supposing that you are thinking of recommending him to Susan?"

"We can't let a good waiter go to waste," he replied with a smile. "She wants to bring in two or three more people so they can open for lunch as well. I thought the timing would be perfect and I think he'd do well. We have to keep Susan's Place on top."

"Susan's Place?" Jim asked, serving Mallory's lemonade. "Your salad plates will be up shortly. Pardon me, are you are talking about the small Italian restaurant in the Glen?"

"Uh-huh. Mr. Mallory knows the owners well," I said, skipping over Arlene's connection. "Have you been there?"

"I went with my folks once, right after they opened. They try to get there once a month. I remember the food was really good."

"That it is," Mallory confirmed. "I told Lauren that Susan would like to open for lunch and she's going to be hiring more staff. I thought I'd pass along your name, if that would be agreeable to you."

"Gee, Mr. Mallory! That would be great! Thank you!" He hurried off to the kitchen, beaming.

"Mallory Employment Agency strikes again," I murmured, certain Susan would like the young waiter.

"Good afternoon," Thompson greeted us, coming up to the table. "What is Jim so happy about?"

"I'm going to recommend him for a job in the Glen after your season is over," Mallory replied. "Some friends of mine run a small restaurant and I think it would be solid match for all concerned."

"I'm glad. He's a good kid and a hard worker." Thompson pulled a chair to the table and sat. "How was your dive?"

"We enjoyed it. Lauren did very well."

"I went down to the boathouse to reserve scuba equipment for a lesson for Constance, but it was locked. Do you know where Arlene is?"

"She told me she wanted to get the tanks filled at the fire station in the Glen. Something may be wrong with the compressor here and she doesn't want to take any chances," Mallory told him, surrounding the lie with a truth. "I helped her load the tanks into her car. I'm glad you have managed to talk Constance into trying it."

"The lesson in the pool comes first, hopefully this afternoon. I think watching Lauren's session helped, and so did last night's swim, in spite of what happened." Thompson chuckled, an undeniably irritating sound. He leaned in closer. "Robert, I'd appreciate your help this afternoon. I know she trusts you."

"Well, we've known each other a while," Mallory said. "Arlene probably won't be long,"

"Will you two be attending the dance tonight?" he asked with his cackle, always the eager host. "It's our most popular activity."

"We're looking forward to it," Mallory told him.

"What are the dress guidelines?" I wondered which of Julie's choices I needed to wear.

"We encourage something a little dressier than what you would wear to our weekday dinners," he said, waving Janet over when she entered the dining area. "Your wardrobe is quite fashionable. Constance has commented on it."

Mallory winked. I swallowed lemonade along with the reply I wanted to make.

"Excuse me, Mr. Thompson," Janet interrupted, coming up in time to hear his compliment. She shot me an angry glance, which surprised me. I raised my eyebrow and she sniffed. I wondered what I had done to deserve it. I looked at Mallory, who shrugged.

"Yes, Janet?" her boss asked.

"Do you still want me on the switchboard for part of tonight? My training last night got cut short."

"Yes, if Dorothy can take over in the Lodge. We have more guests coming in this afternoon, though, so I want you on your desk for now."

"Yes, sir!" She flashed him a big smile which he returned, and headed out the door.

"I've come to rely on Janet," he confided, sounding obsequious. "She doesn't know it yet, but I plan to groom her to be our assistant manager next summer. She's good with our members, reliable, and very capable."

"She told me she had been hired originally as a housekeeper," I said.

"Like Robert, I hate seeing talent go to waste," he responded with adding his irksome chuckle. "Janet has a lot of potential and I'm hoping this will be the beginning of a good career for her."

Thompson left us when Jim arrived at the table with a tray.

"I suggested a touch of color to Chef Willard. We thought tomato wedges would be all right," he said, putting the plates in front of us. He smiled and added, "I also brought you some of the house dressing in case you might want it." He set a small dish on the table.

"It looks very appetizing," I complimented. "Will you, Gerald, and George be on-duty this evening?"

"Definitely! We'll be joined by Charlie, Matt, Michael, and Hank—our part-time waiters. They come in for weekends. Matt will also be the deejay for the dance." He glanced around. "The weekend crowd is already starting to show up. Enjoy your lunch."

"That kid has a real future in hospitality," Mallory predicted, spearing a tomato wedge.

"Something Thompson just told us reminded me of a comment Arlene made back at Susan's the other evening," I told him, lowering my voice. "Remember her answer when we asked her about Vera's friends and enemies? 'One of the housekeeping girls, who has a crush on Mr. Thompson...' I wonder if she meant Janet."

"She was certainly eager to stay with Thompson last night," he acknowledged. "I had to sternly insist she leave and get some sleep. I hope she knows how possessive Constance can be, though."

"You noticed the smile Janet gave him a few minutes ago? She's got it bad," I said. "She intimated that you are pursuing me, yet she wasn't pleased when Thompson complimented me."

"I saw that and wondered about it myself. What are you thinking?"

"I'll let you know when I finish working on it," I murmured. "When will Mr. O'Brien be back?"

"Technically, today is a workday for him, so it's up for grabs. He'll get here as soon as he can, and bring the reports with him."

"Thompson could be the rope in a tug of war between Constance and Janet," I contemplated aloud. "That could mean some of these shenanigans are based in jealousy taken to extremes."

"Such as the drugged drinks?"

"I knew you caught that. Yes. It would be comical if it weren't so nasty. Also it doesn't make any sense, unless Constance drank the drink she drugged."

Mallory gave my comment a moment's thought. "I'm confused."

"Constance told you that she spilled her first drink, and Thompson gave her the one he had. She drank his, and then got another one for him. Assuming George and Jim aren't involved and both drinks were drugged, who did it? Constance, Thompson, or Janet?"

"All right, I see your point. However, Janet wasn't there."

"She may not have been there all the time, but she told me she had a dinner break, and I saw her at the Lodge when I went to change for the evening's swim."

"That could let her out," Mallory mused.

"Maybe, maybe not. Immediately prior to Mr. O'Brien's call last night looking for you, Janet told me she would be coming back up to the clubhouse for another training session on the switchboard. So she may have been around, certainly long enough to drug a drink or two. But *why* would she?"

"Just because we can't see a motive doesn't mean there isn't one," he reminded me.

"I'm aware of that. If we remove Janet from the equation, and unless one of the remaining characters drugged his or her own drink and then downed it, none of it is plausible." I started to say something else when he cut me off.

"This tuna salad is quite tasty," he remarked casually, inclining his head slightly toward the side door.

Constance entered the dining room and strolled over to us.

"Good afternoon," she cooed to Mallory, who stood. "How was your dive?"

"I think Lauren enjoyed her first taste of open water scuba diving," he said with a smile at me. He pulled a chair over for her.

"I did," I piped up. "I'm glad Arlene came down with us, too. It would be easy to get disoriented underwater."

"Eddie is going to teach me how to use the gear this afternoon, if Arlene ever gets back with it," she said, petulant and obviously perturbed. "He told me she went to get the tanks filled at the fire station." She sat down and pulled her chair closer to Mallory.

"Arlene was concerned there might be something wrong with the compressor and she didn't want to take any chances with the air. She'll be back soon," Mallory explained. "You should enjoy the experience. I spoke to my daughter earlier, and now she wants to learn!"

"I have a feeling that scuba diving is going to become one of the most popular water sports around," I said. "Although from what you've told me about her, I wouldn't suggest you run out and buy your daughter a set of gear just yet." Julie, always cautious about trying new things, did not enjoy water sports as much as he did.

"It was a thought. Her birthday is coming up at the end of the month," he informed us.

"How old will she be?" inquired Constance. Her syrupy voice dripped and she leaned towards him, ending up with her arm through his.

"Twenty-one." He ruefully smiled. "It's hard for me to realize she's that grown up."

"You hardly seem old enough to have a daughter who's twenty," she murmured, snuggling against his arm like a kitten with a blanket.

"Any ideas as to what I should get her?" He included me in the question while he freed his arm from her grasp. "I'm stumped and I hope you ladies can help me out."

"It's a special birthday, and you should get her a very special gift," Constance told him, putting her hand back on his arm. "Jewelry. It should be something classic and elegant that will remind her of you every time she wears it."

"I agree," I said, startling her. "If you're serious, I do have a suggestion."

"Please, I need ideas," he encouraged.

"A string of pearls," I promptly offered. "A choker or, more appropriately, princess length would be a classic gift."

"Why, that's a wonderful idea, Lauren! I was going to suggest earrings, but pearls would be perfect!" Constance gushed. "Robert, every girl needs pearls and she should get them as a gift! How clever of you to think of it," she told me, rendering the compliment condescending.

"Then a string of pearls it is, especially if you both feel it's appropriate," he beamed, mostly at me to her visible pique. "A friend of mine is a jeweler and I'll put him on it. Thank you! I always get panicky when it comes to gifts for her."

"You can call me anytime," Constance told him, her hand still on his arm.

"If you will both excuse me, I think I'll visit the powder room," I announced. Her attitude bothered me almost as much as Thompson's chafing chortle. "I won't be long."

Constance disappointed me by not saying something along the lines of "take your time." Mallory stood as I left. I might have imagined the slight frown on his face while he watched me leave the table.

Once inside the restroom, I leaned against the wall and took a deep breath. Seeing her cloying behavior evolve into an air of 'take me, I'm yours' wore thin. So did watching her play with Mallory in front of Thompson. I dawdled a bit, hoping she would be gone by the time I returned. No such luck.

They both stood when I approached the table.

"Robert," she told him, her hand resting possessively on his arm, "I promise I'll make sure we have a chance to talk tonight." She turned to me. "Lauren, Robert tells me you two will be at the dance. I'll let you in on a secret: he is one of the best dancers I've ever known! You're in for a real treat, but I warn you, you'll have to share him! See you later!"

Mallory sighed and sat down when I did, his lips pressed into a firm line. He wordlessly picked up his fork. I tried to phrase my thoughts; we did not often get our wires crossed.

"You abandoned me," he gently chastised.

"I wish I could say I was sorry," I returned. "My tolerance for imperial haughtiness stretches only so far and a little of her fawning goes a long way."

"I tried to take the opportunity to remind her of a few things." He shook his head. "She isn't listening." He left anything else unsaid and changed the topic. "About Julie's gift. The pearl necklace was the idea you mentioned at Susan's, correct?"

I nodded. "Expensive and she honestly will love it."

"Would you please explain the difference between a choker and princess length so I know what I'm talking about when I order it?" The humorous glint in his eyes returned.

"Pearls come in varying standard lengths. A choker is about sixteen inches and a princess string is about eighteen inches. I think Julie would prefer princess length; she won't need more than that for years. It's a classic gift. The ones I have belonged to my mother and my grandmother before her."

"Constance was surprised you knew about this sort of thing."

"Mom raised me with a touch of class. Some of it took in spite of my being a tomboy. All Constance can see is a working peon, and I would bet that she's trying to figure out why you are bothering with me. Has she warned you that I'm a reporter?"

He threw back his head and laughed, startling a few of the other guests.

"I'll take that as a yes. Did you thank her for the warning?"

"I did indeed. She thinks you are definitely beneath me."

"From her point of view, she's bound to," I reflected. "She's got her Eddie, and he is improving with her coaching. However he's not in your league. All things considered, she'd much rather have you. Be careful."

"About tonight's dance," he diplomatically broached a new subject. "I suppose I should ask if you know how."

"Oh, bother! Yes, I learned the basics. I haven't had much opportunity to put it to use, though. Evenings in nightclubs are not part of my social calendar."

"I suggest we get some practice. Can you handle a lesson or two?"

"All right. Where and what do we use for music?"

"My cabin and a radio." He stood. "Ready?" He waved his thanks at Jim, who nodded.

"I want to be poolside when Arlene works with Constance," I warned him while we strolled to his cabin.

"Affirmative. I asked Arlene to report to me when she gets back, so we'll also be informed of what's going on there. Meanwhile, how's your box step?"

"What's a box step?" I asked innocently, keeping my eyes wide open.

He gave me a mock groan.

After an hour and a half of his tutelage, I could manage the box and a few other dance moves without stepping on him. Mallory felt I would not disgrace either him or me, although I knew I would never pose a threat to Ginger Rogers or Ann Miller. I figured even Betty Garrett could consider herself safe.

"That's fun, but it is work!" I sank into a convenient chair.

"You'll be fine," he assured me.

"We've had this conversation," I crossly mumbled. "Don't bring up fainting again, please?" I decided not to bring up nightclubs.

"I'm proud of you. You seem to have a knack for this in spite of growing up a tomboy. With more practice, you could rival Julie. Maybe we should work an occasional nightclub evening into your calendar."

Bother! He's reading my mind and not for the first time. "Thanks, I think," I muttered aloud.

"Have you figured out what you're going to wear this evening?"

"Oh, I thought I'd wear something Julie picked out," I said with a careless wave of my hand. I glanced up in time to duck a small pillow headed through the air in my direction. "How about a swim first? Oh, bother! I'll need to change clothes. Again."

We were on the porch of his cabin when Arlene stepped out of the boathouse and trudged in our direction with her head down and shoulders slumped.

"On the other hand," Mallory wryly suggested, "why don't we all go inside."

Once inside his cabin, Arlene sat in an easy chair and stared at the floor, a portrait of dejected resignation.

"Uh-oh, I don't think this is going to be good news," I muttered after a few moments of silence, mostly because I felt someone should say something.

"It isn't. Every tank had the reserve rod problem. We didn't find out about ours in the water because you ran dry." She noticed the confusion on my face. "I gave you the tank you used in the pool yesterday, so you didn't start with a full tank. Mr. Mallory and I started with full tanks, but eventually we would have run into the same problem."

"Mr. O'Brien said he would check to see if Vera's tank had a faulty reserve," I said. "I'll bet it's the same. What about the regulators?"

"The only damaged one was the one with the hole. The dive pro replaced the hose, so it's now usable. All the O-rings have been replaced to be on the safe side, and the rods have been properly reattached, so everything is okay." She shuddered and sighed. "We've been lucky.

The pro was astounded that someone would do this without any regard for who got hurt."

"That's been nagging at me," I said. "Malice is one thing. This goes way beyond it."

"We're ahead of it now," Mallory pointed out. "Arlene, did you know Thompson is looking for you?"

"He stopped me on my way back in. He wants to teach Mrs. Ambrose how to dive. I told him I would feel more comfortable if I did it, but he insists that *she* will be more comfortable if he does it."

"We'll all be there so it should be okay," Mallory reassured her.

"All the same, when it comes to an open-water dive, I'm going to insist I go with them."

"Lauren is heading back to the Lodge to change into swim togs. While she does, let me help you get the gear to the pool."

"Okay." She stood and forced a smile. "We can handle this?"

"Of course we can," I firmly stated. "If I can learn how to dance in ninety minutes, I'm sure the three of us can sit and watch a scuba lesson!"

Arlene laughed. I went to change, pleased she appreciated my comment.

17

An hour later, I watched Constance swimming around the bottom of the pool in full scuba gear. Despite his faults, I conceded Thompson made a decent teacher. Possibly patience played into his confidence scams; nevertheless, he proved both gentle and thorough in handling his skittish partner.

To my surprise, Constance settled down to learn her lessons without dramatics. She mastered the concepts quickly, although she required continual praise from her Eddie and Robert. Arlene and I echoed the men, but we did not count. Back on the deck, Thompson helped her out of the backpack.

"When are you going to take me diving in the Sound?" Constance arrogantly demanded.

"How about tomorrow morning, say around eleven?" Arlene suggested. She collected the gear and loaded her cart.

"Why not now, while I'm in the mood?" she haughtily persevered, hand on her hip. She glared at the girl.

"Constance," broke in Mallory, getting out of the pool, "Arlene has a swimming class scheduled for three-thirty. It wouldn't be fair to your guests to force her to cancel it."

"She doesn't have to come," she sulked, visibly irritated. "Eddie can take me. You can come, too, Robert."

"You should have a guide who knows the waters," Mallory reasoned quietly, "and that's Arlene. It would be better to wait until tomorrow as she suggested."

"Well, if that's the way it has to be—" she said, slightly appeased.

"Besides," Thompson offered thoughtfully, "you want time to get ready for the dance, don't you?"

"I *said* all right," she acidly lashed out with a total change of attitude. "*All right*! Tomorrow, then," she spat and flounced off in the direction of her cabin.

"I don't think I've ever seen anyone flounce in a bathing suit," I murmured to Arlene, who could not quite stifle a giggle. "I'm hot! Heads up! I'm going in."

Mallory joined me. Arlene returned from stowing the gear and reminded us that we owed her a demonstration of our dive trick. She cleared swimmers out of the water and we complied. My dive almost equaled the first one.

"I guess that's my moment of glory for the day," I commented to Mallory once we vacated the pool to make way for Arlene's lesson. "I sure won't have one tonight."

"You never know," he remarked. "You might surprise yourself."

"I'll surprise myself if I don't trip over my own feet, much less yours." I sat to put on my zories. "What time is it?"

"A little after three."

"I suppose I'd better start getting ready. Even if I can't dance well, I should look the part."

Jim stepped out of the clubhouse and hailed Mallory. "Audrey has a telephone call for you, sir. You can take it in here."

"Don't go away," Mallory instructed me, rising. "I have a feeling—"

Moments later he marched out to the terrace and extended his hand. "Come on. We're going to the office."

I heard a tone in his voice he did not often use. The first time I heard it was years back when Julie came home from school upset and crying after a junior high teacher unfairly penalized her. Mrs. Fiddler and I heard his half of the phone conversation with the school's principal. I dubbed it his protective mode. Since the current circumstances did not require it, my curiosity peaked. From his attitude, however, I knew better than to ask. I would find out when he wanted to tell me and not a moment sooner.

Both offices were empty. Mallory strode to the desk and picked up the switchboard telephone.

"Audrey? This is Robert Mallory. I'm in the main office. Would you ring Mr. Thompson's cabin for me and ask him to join me? Thank you." He replaced the handset.

I opened my mouth to speak.

"Not yet," he counseled.

The telephone rang. "Northwoods Resort—" he began. "Yes, Audrey. Thank you. Keep trying to locate him. I'll wait here." He hung up. "Let's sit. My call was from Danny O'Brien."

"I guessed. What did he have to say?"

"You are going to take advantage of Thompson's offer and move into Cabin Four." He stopped my question with a look. "Lauren, this is not a request. O'Brien said he'd give us the details once he gets here, but for now he wants you out of the Lodge. I gathered something turned up in Janet's background."

"Earlier today, he suggested I should stay put."

"Danny is not an alarmist but something has him spooked. All I can tell you is he wants you out of the Lodge and in the cabin as soon as possible. He wouldn't make this a demand unless he believed it was warranted."

199

"How long have you known him?"

"Long enough. He's a top investigator, totally honest, and a bulldog when it comes to justice and fair play." Mallory paused, regarding me. "I know you're independent and you want to stand on your own, but please, Lizzie, go along with this."

He clinched it using my nickname, the one derived from my middle name. Anytime it happened, I figured I had no choice or room for argument. My nickname was a reminder that our acquaintance began the day he caught me trespassing in his out-of-bounds apple tree, helping myself. At the time, he refrained from reporting my transgression to my parents. My nickname signaled the final 'say' on any given subject.

"I surrender." I held up my hands. "If you and Mr. O'Brien feel that strongly about it, I'll move. That's why we're waiting here? To get it arranged?"

The telephone rang again.

He nodded and picked it up. "Northwoods—Yes, Audrey, thank you. I appreciate it. Would it be possible to find Carmella and have her come to the office as well?" He paused. "Fine, and thank you again."

"Carmella?"

"I think she should help you pack."

"Such service." *What in blazes could have unnerved O'Brien? That 'something' in Janet's background must be a real bombshell to cause this furor. Heaven help us.* I shivered, not from my damp hair and bathing suit.

"When Thompson gets here, confirm you want to accept the offer, and I'll take it from there," Mallory suggested. I nodded my agreement.

Carmella entered first. "Hello! What's going on? Audrey called and said you wanted to see me over here."

"Mr. Thompson offered Lauren a cabin for the weekend," Mallory explained easily with his disarming smile. "From what I gathered earlier, Janet is going to be busy checking in new arrivals and I wondered if you might be willing to help Lauren pack and move."

"I'd be happy to." She shyly returned his smile. "Are you two going to the dinner buffet and dance?"

"Definitely," Mallory answered.

Thompson entered the office.

"I just spoke with Constance. We're going to hold a jitterbug contest during the evening!" He gave us the cackle he thought equaled a chuckle. "Now then, Lauren, I understand from Audrey that you wanted to see me?"

"Yes. I've decided if your generous offer of the cabin is still open, I'd like to take you up on it." My smile radiated charm. "I mentioned it to Carmella, and she volunteered to help me move."

"Great! This helps us out, too. It looks like we may need the room in the Lodge. Not for tonight, Carmella," he hastened to assure her. "You'll have tomorrow morning to get it ready. Let me get the key to the cabin, and you can leave the room key with Janet once you've moved out."

He juggled his paperwork, and handed me a key. "Off you two go," he told us, chuckling again. "I want a word with Robert."

Carmella and I walked across the lawn to the Lodge lobby.

"Hello, Janet! Mr. Thompson is moving me to a cabin for the rest of the weekend," I clarified. I gave Carmella my room key and she headed for my room.

"Oh. Mr. Thompson is giving you the cabin?" Suspicion colored her question.

"He told me he wanted to thank me for my help last night and apparently there's also the chance he can fill my room tomorrow night. He knew you were busy with new people coming in, so I asked if Carmella would help me," I continued, taking note of her attitude. "I'd do it myself, but I'm also going to have to get ready for the dance." I grimaced. "Hair and makeup take time. Well, they do for me."

Janet barely smiled.

I found my dresser cleared and Carmella already working on my hanging clothes.

"Janet seemed upset that Mr. Thompson is doing this," Carmella said while we emptied my closet into my borrowed suitcase.

"I noticed that too. I'm not sure what it means, if anything," I told her, closing the bag. "Okay, here we go."

"Let me take this to the cabin and start getting it unpacked," Carmella offered as we approached the desk. I nodded.

"Nice girl," I told Janet as I handed her the room key. "Here. I'm proud of myself, I didn't lose it again!"

She gave me a genuine smile. "Mr. Thompson called to tell me we will need your room tomorrow, so this does help with our bookings."

"Robert Mallory sort of pushed me a bit to do this," I confided. "Cabin Four is close to his, right?" *Always hide a truth within a lie. He did push, after all.*

"That thought occurred to me, too," she responded with a nod. "I'll see you at the dance. We're going to have a contest, too."

"So I've heard." I shook my head. "Robert will undoubtedly be polite and enter with me, although I suspect I'll be hopeless. Does Edward dance?"

"Oh, yes! He's a very good partner." Her expression contained a fair amount of innuendo.

"Mrs. Ambrose already told me I'm going to have to share Robert Mallory with her." I sighed. "I don't mind sharing, but I'd like to make sure I get him back in one piece, if you know what I mean."

"I do," she said with a wink. "I don't think you have to worry about that, though."

"Well, I'd better get going. Hair and makeup. Ugh."

I caught up with Carmella, who turned out to be a whiz with hair styles. After watching me make one attempt to put my hair up, she commandeered the brush.

"I've done Constance's hair for family occasions, and if I can please her, I've got to be good," she giggled while she worked. "If I'm here she can't ask me to do hers. Besides, the two families with kids asked Mr. Thompson if they can hire housekeepers to babysit. If it's all the same to you, I'd rather be here."

"In that case, I'm more than happy for the assistance. All I'd be able to do is put it up in a bun. That's how I wear it to work." I sighed. My brown hair usually fell lank and straight.

Forty-five minutes later, Carmella stood behind me and regarded my reflection. "There! It should stay put at the dance, too." My hair, which she pulled up and away from my face, looked great with twists and braids intertwined. "Now, where is your makeup?"

"You are enjoying this," I commented once she finished her magic. I looked like a professional make-up artist performed wonders on me.

She nodded. "It's fun! Now, what are you planning to wear?"

I pulled a simple brown dress with golden highlights from the closet. "I like this one."

"It's beautiful, but not for tonight. Wear it tomorrow night. A sheath won't give you enough room for dancing," she declared while she studied Julie's other choices in my closet. "Here." She selected a full-skirted, blue dress with small dark blue polka dots and cap sleeves. "Your petticoat and sling-back heels will be perfect with this!"

We assembled my outfit on me. I felt like a department store manikin.

"I love your clothes," she said, bending to make sure my slip did not show.

"I can't take credit for them. Robert Mallory's daughter, Julie, picked out most of them. I wish you two could meet—you'd be great friends."

Earlier in the afternoon, Mallory and O'Brien—dismissing all my objections—insisted I needed an escort to the festivities. The time Carmella saved me turned out to be fortuitous. The men arrived at five-thirty, a full half-hour early.

Entering my cabin, O'Brien smiled and addressed her. "Carmella, you saved me the trouble of finding you. Would you like to join us for dinner? That is, if you won't be breaking any rules."

"Oh, thank you! I'd like that very much. Mr. Thompson told us this morning that if our duties permitted it, we could join the guests this evening."

"I'd appreciate it. Will it take long for you to change?" he asked, eyeing her polo shirt and skirt.

"Give me fifteen minutes," she said with a grin and dashed out the door.

"I've got to ask why," Mallory questioned the police captain. "She's a lovely girl, yet she's not involved in this."

"Why did you invite Lauren to be your dinner partner last night?" O'Brien blandly returned question for question.

"She was my plausible diversion."

"Same thing. You're the one who told me I had to try to blend in with the other guests. I chatted with her earlier while I was unpacking." O'Brien regarded me curiously and asked, "why the look of surprise?"

"You are being nice."

Mallory laughed. "He is human, at least occasionally."

Carmella returned in record time, slightly flushed, in a lovely full-skirted rose dress which set off her coloring. "I hope Jim doesn't get the wrong idea," she confided to me while we walked to the clubhouse. "I think you're right that he wants to ask me out."

"I'll have a word with him," I said. "Don't worry."

18

We found a banner stretched across the entrance to the clubhouse announcing *"Glenn Miller Night: In the Mood"*. On the terrace, small bistro tables and chairs surrounded an area set aside for dancing. Jim did appear slightly annoyed to see Carmella with us.

"Relax. Mr. O'Brien asked her to make a foursome, nothing more," I assured him when he took my drink order. "It's also a thank you because she helped me get ready."

Dinner seemed inconsequential compared to the anticipation of the dance for most of the members. Even with a buffet, the waiters worked drinks and kept things moving. At eight o'clock, George moved the bar outside and two of the part-time waiters set up a record player and speakers. The golden globes of the lights came on, bathing the outside setting in a glow against the gathering dusk of the warm evening.Big band music drifted inside the open doors. We finished dinner and the four of us proceeded outside. We staked out one of the small tables set around the makeshift dance floor.

My first attempt at dancing, to *Little Brown Jug,* resulted in disaster. I stayed upright only because Mallory held on to me.

"I would rather have partaken from that little brown jug than danced to it," I muttered tartly while we waited for the next song. "Did I tread on your toes?"

"There's always the possibility that the former might help the latter," he conceded while he laughed, "and my toes are fine. Lauren, stop thinking about what you're doing. Feel the music and let me lead."

He swept me into his arms and led me off. I got better at it, although I suspected my partner did most of the work. Not that it mattered. *Eat your heart out, Mr. Gene Kelly! I have a great partner!* I felt a bit like Cinderella after all.

We danced to *Tuxedo Junction* and I made it through S*tring of Pearls*. When Matt, the deejay, announced *In the Mood,* Constance cut in between us without a word, rudely shouldering me aside with enough force I stumbled. Mallory glanced at me, checking my reaction; I shrugged and shook my head, not wanting to confront her.He winked at me over her shoulder.

I started to work my way through the crowd to our table. Thompson stopped me.

"Care to give it a try?"

"Only if you promise you won't complain when I spend more time on your feet than mine," I warned him.

"Promise," he chuckled.

Thompson guided me through a couple of turns while he kept an eye on Constance. With an admitted touch of envy, I noticed she and her new partner ably demonstrated how the dance moves should be done. The deejay announced *Moonlight Serenade.* Constance pulled herself closer to Mallory, clinging to him like ivy climbing bricks. Thompson frowned. He glanced down at me and his face flushed when he realized I saw his reaction. I figured I didn't need to underline it with a comment.

"Still game?" he asked, struggling not to rubberneck at the other couple.

"Janet is staring at us. Are you sure you don't want to change partners?"

"I'm happy with the one I have," he assured me, his annoying cackle sounding again. "I'll make sure she gets her turn."

We slowly rotated around the dance floor. I noticed Janet cut out Carmella to dance with Jim, after which O'Brien offered his arm to Carmella. Other guests paired up, with Hank, Michael, and Charlie filling in here and there. I wondered if the resort's job application listed the ability to dance as a necessary qualification.

I soon found my attention drawn to something other than my feet: my partner developed a bad case of wandering hands. More than perturbed, I discovered not only did I have to deal with it, I saw Janet spot it and scowl. *Great, one more problem.*

"You do better when you're not paying attention to it," Thompson told me when we finished.

"That's what Robert told me," I answered vaguely, watching couples shift and reform.

The Nearness of You came up next. O'Brien turned Carmella over to Jim.

"Let's see if we can swap with Constance and Robert," Thompson eagerly suggested.

"That's fine with me."

We extricated Mallory from Constance's grasp and he swept me away before she could do more than pout.

"Swing around and take a look at Janet," I told Mallory. I nodded to where Janet stood off to the side, gazing wistfully at Thompson dancing with Constance.

"She does not look happy," he agreed, steering me in a half circle.

We watched O'Brien offer his arm to take Janet onto the floor. She accepted with a decided lack of grace.

"We still don't know what he found out," I murmured. We nodded to Jim and Carmella in passing.

"Meanwhile, you are safely in the cabin."

"Which is going to be widely interpreted as a lascivious move on your part," I added. "Janet already mentioned it."

"Do you mind?" he inquired. He twirled me around under his arm.

"Not if it keeps Thompson's hands where they should be rather than where they want to go."

He raised an eyebrow. "I would have thought Constance and Janet would be enough for him."

"Apparently not. I'd take it as a compliment but unfortunately Janet spotted him doing it. We certainly don't need any more complications to this morass. It already has enough angles to satisfy a geometry teacher."

"You do have a way with words."

The record changed to *Polka Dots and Moonbeams*. Constance approached Mallory, intent on trading again. Thompson, frowning at her attempt, overruled her by leading her into the dance. She aimed a glare at me when we went by. Janet, back on the sidelines after her dance with O'Brien, altered her expression from wistful to outright petulance.

"This is getting to be a real-life soap opera," I observed. "Janet wants Thompson, Thompson wants Constance, and Constance wants you. Bother!"

"I wouldn't have let Constance cut in anyway. I couldn't miss this number with you in that dress," he murmured, his eyes smiling into mine. "Although I have always appreciated the independent tomboy, I could get accustomed to this side of you. Lauren, you look wonderful tonight."

I felt my face blush and turned my head away from his hypnotic eyes. My gaze happened to fall on Constance's face at the moment Mallory chose to pull me in closer. Her eyes shot daggers at me. *If looks could stab, I'd need a blood transfusion.*

"According to Carmella," I broached a new subject, "if Constance suspected Janet had designs on her Eddie, Janet would be out on her rear." I filled in more of that conversation. "This may set a new record on triangles."

The strains of *Chattanooga Choo Choo* began and I begged off. I wanted a break from the theatrics, a drink, and a chance to sit down. At the bar, George asked if I wanted my 'usual.'

"Do I ever!"

"I'm going to call it a C&T, for "Club and Twist," he announced, handing me the refreshing drink. I found my seat and sipped.

Out of habit, I kept an eye on the players involved in our little game of musical partners. Constance and Thompson stayed paired on the dance floor. Mallory disappeared into the building. Janet, standing like her feet had grown roots into the concrete, scowled. The expression on her face eased only when Thompson smiled at her over his partner's shoulder.

O'Brien, free at the moment, joined me at our table.

"You cut a mean rug," I complimented him.

"Thank you. You're improving. What are you drinking?"

"One of my camouflage drinks," I said. I described its origins.

"Beautiful! I'll have to file it for official social events," he said, treating me to a genuine grin. "Meanwhile, I think I'll try one."

"Ask George for a C&T." I caught George's eye at the bar and raised my glass. The bartender saluted and nodded when the policeman approached the bar.

Matt announced a ten minute break, which triggered a shuffle in our players. O'Brien came back with his drink. Constance and Thompson headed to the bar, where they separated. Mallory reappeared, paused for a word with the deejay, stopped by the bar, and eventually joined us with his own C&T. Thompson and Janet were absent. Constance glanced around, spotted us at the table, and quickly made a bee-line for Mallory.

"You requested a song?" she inquired with a hand on his shoulder, preventing him from rising.

"Yes, I want to hear one of my Miller favorites from the war," he replied. "Lauren will enjoy it," he added, his blue eyes glinting with mischief.

"Do you remember the war?" Constance asked me, full of contrived and maudlin innocence. "You must have been very young."

"I wasn't too young to mourn when my father died during the landings on D-Day. The war ended less than five years ago, Constance," I reminded her, squelching a scathing reply.

Taking the hint, Constance scanned the lamp lighted terrace. "I think we've got about sixty people here! We always get a good turnout for our dances. Where did Eddie go?" she finished with another pout.

"He could be taking a break inside," Mallory said. "Oh, here he comes."

"We have a request for one of Glenn Miller's wartime classics," announced Matt when he resumed his place by the record player a few minutes later. "Take the floor for *Don't Sit Under the Apple Tree*."

Mallory, smiling broadly at my groan, took my hand. "I could change the line to, 'don't climb up in the apple tree', if you'd prefer that," he said, referring to the day we met.

I laughed and followed him out to the floor for an extended romp. *Perfidia* and *Pennsylvania 6-5000* followed. Matt announced *Sentimental Journey* next. Mallory fended off attempts from both Constance and Thompson to cut in for that one.

"You're relaxing," he told me after he twirled me again. "Good!" The laughter in his eyes matched his smile.

"You're making her mad, you know," I told him as *Begin the Beguine* started.

"I'm trying to make a point. Unfortunately she's not paying attention," he murmured while Constance danced by with O'Brien. "She's used to having everything her own way and her temper flares when she's thwarted. That was one of the serious doubts I had prior to my talk with her father. Change of subject. Is anyone missing?"

"You mean from our primary cast of characters?" I surveyed the crowded terrace when he nodded. "Thompson is dancing with Arlene. Janet isn't out here."

The song ended. Thompson moved to stand in front of the clubhouse door and called for the crowd's attention. Everyone quieted down and turned toward the resort's manager.

"I don't know if you've noticed, but we are being threatened with rain," he said. A rumble of thunder emphasized the point. "Thank you," he quipped looking up at the sky. Everyone laughed. "We are moving the record player and the bar inside."

"Don't worry, we'll follow," yelled Doug Tyler, one of the cabin residents.

"Oh, yeah! You know we'll always follow the bar!" added Peter Watson, raising his glass. He and Tyler 'clinked' their glasses. Their wives rolled their eyes in resignation.

"I was counting on it," Thompson responded to more laughter. "Give us a few minutes and we'll have more dancing. First, though," he paused for another rumble of thunder, "I'll take that as a drum roll. First will be the dance contest! The song will be *In the Mood*. Choose your partner for your best chance to win!"

"What's the prize?" called out Doris Rosen, one of the water skiers from yesterday.

"The couple who receives the most applause wins a certificate for a free Italian night dinner," he answered. He bowed to cheers from the gathered guests.

"Robert, I can help you win the prize," Constance purred, materializing beside him. "You know we are always good together, not only on the dance floor." She sent me a glance so full of innuendo it would have overflowed a pitcher.

"Constance, thank you. However, the prize isn't important to me," he said. "Besides, I already asked Lauren." His gaze shifted to me and he smiled.

That's news to me, Mr. Mallory, but not unexpected. I smiled at her and slipped my arm inside his.

"Do your best, dear," she pouted. With another flounce, more effective in her dress than her bathing suit, she left us.

The gathered members slowly filed into the clubhouse. The waiters were still moving tables to clear an area for the dance floor. O'Brien, Carmella, Mallory, and I grabbed one next to the window at the head of the now-empty space. Matt, the deejay, moved the record player to a spot not far from us while Charlie set up the speakers.

"All those who are entering the contest come forward," Thompson called once the crowd reassembled inside the clubhouse.

"Mrs. Ambrose graciously invites staff members to enter," announced Thompson. He stood a few feet away from us. "Those of you too chicken to participate, please move to the edge of the dance floor."

That elicited a few laughs along with a couple of chicken cluck noises from Ed Stevenson, another of the cabin residents.

"You're nuts, you know," I told Mallory. "Carmella would be able to keep up."

"I have chosen my partner." Mallory rose from the table and took my hand, gazing down at me. The warm, deep look in his eyes gave me goosebumps and I shivered slightly when he slid his arm around my waist. *Plausible diversion, remember you're his plausible diversion.*

He steered me to the middle of the forming circle, where we joined four other couples: Jim and Carmella, the Tylers, the Rosens, and the Watsons. Janet approached Thompson and whispered something to him; he shook his head. She stayed by him until Constance claimed him, then turned and stalked out of the immediate area. O'Brien caught Mallory's eye, nodded, and followed Janet.

The contest music started.

Mallory led off, guiding me through several moves I never dreamed I could make. My foot slipped and he swung me in mid-air sideways. I managed to regain my footing briefly beforehe lifted me off the ground and spun me completely around him. I followed his lead the best I could, locking my eyes on his throughout the blur of the number. The music ended and we joined the other couples taking bows.

Thompson stood by each couple in turn and asked for applause. To my amazement, we placed second. Jim and Carmella, who wiped the floor deliberately, placed first. Thompson announced for the following week's Italian night, Jim could skip his duties and take Carmella as his dinner guest; everyone applauded the popular staff members.

O'Brien slipped back in unobtrusively, although Janet did not reappear. We grabbed a table by the poolside window.

"Well, where did she go?" I asked.

"Later."

Matt announced *Blue Moon*. Mallory cocked his head at me, inviting me to dance again. I shook my head and he agreed with a smile. Constance and Thompson went out on the dance floor.

"How soon can we gracefully leave?" O'Brien inquired of Mallory; his voice barely audible above the music.

"Not yet," Mallory told him. "Constance is still prowling, and I'd prefer not to have her show up at my cabin."

The song ended and he nodded towards the dance floor. Constance, once more draped over Thompson, sent repeated surreptitious glances at Mallory. Two couples, the Tylers and the Shaws, stopped for a few words with them. The deejay introduced *I'll Be Seeing You.*

In the pause between the announcement and the start of the music, a bright flash of lightning lit the sky followed by a booming clap of thunder. The building shook. Pelting rain started falling seconds after it faded. The lights went out.

19

"That's a cue for a scream," I quipped while people groaned at the power loss. Both of my companions laughed. "It's a B-movie formula. A flash of lightning, clap of thunder, a downpour, the lights go out, and somebody screams. It always happens that way—"

A scream cut me off. A man's voice full of panic resounded through the dark room.

"Thompson! We need flashlights and lanterns!" Mallory spoke up in the stunned silence following the scream. Another scream, longer and higher pitched, echoed while someone began moaning and sobbing.

A general babble built, accompanied by the raging thunderstorm outside and punctuated by the scraping sound of chairs moving. Voices called out as guests tried to find each other in the dark.

"*Quiet, please!* Everyone, stay where you are!" roared O'Brien. "Sit down in the nearest chair or on the floor. Moving around will only cause more problems. Where's Thompson?"

"*Robert!*" Constance shrieked hysterically, "help me, Robert, please! *Eddie's hurt!*"

"Stay put," commanded Mallory and O'Brien as they stood.

"Promise." I figured staying put meant I would avoid tripping over something.

I thought I heard Mallory mutter, "For once—"

"Mrs. Ambrose? I have called the power company," Mildred Abernathy's calm voice cut through the subdued background conversations. "The operator said they'll have a repairman out as soon as they can."

"Thank you, Mrs. Abernathy," replied the deep voice I trusted most in the world.

"Mr. Mallory, sir," Jim's voice came from the kitchen doorway, "I have a couple of flashlights." The light from his torch played around the room until it rested on Mallory. "Gerald has gone to see if it's a fuse."

"Mrs. Abernathy, do you have a flashlight?" Mallory asked.

"Yes, sir." the switchboard operator responded.

"Keep it and stay by your board," Mallory ordered.

O'Brien and Mallory took the flashlights from Jim.

"Constance, where are you?" the latter asked. "Where's Thompson?"

Guided by the flashlight in his hand, Constance threw herself into Mallory's arms. "Help me! Eddie is *bleeding!*"

She dragged Mallory over to the edge of the dance floor not far from where I sat. I only needed to crane my neck to see the activity. In the light provided by the two torches, combined with flashes of lightning, I saw Thompson lying on the floor. His moans and sobs filled the gaps between rumbles of thunder.

"We need a doctor." O'Brien announced, bending over him. Thompson's moans continued.

"I'm a physician, perhaps I can help?" A tall, middle-aged man came forward in the intermittent flashes playing outside. "Harlan James."

"Please, if you would, Dr. James," O'Brien said, holding his flashlight steady, "take a look at him." The doctor knelt to examine the wound.

"I don't wish to alarm you, but from what I can see, he's been stabbed," the doctor declared a moment later, straightening up and addressing O'Brien. "I'll need to examine him more thoroughly in better light to be certain."

Thompson's moaning increased. No words, just moans from what I could hear.

"Let's get him moved to his cabin," O'Brien ordered, standing up. "Jim? Robert? Give us a hand."

The two men obeyed. I noticed not only did Mallory and O'Brien behave like a well-rehearsed act, but everyone obeyed them.

"Constance, if Edward has been stabbed, don't you think we should call the police?" a woman's voice asked.

"The police are already here." O'Brien turned to the guests. "Ladies and gentlemen, I am Daniel O'Brien, Captain of the Northwoods Glen Police Department."

Mallory and Jim managed to get the groaning Thompson upright between them. Dr. James held a flashlight to guide their way. They were four feet from the door when the lights suddenly flared back to life. Gerald came out of the kitchen.

"Someone pulled out one of the fuses," he announced. "I'm sorry it took me so long to find it."

"Thank you. Have Mrs. Abernathy cancel the repair request," Mallory told him.

Constance shrieked—again—and threw herself—again—at Mallory, forcing him to let go of Thompson. "Robert, it's so awful!" she sobbed, clinging to him and burying her face against him.

I bit my tongue when he patted her on her shoulder. Her sobs were phony.

"Constance, he's going to be all right. Doctor?"

"Oh, yes, no question," James immediately confirmed. "I can help Jim get him to the cabin if you're needed here. I have an umbrella."

"Thank you," Mallory told the doctor while he attempted to disengage himself. "Constance, what's wrong?"

"This! All this!" She let out one more anguished cry and melted against him. Left with no choice, he guided her to our table and got her into a chair. She leaned against his legs.

"Captain?" I spoke for the first time since Thompson's scream cut me off.

"Yes?" It came out as a growl.

"You're going to need statements, and people are getting restless." He glared at me and I shrugged. "I'm only trying to be helpful." I nodded to the guests.

He scanned the room. A few women started gathering purses, preparing to leave.

"Everyone, please stay here." O'Brien ordered. He disappeared into the switchboard office.

Constance whimpered. Her elegantly coiffed hair, elaborately done with hair picks and combs, showed signs of coming down. Somehow or other she managed to get her dress dirty, too. I noticed a dark stain on the shoulder of her white dress.

"Calling for reinforcements?" I nodded to the office.

"A fair guess. There are about sixty people here and his first step will be getting their statements. He can't do that and question the top five by himself," Mallory confirmed. He gazed down at Constance, shaking his head in resignation.

Constance seemed content as long as she could lean against Mallory. I glanced around the room, noticing small groups of members standing around, conversing in low tones. The indistinct chatter increased, getting stronger until O'Brien returned, Mrs. Abernathy behind him in her doorway.

"Ladies and gentlemen, may I have your attention?" O'Brien moved to one end of the dance floor. "Mr. Thompson has been stabbed and is now under a doctor's care. We are going to need your cooperation to find the person responsible. I'd like you to find seats and try to avoid discussing these events among yourselves more than you have already. Please remain here until you have given your statement to one of my three officers, who will arrive soon. Does anyone have questions that can't wait?"

"There are two families here. Can we check with our babysitters?" Mrs. Tyler, whom I saw with three children Wednesday night, asked. Her voice sounded like the one which suggested calling the police.

"Your name and cabin?"

"Geraldine Tyler, Cabin Six. My husband is Doug Tyler."

"The other family?"

"John and Stephanie Shaw, Cabin Eight," a man of about thirty spoke up. "My wife and I hired one of the housekeepers to watch our kids while we attended the dance. So did the Tylers. The babysitters are in our cabins staying with the kids."

"Once my officers get here, we'll take you first," O'Brien decided. "In the meantime, I'll have the operator call your cabins to check for you." He nodded to Mrs. Abernathy. "Will that be satisfactory?" he asked the concerned parents.

"Yes, sir, and thank you." Shaw's arm tightened around his wife's shoulders.

Carmella slipped through the crowd to our table and hesitated with a look at Constance.

I indicated an empty chair. "Congratulations on your win. You and Jim make a great team."

She beamed, nodding her thanks. Constance ignored her.

O'Brien pulled up a chair and faced Constance. Mallory took the seat next to her and she leaned her head on his shoulder, clutching his arm.

"Mrs. Ambrose, I'd like you to tell me exactly what happened when the lights went out," O'Brien requested, more agreeably than I expected.

"Janet stabbed him. It had to be Janet," she said.

The tone of her voice did not match her body language. Her statement came out with too much force, belying the helpless female she attempted to portray.

"You saw her stab him?" O'Brien's tone stayed neutral.

"No, I just know she did it."

"You didn't see her with a knife?" persisted the policeman.

"I had my eyes closed. I hate thunder and lightning, so my eyes were closed when the lights went out," she explained with an over-exaggerated shudder. "I heard Eddie scream, and opened my eyes. He fell against me and we sank to the floor."

"You didn't actually see anyone approach him, or inflict a wound?"

"How could I? I had my eyes shut," she said contemptuously, treating O'Brien like a lowly servant. "Why are you asking all these questions? I've already told you. Janet did it," she irritably insisted.

"You seem sure of that. Why would she hurt him?" O'Brien questioned.

"He was ignoring her. She wanted to dance with him, and he wouldn't pay any attention to her, so she wanted to hurt him, and she stabbed him," Constance explained like she would to a child.

Abruptly, her demeanor altered, flipping one hundred and eighty degrees.

"Find her!" she snarled belligerently, leaning forward to confront the policeman. "You want to get the person who did this, find Janet and arrest her!" Her voice grew wilder, and she yelled, "She stabbed Eddie and she'll come after me next!" Constance half-rose out of her seat and screeched, "I'll be next—you'll see!"

Less than three seconds later, her mood seesawed again.

"I want to go to my cabin. Robert," she whimpered, sinking back into her chair. "Take me to my cabin." Constance covered her face with her hands, and her shoulders shook.

Heaven help us! From what I could see, Janet was not even in the room. I glanced at Mallory, who gave me the faintest of negative head shakes. *Okay, not now.*

O'Brien frowned at Mallory, then me, then Carmella. "I want someone to stay with her."

"I concur." Mallory stood and solicitously raised her up; she leaned into him. "Constance, I'll take you to your cabin, but I'll have to come back up here."

"Why can't you stay with me? I want you to stay with me." Peevish and whining, Constance tightened her grip on his arm. "I need you. I want you. I always have. Robert, please?" she pleaded.

"Danny is going to need my help up here. Lauren or Carmella can stay with you." He took one of the umbrellas Mrs. Abernathy produced, and the four of us proceeded.

Meekly, Constance offered no protest.

Too meekly.

Constance's acquiescence lasted from the time we left the clubhouse until the moment the door shut behind Mallory when he left her cabin. Once he departed, she went into a hysterical rage. She struck out at us, threw whatever objects she could grasp, and screamed at us to leave her alone in a tantrum rivaling Judy Garland's outburst in *The Pirate*.

"Get Dr. James!" I ordered Carmella, turning to one side with my forearm raised to deflect an ashtray. Carmella dodged around a table and left. The door closed an instant before a glass hit. It bounced and landed on a rug.

I fended off more flying objects while Constance screeched at me in a language I did not understand.She picked up a heavy vase by its neck and started using it as a club. I retreated behind a chair, dancing around it to avoid her swings. Dr. James arrived on the hop, bag in hand. Taking in the scene, he quickly filled a syringe. Carmella and I wrestled Constance to the settee and resolutely held her. She hurled more abuse at us while the doctor jabbed her with the needle. We stayed with her on the settee for an interminable five minutes, letting go only when she started to calm down.

"Thank you! I was getting tired of dodging," I told him wearily, standing up and straightening my dress.

The three of us moved her into the bedroom. Constance, no longer combative, accepted our assistance after she pompously dismissed the physician. We got her undressed and into a nightgown. Carmella undid her hairstyle.

"You're frowning," I said to Dr. James once he rejoined us in the bedroom. "Why?"

"The shot should have knocked her completely out. Does she take any medication?"

"Check the bathroom cabinet." I gathered up the hair ornaments into a hand towel and folded her dress.

Dr. James emerged from the bathroom shaking his head. "She should fall asleep shortly. Judging by the bottles in her cabinet, she may have a very high tolerance for drugs."

"Doctor, how is Eddie?" Constance's words slurred.

The drug finally took full effect, I realized with relief.

"He's going to be fine," James assured her. "He's resting. Someone will be staying with you for the night if you need anything. You should rest, too."

"I think I will," she responded, once more meek and mild.

We left her tucked in bed. Back in the main room, I noticed one of the hair picks looked dirty and I decided I wanted to get the spot out of her dress. I bundled it with ornaments to take them back to my cabin for cleaning.

"This is getting to be a habit," I remarked to Carmella. "She should consider a paid companion."

"You stayed last night," she said. "I'll stay tonight. Jim has offered to stay with Mr. Thompson."

"Mrs. Abernathy will be on the switchboard," I told her. "Yell if you need something. Dr. James, I'm heading back to the clubhouse. If you can leave your patients, I suggest you accompany me."

"I'll be right with you." He gave Carmella a few instructions and followed me.

20

The storm over, we walked back under a clearing sky to the accompaniment of crickets. Twinkling stars peeked out to play hide and seek among the remaining clouds.

In the clubhouse, O'Brien's three officers took statements while two typists struggled to keep up. Mallory waved us over to the familiar window table. More than ready to get off my feet, I dropped my bundle on a spare chair and glanced around the room. Seeing no sign of the Tylers and the Shaws, I assumed O'Brien kept his word. George and Gerald stayed busy running drinks to various tables. Dr. James gratefully sank into the chair next to mine.

"Maybe there should be some snacks or food available to offset the liquor," I quietly suggested to Mallory.

"An excellent thought. I'll be right back."

He held a brief conference with Gerald, who disappeared into the kitchen. Within ten minutes, Michael and Gerald brought trays of cheese and crackers and bowls of nuts to the buffet table. Chef Willard entered shortly and set out a platter of cut sandwiches. Mallory grabbed a plate and piled on several sandwiches together with some cheese and returned to our table.

"Danny is trying to determine who was standing nearest to Constance and Thompson," Mallory confided, placing the snacks in the middle. "Ah, here he comes."

I moved the chair with the bundle back and O'Brien pulled up one for himself. Notebook out, he glanced at me with a decided lack of enthusiasm. I wondered if he wanted to tell me to get lost.

"You haven't questioned anyone," he challenged. I shook my head. "Good."

We helped ourselves to the sandwiches.

"Dr. James, what type of knife was used to stab Edward Thompson?" the policeman asked.

"My best guess is the blade was long and thin," said James. "It's more of a deep wound than a slice. Whatever it was, it didn't hit anything except muscle in his upper arm and it didn't go all the way through. From what I saw, it looked as if the blade was plunged in from above his arm and immediately pulled out, like this." He demonstrated. "However, I'm a family doctor, Captain, not an expert."

"You'll do." O'Brien scribbled in his notebook. "I have a few questions, if you don't mind?"

"Of course not."

"You're a member here?"

"Oh yes. We joined when it first opened in May. My wife and I enjoy coming here for dinner about once a week and she comes during the day to swim at least twice a week. We don't stay the night, as a rule." Dr. James glanced at his watch.

I glanced at my own wrist before I remembered taking off my watch prior to the dance. Mallory held out his. *A bit after eleven? After last night's fitful rest, the dive, the dance, and now this - no wonder I'm tired. Bother!*

"Can you tell me your movements from the time the contest ended until the lights came back on?" O'Brien looked up from his notes.

"Certainly. I had just re-entered the building and I was standing at the edge of the dance floor, near the windows overlooking the Sound. I went out because I wanted to make sure that the windows of my car were up before the rain started. I brought my bag back with me so I could put a Band-Aid on a paper cut." He held up his left hand; the ring finger sported a small bandage. "I was waiting for my wife to come out of the ladies' room when the loud boom sounded, and the lights went out. When you called for a doctor, I stepped forward."

"Thompson will recover?" Mallory asked.

"The wound isn't dangerous, if that's what you mean," the physician answered. "I cleaned it and bound it. No stitches were required. However, I am a little concerned because he's not as alert as I would expect."

"I don't understand," O'Brien said, puzzled.

"I know he's had a couple of drinks," Dr. James began, "but he's a bit vague in his reactions and responses. Almost—" He let it hang.

"Almost like he's been drugged?" I suggested. It popped out and earned me a glower from O'Brien. *Here we go again, in more ways than one.*

"Well, yes. Without running tests, though, it's no more than an educated guess. I can't be sure."

"I understand. Thank you, Dr. James. If you and your wife will give us your statements, we won't keep you much longer." O'Brien stood and offered his hand.

"Pardon me, Doctor," Mallory spoke when the doctor rose, "will you be available to check on Mrs. Ambrose and Mr. Thompson in the morning?"

"Of course." The physician gave his telephone and his answering service numbers to O'Brien. "I live between here and the Glen, so I won't be far away."

"Hanlon!" O'Brien barked. An officer jumped to his feet. "Take Dr. James' statement next. Do we already have his wife's?"

"It's being typed now." Hanlon, one of the tallest, thinnest men I ever saw, replied. "If you will have a seat, Doctor, I've about finished with Mr. Rosen."

"I'll stop by the cabins on my way out," Dr. James told us. "If anything has changed, I'll call up here."

"Doctor, thank you again for your help with Constance," I sincerely told him. After he left, I stretched and yawned.

Mallory looked at me, frowning. "Help?"

"I had to call him over after you left," I explained. "Constance pitched a major tantrum. She was totally out of control and she tried to bean me with a vase."

"What?" Startled, O'Brien glanced up from his notes.

"She threw a vase at you?" Mallory's eyebrows climbed his forehead, trying to reach his hairline.

"She didn't throw it, exactly. She came at me swinging it like a club while she screamed all sorts of words I didn't understand. She threw other things, like ashtrays and glasses, but the vase was bronze." I grimaced, rubbing the bruise on my forearm where the ashtray hit. "Dr. James got to her before it landed."

"She *swore* at you?" O'Brien asked.

"You've got me," I said with a shrug. "From my viewpoint, I'd guess definitely. The inflections and gestures were all there. My memory for spoken words doesn't extend to languages I don't have in stock. To me it sounded like noise. To her it probably constituted a diatribe. Check with Carmella. I sent her after the doctor, but she heard part of it. All I can tell you is I wasn't going to ask for a translation—I was too busy ducking." I shuddered. "No matter what the reason, you should be grateful her father had that chat with you," I told Mallory.

"She's always been highly strung, but she was never violent," he sadly murmured.

"Mr. O'Brien? There are a few things I'd like to know."

"Such as."

"What did you turn up in Janet Benedict's background which spooked you so badly I had to move out of the Lodge?"

"That will have to wait for a less public conference. What else do you have to know right now?"

"You slipped out after Janet left during the dance and came back without her. Where did she go?"

"She went back to the Lodge for a while and went off to the staff quarters. After a few minutes, I decided to come back here rather than be seen loitering. Why ask?"

"From my position here, as far as I could tell Janet wasn't even in the room when Thompson was stabbed," I told him. "Unless—"

"Unless what?" The men voiced the question in unison.

"We know someone pulled the fuse out to turn the lights off. The fuse box is in the kitchen area, which presumably has an outside entrance. Janet could have entered there, pulled the fuse, darted into the main room, stabbed him, and exited."

"In the dark? With people and tables and chairs in the way?" O'Brien scoffed. "Not feasible."

"I didn't say it was a good explanation," I shrugged. "I'm only offering it as a possibility. I know it's lame enough to need crutches."

"That's a colorful way to put it," remarked Mallory.

"Any other not-so-bright ideas?" the police official inquired, his voice dripping with sarcasm.

"One that may be closer," I retorted. "I honestly think Janet pulled the fuse."

"Why?" O'Brien fired at me.

"We know someone did. Maybe she was doing Thompson's bidding."

"Why?" This one came from Mallory.

"My reasons go back to last night. I'm sure you've noticed there have been quite a few drugged drinks around." I shook my head. "Janet may have been helping Thompson subdue Constance so they could spend some time together."

"Okay, that one's just limping," O'Brien said. He glanced over at his men to check their progress. About fifteen people waited to give statements. Dr. James and his wife were gone. He turned back to me. "I don't suppose you noticed who was standing near Thompson when the lights went out."

"Constance, the Tylers, and the Shaws," I promptly furnished the names. "They were the couples with the babysitters," I offered to be helpful when he looked blank.

"Take her back to your cabin," he instructed Mallory. "I'll meet you there."

I heard a phone ring. Mrs. Abernathy stepped out of her office and gestured to O'Brien. Mallory and I exchanged looks and moved to the door. Sure enough, O'Brien came striding out, heading for us.

"Come on," he growled at Mallory. I started to follow, and he hesitated for a second. Nodding his assent, he grumbled, "Okay."

We ran down past one cabin, darted between the croquet field and Lodge Two, and turned toward the manager's cabin. Jim and the doctor waited between it and the owner's cabin. Jim looked wan, clammy, and shaky.

"Thank you for coming so quickly." Dr. James indicated the owner's cabin. "Mrs. Ambrose has taken an overdose. I induced vomiting, and she should be okay, but I'd rather have her in the hospital. She flatly refused the suggestion."

"When you called, you mentioned a problem with Thompson," O'Brien said, his voice sharp. "What's wrong?"

"Captain, he's dead," Jim informed us, his voice trembling. "I found him a few minutes ago. The doctor said—well, he told me—"

"I believe he was poisoned," finished the physician.

21

"*Poisoned?*"

The three of us spoke the word like a rehearsed Greek chorus and immediately diverged. O'Brien wanted to know when, Mallory asked how, and I wanted to know why. I felt sorry for Dr. James. Our questions piled on top of each other, and he couldn't answer any of them. It got us exactly nowhere.

"Hold!" Mallory sharply broke the logjam. "Danny, do you want some officers down here?"

"One to take statements, and two to process the scene." O'Brien closed his eyes for a moment, regrouping. "Let's go inside and see what I'm dealing with. You," he ordered, meaning me, "stay here."

"No." Mallory snapped the word out like a command.

"*What?*" O'Brien stopped in mid-stride and pivoted, glowering at his friend. His voice held enough ice to cover a skating rink.

"You want her inside. Let her look around. The doctor and I will check on Constance. Jim needs to remain here and keep people out of our way." Mallory's attitude did not invite discussion or leave room for negotiations. He wanted me inside. Period.

"Amateurs. I hate amateurs," O'Brien groused while Mallory and the doctor left to visit Constance. "Okay. I'll take Mallory's word, but don't touch *anything*," he sternly warned me.

I meekly nodded and followed him.

Inside the cabin, I did exactly what Mallory suggested: I looked around. The living area appeared smaller than the owner's cabin although bigger than the one where I parked my things. I saw the same rustic-looking furniture with area rugs on the floor. A small end table paired with two easy chairs held magazines. The kitchenette consisted of the same table, chairs, sink, and refrigerator as the owner's digs, with fewer cupboards. Three bookshelves, housing books and a few knick-knacks, lined up against a wall. His desk, with a matching pen and pencil set resting on the blotter, seemed more utilitarian than the roll-top one in Constance's cabin, with a swivel chair behind it. I noticed an open box of Schrafft's assorted candy; the lid sat slightly askew. Two phones sat side by side.

I walked to the bedroom doorway and peered inside. O'Brien, standing in the middle of the room, scowled at me. I ignored him, primarily because my attention immediately focused on something else.

Thompson's body lay sprawled on the bed. It looked like he fell over while sitting. A copy of Agatha Christie's *The Moving Finger*, with a bookmark about half-way, sat undisturbed on the bedside table next to a drinking glass. I saw a Bible on the lower shelf.

I clearly showed O'Brien I held my hands carefully clasped behind my back and moved through the bedroom to the bathroom.

"May I open the cabinet?" I asked.

"Let me." Standing beside me, he reached up and used his handkerchief to pull on the inner third of the upper edge. The mirrored door swung open.

"Since that's not the normal way to open it," I said thoughtfully, "it won't ruin any prints?"

He regarded me like he might be willing to admit I belonged to the human race.

"Right," he nodded. "Remember that."

"I will," I vaguely promised. Something in the cabinet caught my attention. "Captain? You might want to have Mr. Mallory take a look at this."

"Why?" He asked a genuine question instead of barking or snapping.

I wondered if 'why' was his favorite word.

"Last night, Mr. Mallory checked this cabinet after we decided that the butler had slipped something into Thompson's drink. He reported enough vitamins, aspirin, and cough syrup to stock a drug store yet nothing requiring a prescription. Which means that," I pointed to a pharmacy bottle, "wasn't here. He would be able to tell you for certain."

"I'll check with him."

We went back into the bedroom and I took a better gander at Exhibit A.

Contorted facial features indicated a painful death. Dressed in only pajama bottoms, the bandage over the stab wound in his upper left arm appeared intact. I moved closer, with my hands still clasped behind my back. Thompson's right hand lay across his chest, like it had been up around his neck when he died, yet his arm rested at a weird angle. All his muscles were clenched: his legs pulled up toward his chest and his back slightly arched. I noticed dark smudges on the thumb and middle finger of his right hand while his left one gripped the bedclothes.

All of a sudden, the world started to spin. I straightened up and stumbled backward into O'Brien, who steadied me while he turned me around.

"Easy! Take deep breaths," he encouraged, surprisingly reassuring. "It's okay." His hands rested on my shoulders while he studied my face.

"Sorry," I said, my voice and body trembling. I shut my eyes, but the sight of the body remained in my mind.

"Your first fresh corpse," he shrewdly guessed and I nodded. "It's a normal reaction. Don't worry, it happens. Let's go into the main room."

Mallory waited for us with Dr. James. Mallory immediately put me in one of the easy chairs and dragged one of the kitchen chairs over to sit near me. I did not lean against him, although the thought crossed my mind.

"Constance adamantly refuses to go to a hospital," he reported to O'Brien. "I tried. I couldn't get her to budge. She swears she only took a couple of pills and promised me it wasn't a suicide attempt. She told me she woke up and, wanting to go back to sleep, she took two of her sleepers. It proved a bit too much on top of the sedation."

"Is Carmella with her?" O'Brien asked.

"Affirmative and she has offered to stay until she's not needed." Mallory cocked his head sideways toward me. "You look about like Jim does."

"Jim found the body." I grimaced. I took more deep breaths, letting them out slowly; my shakes subsided. "I only looked at it."

"Danny, I sent Jim to the parking area to tell Mrs. James to go back to the clubhouse. Don't you need your people here?" Mallory's question eerily resembled a command.

"Dr. James, what phone did you use to call the clubhouse?" O'Brien asked, not bothering to quibble with Mallory.

"The one closest to the corner."

O'Brien picked up the receiver. "Mrs. Abernathy, I need a line to the police station."

We listened to him giving a stream of orders. He hung up and called the switchboard again, asking for

Hanlon. More orders followed, including getting three of his men down from the clubhouse.

Mallory reached over and placed his hand on my arm. "Are you alright?" he quietly asked.

"It crept up on me kind of sudden-like," I told him. "I'll be okay. I do have a question."

"There's a surprise," muttered O'Brien while he waited to be connected to the coroner's office.

"Does Constance know Thompson is dead?" I asked Mallory.

"I certainly didn't mention it," he replied, "and neither did she. Doctor, did you tell her?"

James shook his head. "I wasn't about to risk triggering another tantrum. I wanted—"

"Doctor, I'm afraid we're going to need another statement from you," O'Brien interrupted, hanging up the telephone. "You can start by telling us what happened." O'Brien's gaze measured me while he took his notepad out of his jacket pocket. "How good is your memory?"

"Good enough." I considered asking if I would have to relay it to Hanlon, but the expression on his face quelled the notion.

"Doctor, go ahead. When you left the clubhouse, you said you would stop by the two cabins on your way out."

"I walked my wife to the parking lot and unlocked our car. I told her I'd be right back, and I went to Mrs. Ambrose's cabin. Carmella was about to telephone the clubhouse, because she had checked on Mrs. Ambrose and found her unresponsive." He swallowed. "May I have a glass of water, please?"

Mallory took care of that and got one for me. I gratefully accepted it.

"Thank you." He sipped. "I found a bottle of sleeping tablets open in the bathroom, with a glass on the sink. I still had my bag and I induced vomiting since I didn't know how much of the drug she had taken on top of the shot I gave her. Carmella and I got her cleaned up and back in bed. I sent Carmella to the parking lot to suggest my wife go back to the clubhouse because I was going to be a while longer. When Carmella returned, I thought I'd check on Mr. Thompson before calling you about Mrs. Ambrose."

"How long did all that take?" O'Brien asked.

"About fifteen minutes, not much more."

"What did you do next?"

"I left Carmella with Mrs. Ambrose and came over here," he stated. "There was no one in this room when—"

A knock interrupted. O'Brien answered it and showed his men into the bedroom. "Make it more than thorough."

"Captain, we didn't bring a camera." I recognized the officer as one of the men in the clubhouse.

"I have one." I handed the officer my cabin key. "Come with me."

I ran outside, told Jim to follow me, and got Carmella. Leaving Jim to keep an eye on Constance, I sent Carmella and the officer for my equipment.

"Carmella helped me move to the cabin earlier and she knows where my camera bag is," I explained, re-entering Thompson's cabin. I resumed my seat.

O'Brien started to say something, undoubtedly a snide comment about me, but Mallory shook his head. O'Brien didn't utter a sound.

These guys make quite a team, but Mallory leads.

"Doctor, you were saying no one was in here when you came in." O'Brien picked up his thread.

"That's right. I heard retching, so I went to the bedroom. I was checking Thompson when Jim came out of the bathroom," the doctor explained. "Jim told me he found Thompson like that."

"Did he hear anything to make him think he should check on Thompson?" I asked, forgetting my position as the tape recorder for a moment. O'Brien's nod surprised me; I anticipated another glare. If 'why' topped his list of favorite words, glares ranked as his favorite expression.

"Yes, he mentioned he thought he heard a coughing sound or something," the physician answered my query.

"As soon as Carmella gets back, we'll get Jim's statement," O'Brien acknowledged. "Did you examine Thompson?"

"I only confirmed the death. I saw no overt signs of violence, and under the circumstances, his death was highly suspicious. The facial contortion, the position he was in, and the muscular contractions of his limbs all suggested an unnatural death. I left him as he was rather than move the body."

"I appreciate that. What makes you suspect poisoning?"

"It's mostly a matter of deduction. An otherwise healthy man in his late thirties does not die from a simple stab wound. I had examined him less than an hour before. His wound was not serious, and even assuming he was slightly drugged it was not life-threatening. With no other obvious causes, poison seemed probable."

We considered the theory. When the officer came back with my camera bag, I quickly rewound my film in the Kodak, inserted a new roll, and showed it to O'Brien. "Will this do?"

"Randolph?" O'Brien nodded to the first officer.

"It should." Randolph took it with the flash attachment into the bedroom. The other officer came out.

"Captain, I took his prints. There was something on two of the fingers of his right hand."

"Which ones?"

"Thumb and index finger," the second officer reported.

"Excuse me! Thumb and *middle* finger," I corrected. "Brownish. My guess is chocolate."

O'Brien glowered at me. "I told you not to touch anything," he growled.

"I didn't," I objected, growling back. "I only did what I was told. I simply looked."

The second officer held out a small evidence bag with what looked like a tissue in it. "I apologize, sir, she's correct about the middle finger. I'll get it to the lab, but she could be right about chocolate." That earned him a glare from the captain.

"Captain?If I could give you my statement, I'd really like to get out of here," Dr. James said.

"Where's Hanlon?" O'Brien asked the officer in front of him.

"He's in the other cabin, getting a statement from the girl Carmella."

"Doctor, you've been very helpful. If you will give your statement to Hanlon, the man who took your other one," O'Brien told him graciously, "you and your wife can leave. I'll call the clubhouse and have her escorted to your car."

"Thank you, I'd appreciate that. I'd like one more look at Mrs. Ambrose, too." He left.

"Hopefully, she's still breathing," I mumbled, while O'Brien used the phone again."What a convoluted mess."

"Chocolate, eh?" Mallory commented softly to avoid disturbing O'Brien's conversation with his remaining officer.

"Let's wait a minute," I murmured, nodding at the captain. "I only want to relate this once."

"The ambulance is on its way to pick up Thompson. My man will wait for it after he sees Mrs. James to the parking lot." O'Brien sat down. "Now, what's this about chocolate?"

"I saw something brownish on his fingers. There's an open box of candy on the desk."I pointed to it. "Let's say it fits together. Mr. Mallory, did you see that box of candy on the desk last night?"

"No. I'm not as good as you are, but I would have noticed that," he firmly stated.

"Was there any bottle of prescription medication in the bathroom cabinet last night?" I continued with questions while O'Brien allowed it.

"No."

"Evans!"O'Brien yelled.

"Sir?" The second officer leaned out of the bedroom doorway.

"In the medicine cabinet, you'll find a prescription bottle of pills. Dust it for prints. When you're done, I want the kit."

Evans nodded and returned to the bedroom. O'Brien swiveled in his seat. "I'll take Mrs. Ambrose's prints myself, Robert, if you'll help smooth the way."

"I'll do my best."

"Can we get back to Janet for a moment?" I asked. "You have a chunk of information about her you haven't divulged, specifically whatever you discovered before you ordered me to move from the Lodge to the cabin. Care to give it to us now?"

He hesitated; his lips pursed together. I waited, hoping he would flip a coin or something to decide whether to let loose or not. After a minute of silence, I risked a guess.

"Was Thompson a bigamist or is Janet related to Constance's late husband?"

"Cheese and rice!" exploded O'Brien; his broad, craggy face turned red. "How in blazing Hades did you know?"

"Which is it?" I scrupulously controlled the urge to sound smug.

"Her legal name is Janet Benedict Ambrose. She's Doug Ambrose's kid sister."O'Brien attempted to intimidate me by glaring holes in me; his glower came naturally. "I want to know how *you* knew."

"Captain, I promise it was only an educated guess," I placated. "Those were the only two circumstances I could conceive which would spook you into summarily ordering me to vacate her area. Plus, it fits the overall picture." I paused for a moment. "I wonder, though, if Thompson knew. He kept pulling Janet out of Constance's way, even while he toyed with her. Or maybe he was trying to protect Constance from her late husband's sister."

Mallory smiled at the expression on O'Brien's face, which looked like a mix of exasperation and disdain tempered by a tiny smidgen of approval.

"Danny, relax. Be thankful she's on your side."

"Smart-aleck amateur! Just what I need," he beefed. "I need Janet's statement. Blast it! I need Janet, period."

"What I need is to go back up to the clubhouse," I announced, taking the cue. I rose and stretched. "I left a couple of things up there when we bolted down here."

"Like what?" O'Brien did not sound sympathetic. "You haven't lost your key again, have you?"

"I put that in my pocket. I do learn my lessons," I retorted, patting the side-seam pocket in my dress. "I took Constance's white dress and her hair ornaments up there after Carmella and I got her to bed. They need some spot cleaning and I thought I'd take care of it in my cabin. I'd also like to spend a bit of time there. After all, it was free." I yawned. "I'd especially enjoy sleeping. The bed looks comfortable."

"Do we have your statement for earlier this evening?"

"Nope. Or one for this latest fracas. I warn you though, if I don't get some sleep, all Hanlon will be able to write down is 'snoring sounds.' Besides, I didn't see anything you two didn't see."

"I'm beginning to get the feeling that you see more than I ever will," O'Brien grumpily complained. "By the way, who taught you how to do that?"

"Do what?" I yawned again. "Excuse me."

"I think Danny wants to know how you learned to remember all the little details of what you see," Mallory generously interpreted. "I've never asked but I'd be interested too."

"From the time I was a little girl, my parents and I used to play a game. We'd go somewhere and study something like a display, then walk off and try to remember everything about it. My favorites were store windows at Christmas." The recollections brought a faint smile to my face. "My dad was good at it, but my mom reigned as the family champion. I learned to associate items with each other to form patterns."

"You're wasted on journalism," O'Brien acerbically conceded, "but stay out of my investigation!"

"I didn't horn in for the fun of it, you know," I pointed out, tired enough to show my aggravation at his harping. "I told you I'm here doing a job while I attempt to work in a favor for a friend. Oh! Speaking of my job. If things ever calm down enough, Mr. Mallory, I'll need that typewriter. If I don't show up with an article, my boss is going to toss me out on my rear."

"Typewriter?" O'Brien questioned.

"Mr. Slater sent it out here with Mr. Mallory. It's one of the ones your typists are using." I aimed a warning at O'Brien. "Don't run off with it. It belongs to the *Gleaner*. Can I go now?"

"I suppose. You're not going to vanish on me, are you?"

"You mean like Janet did? I don't plan on it, I promise."

"You promise," he scorned.

"I would like to point out I promised I'd stay at the table after the lights went out," I objected, "and I'll have you know I did."

"Evans!" O'Brien sang out again.

The police officer came out of the bedroom, briefcase and bag in hand. "Captain?"

"You're finished?"

"Yes, sir." He extended the small bag. "Here's the kit."

O'Brien took it just when a knock sounded on the door. I opened it. Two attendants with a stretcher entered.

"Bedroom, that door," I instructed, pointing. "Captain O'Brien? Will you have the candy in the box analyzed?"

"Believe it or not," he snapped, "it *had* occurred to me. After it gets dusted for prints." He handed the kit back to Evans. "Do it and bag it."

The attendants removed Thompson's body while Evans finished with the candy box. Hanlon and Randolph showed up at the door in time to hold it open. O'Brien proceeded to issue more orders.

"Evans, take Kaye up to the clubhouse. Let her collect a couple of things and make sure she doesn't fall into the pool. Once she retrieves her things, escort her to her cabin and make sure she doesn't get lost." O'Brien looked at the other two. "Seal this cabin. No one in without my okay."

"Yes, sir." Evans did not smile, although I thought I caught a glint of humor in his eyes.

"Mr. Mallory? Would you take charge of the typewriter? I'm going to need it tomorrow afternoon." I yawned again.

"Not in the morning?" he teased, nodding.

"Definitely not! I plan to sleep all morning." I smiled at Evans. "Ready?"

"Yes, ma'am." He gave me a smile and held the door open for me.

"You're more polite than your boss," I complimented him while we exited.

"*I heard that!*" boomed O'Brien's voice from behind us.

"I meant you to," I shot back over my shoulder. I heard Mallory laugh while the door closed.

Evans grinned. We started past the croquet field. I took in his appearance. A good-looking man, a few inches taller than me in my heels, and approximately my age, he had sandy blond hair and brown eyes.

"Do you have a first name?" I asked, attempting to be sociable in spite of the circumstances.

"Walter. Most of my friends call me Walt."

"Walt, I hope you don't get the wrong impression about me."

"Oh, no, Miss Kaye. Captain O'Brien is one of the finest officers I've ever met. It's just he's always so serious. We never see him joking around." He regarded me. "Are you in law enforcement?"

"Heaven help us, no! I'm a reporter for the *Daily Gleaner*. I'm actually here to do a piece on the resort for our Sunday edition."

"That's going to be some story," he observed.

Resort to Murder

22

The bundle with the dress and hair ornaments lay exactly where I left it. The dining area had been restored to its normal appearance, with no signs remaining of the dance festivities or police activity. Gerald, alone in the room, glanced up from putting chairs under the tables and smiled.

"How's Jim doing?" he asked.

"He's shaky. It was quite a shock," I replied.

George came out of the kitchen. "I thought I heard your voice. I have something for you if you can wait a minute."

I nodded. He retreated, returning in less than two minutes. Smiling broadly, the bartender handed me a paper bag.

I unfolded the top and peered inside. I possessed two bottles of club soda and a small packet of lime slices. "Thank you!" I showed my escort my new treasures and explained them.

Mrs. Abernathy came out of her office and beckoned to me. "Phone call, Miss Kaye."

I turned my loot and the bundle over to Evans and stepped into the tiny office.

"Hello." I adjusted the headset.

"Glad I caught you," O'Brien's gruff voice sounded in my ear. "I'm sending Mallory up to you."

"To use your favorite word, why? What's wrong now?"

"Nothing more, not yet anyway. Mallory wants you protected, and I think I concur."

"All I'm planning on doing when I get to the cabin is get out of my finery and into bed. I figure I'll be asleep about fifteen seconds before my head makes it to the pillow." I yawned.

He made a noise that sounded like a muffled snort.

"Captain, while I appreciate the thought, I don't consider it necessary. Once I'm inside my cabin, I'll send Evans back to you. Please tell Mr. Mallory he should follow my example and find his own bed." I heaved a tired sigh, weary to the bone. "Any sign of the missing lady?"

"Not a whisper, and that's only one of the other things I don't like about this."

"Has Constance been told about Thompson's death?"

"No. Dr. James called here to let me know he was home, and we discussed that. He feels she shouldn't be told until she's more stable."

"Swell. That could be some time around Christmas. How are Jim and Carmella?"

"Holding up, barely."

"Any surprises in their statements?" I yawned. "Excuse me."

"You know, you're not one of my officers," he dryly reminded me. "Can you give me a good reason why I should keep you informed?"

"Honestly? Not a solitary one. However, cutting me off now would make less sense than answering me." I hesitated a second and added, "You do realize I might be of some help."

"Okay, okay. Miracles do happen. But nothing, and I mean *nothing*, gets printed without my say-so."

"Check—no arguments." *Not with who is involved in this.* "I need to file a story as soon as you're ready to let me, though. I do have to keep my job."

"I'm going to release a statement in the morning. I'll let you call your editor then."

"It's a deal. You may have to wake me up." I smiled to myself at the mind-image of that scene. "About the statements?" I prompted.

"Jim said he stepped outside at midnight to stretch his legs for not more than three minutes," O'Brien related, "and when he came back in, he sat in one of the easy chairs and picked up a *New Yorker* from the table. He had started to read when he heard some kind of noise from the bedroom. He described it as not quite an outcry or yell, not quite a strangled gargle. He put the magazine down and walked to the bedroom." He paused. "You know what he found."

"Will you post an officer down there for the night?"

"Already done. Once you are back in your cabin, I'll station Evans in Constance's cabin so Carmella can go back to her quarters." O'Brien paused. "You are telling me you don't want anyone with you?"

"I don't think I'm a target. If I thought otherwise, I'd consider it." Another yawn escaped. "I want to get some sleep. I spent last night on the settee in the owner's cabin. I want a bed. All to myself. For the next three days."

He chuckled, not as warmly as Mallory would have, but closer than a cackle. I definitely heard a chuckle. "All right, you win. I'll tell Robert you'll yell if you need something."

"George, the bartender, has already given me what I wanted most. Two bottles of club soda and a packet of lime slices. I'm all set."

"See you in the morning."

"In case you haven't noticed, it's morning already." I heard another chuckle followed by a click. I gave the headset back to Mrs. Abernathy. "If I close my eyes and wish really, really hard, I might be able to make the world leave me alone for ten hours."

"If it works, let me know how it's done," she laughed.

"I promise. Thanks for all your help. You've been swell."

Evans joined me. "Ready?"

"More than."

When we arrived at Cabin Four, he left me on the porch, after making sure I got the door unlocked, and wished me a good night.

I stepped inside, closed the door, and reached for the light switch. Before I could flick it on, someone grabbed me from behind. I felt a sharp prick on my throat and simultaneously a hand went over my mouth.

My fatigue vanished in a split second. My heart pounded in my ears. I trembled.

Don't give in to fear, don't give into fear, don't give into fear, I repeated to myself. I fought down the panic threatening to engulf me. Instinctively, I inhaled and tried to free myself, reaching up to my neck with one hand. I felt a small knife with its point against my throat.

"Don't yell." Janet hissed in my ear. "You scream and it will be the last thing you do," she warned. She increased the pressure of the knife. I took my hand away. A small drip of something warm slid down my neck. I guessed it was blood. Mine. I fought down a shiver.

Janet? What is going on here? Heaven help me, I cannot afford to panic!

I took slow, deep breaths without moving my neck. The knife stayed poised but she did not increase the pressure. She reached around me and locked the door.

I wanted to faint, or scream, but I knew I could not afford the luxury. I forced myself to remain calm. The adrenaline rush slowly receded and fatigue returned.

"You can let go. I'm too tired to fight with you." I struggled to keep my voice steady.

"Good. I want to talk to you." She shifted her grip on the knife.

"You realize the police would love to have a chat with you."

"I'll talk to you, not the police. But not here. You have a car, and we're leaving. I want to get out of this place before I get killed." She twisted my arm behind my back without lowering the knife.

"Believe me, I don't want to see any more bodies, much less become one. Can we sit down?"

"No!" she snapped. "I told you! We're leaving." She eased the pressure of the knife at my throat. "What bodies? You weren't here when Vera died."

"Janet, how long have you been here?"

"Since the resort opened in mid-May."

"Sorry, I didn't word that right." I sighed deeply, trying to regroup my scattered thoughts. "I meant how long have you been here in my cabin tonight?"

"Since I heard Mrs. Ambrose call out that Edward was hurt. I used my keys to get in."

"Why did you hide?" *Bother! She doesn't know about Thompson's death, only the stabbing.*

"I know she's going to blame me for stabbing Edward, and I wanted to talk to you before I got arrested or killed." Her grip relaxed.

"I'm going to turn around," I told her. "I'm not your enemy, I'm certainly not a rival, and I'm played out." Fatigue replaced the surge of panic.

She lowered the knife and released my arm. I reached for the lamp by the chairs and turned it on.

The composure I admired when I first saw her at the Lodge no longer existed. Dressed for the dance, her disheveled appearance took second place to her expression. She was abjectly terrified.

"Let me put these things away." I slowly walked to the kitchenette to put the paper bag and the bundle on the counter. "Now, can we sit down?" I quietly asked. "Just out of curiosity, when Carmella and the police officer came to get my camera, where were you?"

"I heard them unlocking the door and I hid in the bathroom." She perched on the edge of one of the easy chairs. "The man was a policeman?"

"The police needed my camera to photograph the crime scene. It was faster than sending back to the station for their equipment." I slowly and carefully moved to a chair and sat down.

A knock sounded at the door. Janet sprang up with a grace I did not possess, knife in hand, and moved towards me.

"Lauren?" Arlene called. "May I come in?" The doorknob jiggled.

Janet shushed me, once more holding the knife at my throat. I remained absolutely motionless to avoid another knife prick.

"Lauren?" Arlene repeated and paused, waiting for a response. After a full minute, we heard her footsteps fade when she left the porch.

"We can't talk here," Janet muttered. "Come on, we're leaving. Where is your car parked?"

"It's in the residents' parking lot, but I am way too tired to consider driving," I argued. "I can barely keep my eyes open." I slumped to emphasize it.

"All right, there's someplace else we can go." She grabbed my arm and pulled me to my feet. "Move! We're going to walk along the beach to the other side of the resort."

"I want a sweater." I stepped into the bedroom and picked up my sweater with shaking hands. I would have given anything to burrow into the inviting bed and pull the covers up over my head.

"Come *on!*" she harshly ordered.

I forced my attention back to my predicament.

Impatiently, she grabbed my arm and pulled me out onto the porch. I locked the door. Janet kept her knife close enough to keep me threatened. I did not have the energy or inclination to fight or argue. We walked along the beach past the clubhouse, between the cabins, around the croquet field, and finally to the rear of the women's dorm. She unlocked the west end door and we slipped into room eight. I found myself back where I started on Wednesday. That seemed like a month ago.

"Okay," she began, sitting on the chair and waving me to the bed, "we can talk. No one will think of looking for us here, and there's no one next door to hear us. Has Mrs. Ambrose accused me of hurting Edward?"

"Yes, but—"

"I tell you I didn't do it," she insisted. "I wasn't—"

"You weren't in the room," I finished. "Yes, I know. Did you pull the fuse out?"

"What? How did you—? Oh, okay." She sighed, scowling. "Yes, I did. Edward asked me to. Tomorrow is Mrs. Ambrose's birthday. Edward planned to slip into the kitchen, and we were going to bring out a special cake he had Chef Willard make. I was waiting for him to come in when I heard him scream. I knew something terrible had happened, so I ran. I knew she'd try to blame me."

"She did. I informed the police you weren't in the room when the lights went out, and the chances of you being able to run in, stab him, and run out again without bumping into someone or the furniture were slim to none."

"All I did was pull the fuse. I don't think any of the kitchen people even saw me."

"No one came forward to report you, so presumably not."

"If they believed you—if they know I didn't stab Edward—then why are the police looking for me?"

"They have to get statements from everyone at the dance, and you *were* there," I replied, taking comfort from speaking the truth if not the whole truth. "Now that we have that out of the way, why are you afraid that Constance Ambrose is going to have you arrested? Is it because she believes you stabbed him?"

"No, not exactly." Janet shuddered.

"Then why would she want to kill you?"

Janet's face hardened; the knife she held shook a little. "Mrs. Ambrose is very jealous; insanely jealous. She saw Edward giving me a hug this morning when we were planning the birthday surprise. She pulled me to one side and told me to keep my hands off him or she'd make me regret it." Janet grimaced and sighed. The hand holding the knife dropped to her lap and she let go of it. I decided not to try for it.

"Do you scuba dive?" I posed the left-field question while I could.

"What?" It startled her. "What's that got to do with it?"

"Nothing. I'm curious. Do you know how to scuba dive?"

"Not really. Vera took me diving once but I'm not crazy about it."

"Who tampered with the diving equipment?"

"What do you mean?" she shot back, defensive. She folded her arms around her chest, hugging herself.

"Janet, I know Vera was married to Edward Thompson. Someone tampered with all the diving equipment. I'm guessing it was to scare Vera off."

"Okay, since you know that much," she mumbled, her face sullen. "Edward told me that he hired Vera because she threatened to tell Mrs. Ambrose about their marriage. It's like you said— Edward just wanted to scare her off. He didn't mean for her to die. She was a diver! I mean, for crying out loud, she taught Edward how to dive! Edward told me that he had fiddled with some of the scuba gear, but he could never kill someone." She shivered. "I never expected her to die! I'm not a murderer!"

"Who loosened the reserve rods on the tanks?"

"Edward did that himself. It was part of the things he did with the gear." She hesitated. "He also told me he had agreed to go diving with her but then he changed his mind. You can check all that with him."

I let that ride. Once I told her about his death, she would probably go into hysterics and turn into a clam. I wondered about the abandoned dive, but I changed tacks.

"Who drugged the drinks the night of the pool party?"

"Oh, God," she moaned, nervously twisting her fingers. "That was so scary! It almost killed them both!"

"Only because there were a lot of drugged drinks floating around," I acknowledged. "What do you know about it?"

"Since everything worked out, I suppose I could tell you about some of that," she reluctantly admitted. "It was confusing."

"That's an understatement. I didn't see you around the bar, but I left the pool area with Robert Mallory before Constance and Edward got out of the water. Constance told Mallory she spilled her first drink and Edward gave her his. She also said she got him another one. Who drugged Edward's drink?"

"*I don't know!*" she cried. She jumped to her feet and began to pace. "All I can tell you is what I did. I went past the pool on my break between working the Lodge desk and my session at the switchboard. I put a sleeping pill in the drink that got spilled, the one supposed to be for Constance. Edward and I wanted to spend some time together, and he gave me a pill to put into her drink. He told me it was one of her sleeping pills and it was only meant to put her to sleep." She sank back into the chair and buried her face in her hands for a moment. "Edward's been good to me. When I saw him in his cabin last night, how bad he was after you got him out of the water, I was really frightened. Later he made me promise I wouldn't tell anyone about the drinks."

"You can relax. I knew someone put a pill into one of the drinks. I didn't know it was you. Who drugged the one he drank?"

"I tell you *I don't know!*" she whined. "I was with Mrs. Abernathy at the switchboard. You saw me when you came up from the beach." Her expression became cagey, and she carefully studied me. "This morning, Edward started flirting with you, and he had his hands all over you while you two were dancing."

258

"Honestly, I would have thought Edward had enough to deal with juggling you and Constance," I said, echoing Mallory's comment. "If you saw him try that on the dance floor, I hope you also noticed I kept moving his hands to where they belonged. I repeat, I'm not a rival. Believe me, he's not my type," I assured her, "and I promise I'm not interested." *Bother! I have to keep the references in the present tense!*

"You are fighting with Mrs. Ambrose over Mr. Mallory."

"That's not my style, Janet. I don't play those games," I truthfully told her. "I also doubt that Mr. Mallory is interested in renewing their relationship. He told me they dated a long time ago. I do know she has made all the overtures here. Frankly, I've gotten a bit tired of seeing her drape herself all over him at every opportunity. You must have seen him try to wiggle free."

She nodded. "I thought he did it to play hard to get. She's very rich."

"Believe me, he's no pauper. He doesn't need the money, and even if he did, that's not *his* style."

"Constance likes getting her own way," Janet glumly said. "She wants him, but she won't give up Edward. She can't have them both," she savagely spat.

"While we're on the subject of Constance Ambrose, did you tell Edward why you wanted to work here?"

"What?" she asked fearfully, on guard again.

"Since last night's incidents, the police have been digging into the backgrounds of everyone involved." I gazed steadily at her. "They uncovered your full name."

"You know." Resigned and subdued, she stared back at me.

"Yes. I found out for certain about an hour ago, although I had my suspicions."

"Constance was horrible to Doug. She dazzled him when they met, and he adored her. Her father forced her to marry him, and she hated that. It wasn't long until she began to belittle him. She goaded him constantly, telling him he wasn't as good to her as the man her father wouldn't let her marry. She never forgave her father, and she grew to hate Doug because of it." Bitter and resentful, Janet's words tumbled out like a torrent of water rushing over rocks. "His death was ruled as an accident and I can't prove otherwise, but I wouldn't put it past her to have paid someone to tinker with his car."

"I'm sorry your brother died," I sincerely told her. "You got a job here, hoping to—what? Find evidence that she killed him or had him killed?" *Oh, bother! I hope she doesn't find out the other man was Robert Mallory.*

"No, I've given up on that. I wanted to meet her. I never did because he wouldn't let me. Doug and I were close, but he kept me away from her. When this place opened up, I took the chance. Did you know that it was Doug's money she used to build this? Money she inherited from him?"

"Constance told me that herself."

"She would have. Anyway, I decided to apply. Besides, I did need the job." She sat up straight, and her expression softened. "When I started here, I met Edward and we hit it off right away. I saw Constance was really possessive, extremely jealous of any woman he might even smile at, but I couldn't help myself. It was hard to find time to be together, but I could help him relax."

"Earlier today Edward told Mr. Mallory and me that he relies on you." I caught myself before I slipped and used the past tense, covering with a yawn. "He confided he is grooming you for assistant manager." I sighed. "Janet, it seems you got caught up in a lot of tangles here. Did you tell Edward about your brother?"

"No. I was going to but after I saw how he treated Mrs. Ambrose I couldn't. He caters to her every whim and won't hear a word against her. He always made excuses for her fits of temper, too. I decided I had to settle for being close to him in whatever way he'd let me."

"You do love him?" *Bother! I almost used past tense again.*

"Oh yes, and I have told him that many times. But he's been very careful. He told me that he needs me, but that's all. He explained Mrs. Ambrose owns the resort and he warned me she would fire me if she found out I was in love with him." She shook her head in disgust.

"Edward is always a gentleman, and he said he wanted me as a friend. He can vouch that all I did was try to help him deal with her," she proudly stated. "There were times he felt she was suffocating him. No woman could get near him without her going crazy. I'm surprised she didn't warn you off. You've been with Mr. Mallory a lot, and she wants him, too. She is very spoiled, and I've seen the way she cozies up to Mr. Mallory."

Janet shot me a sly glance. "I also saw the way she looked at you while you were dancing with Mr. Mallory. She doesn't like you. You might want to be careful," she finished with a knowing nod.

"I assure you I'm aware of it," I acknowledged, "although I'm not overly concerned about it. I know she warned him about me. From what he told me, she said something about my being beneath him."

"He's still chasing you, though. Whatever she told him didn't work."

"I don't think anyone can tell Robert Mallory what to do." I smiled to myself—that was an absolute. "Edward does seem devoted to Constance. By the way, earlier this evening I was in his cabin to check on him after he was stabbed." *True enough in a literal sense.* "Do you happen to know where the box of candy came from? Did he buy it?" *If she answers this one—*

"No, he loves chocolates so—"

A knock sounded on the door. No, not a knock. It sounded more like a sledgehammer enthusiastically applied to a wooden door, and it echoed in the room.

"Police! Open up, Janet," hollered O'Brien, "or I swear I will break down the door!"

23

The pounding increased.

"O'Brien! Hold a moment!" I yelled back. "Janet, it seems the police have found us." *O'Brien, your timing stinks! This had better be worth it.* I grabbed a tissue from the box on the dresser and extended my hand for her knife. She did not resist; she relinquished it and I opened the door.

O'Brien and Mallory faced me with a very frightened Dorothy behind them. Mallory's eyes took in the small wound on my neck and started to speak. O'Brien cut him off.

"Out! Both of you," O'Brien ordered with a growl. He waggled a finger at me accusingly, griping, "You disappeared."

"Not of my own volition," I snapped, trying not to growl. "However, you found us. Janet, I don't know if you heard it earlier, but this is Captain Danny O'Brien of the Northwoods Glen Police Department." I offered him the wrapped knife. "She used this to convince me to disappear. It's not the one that stabbed Thompson. Before you start barking and intimidating her, she's got information for you. Try not to scare her, okay? Go easy!"

"Does she know?" He still growled but with less force and lower volume.

"No." *Assuming you mean Thompson's death.* I looked at Janet. "I hope you'll cooperate."

"There's no reason I should," she retorted defiantly as we left the Lodge. "This whole thing was a stall to give them time to find us."

O'Brien led the party outside into the dark night. After searching for her all evening, he made sure he had a firm grip on Janet's arm.

"Not entirely," I refuted. I sounded exhausted, which matched how I felt. "I meant it when I said I'm not your enemy. You gave me my first clues about what kind of a woman Constance Ambrose really is," handing her the white lie for comfort. *Mental apologies, Arlene.* "I don't like seeing anyone hurt, and you are clearly terrified. Don't you want to get to the bottom of this mess?"

"I suppose so." Her morose tone matched her facial expression.

I tripped over the edge of a walkway, and Mallory steadied me. "Sorry, I'm wiped out," I mumbled. He gently squeezed my shoulders before putting his arm around my waist. "Do I get to know where we are going?" I asked, grateful for his support.

"Your cabin. Arlene is waiting," he said. "She got worried when you didn't answer the door and came to my cabin to see if you were with me. That's what started our search for you."

"That nosy little brat," Janet grumbled.

"Janet, I've known Arlene for over five years now," Mallory told her. "She's a hard-working girl."

"Her grandparents own one of the best restaurants in Northwoods Glen," she said, with a smug attitude. "Edward told me."

"They also run it," I said. "Her grandfather cooks and her grandmother waits on the tables. Arlene is working to put herself through college."

"Oh. You know her too?"

"We've met." *Keep it simple.* "Where is Constance?" I asked our escorts.

"Her cabin." O'Brien did not elaborate.

"Does she know?"

"No."

"Carmella? Jim? Are they okay?" I continued, running down our established list of participants.

"We sent them back to the staff quarters. Hopefully, they are in their own beds," Mallory informed me. "They were both exhausted."

"Why are you asking all this? Don't try to tell me you really care about these people," Janet dolefully said.

"You said it yourself when I checked in: I treat the staff like people. That still goes," I replied. "Here," I extended my key to Mallory. "You open it."

"No need." He knocked, far more considerately than O'Brien's assault on room eight, and called to Arlene. "Robert Mallory and Danny O'Brien. We found them."

Arlene threw the door open. "Thanks be to the Almighty!" she exclaimed.

"You sound like your grandmother," I told her, giving her a hug.

O'Brien cut through the greetings. "Inside. Janet, I want a statement from you covering your movements at the time Edward Thompson was stabbed." He picked up the phone. "Mrs. Abernathy? O'Brien. We found both Lauren and Janet; they're safe. We're in Cabin Four."

Once settled, Janet related the aborted birthday surprise plan. "I ran when I heard Edward scream. I knew I'd be blamed for whatever had happened."

"Where did you go?" O'Brien took it easy although his frown indicated it required effort.

"I came here. I wanted to talk to Lauren." Janet aimed a scathing look at me. "I didn't know she was a police patsy."

"She's not. She's something much worse," O'Brien advised her with a sharp glare at me. "She's a newspaper reporter."

"What?" Janet stared at me. "You're a reporter?"

"Guilty. My editor sent me here for a few days so I could do a full story about the resort for the *Daily Gleaner.*"

"Edward knows?"

"Of course. He okayed the arrangements, and after I pulled him out of the water, he offered me this cabin. It wasn't personal, just a thank you." I shook my head ever so slightly at O'Brien. *Not yet.* "Constance Ambrose also knows who I am and why I'm here. My editor assigned me to do a Sunday feature on it."

"So, you work for a living?"

"Absolutely."

"Then I apologize. I thought you were a society chicken being nice to the staff while you went slumming." Janet sank back into the easy chair. "No wonder Mrs. Ambrose warned him about you," she reflected, nodding to Mallory. "She probably thinks you're a fortune-hunter."

"Let's back up to what happened on Thursday night," Mallory suggested, "at the pool party."

"I only put a sleeping pill into Mrs. Ambrose's drink. Edward gave it to me," Janet asserted defensively, "and told me it was one of hers. I slipped over to the pool area to do it. He needed a break from her because lately her possessiveness has gotten a lot worse. Her jealousy drives him crazy. Plus, I wanted some time alone with him. The only way we could do that was if she was sleeping." She defiantly raised her chin. "You can ask him."

Mallory started to speak but O'Brien caught his eye and shook his head.

Teamwork.

"Who drugged his drink?" Mallory asked instead.

"We're talking about the drinks after you and I left the pool party and went to the float, right?" I yawned.*Let's skip the scene at the boathouse for now.*

"Yes."

"I think I have most of this worked out," I said. "It's a matter of tracing the drinks. I believe the first three were all drugged."

"*Three* drugged drinks?" O'Brien asked, startled.

I nodded. "After Constance jumped off Robert's shoulders, she waved the guests into the water. He and I left the area, heading for the beach. I don't know how long everyone stayed in the pool, but when she and Edward got out, Constance took the first drink, the one with the sleeping pill and handed Edward a drink. According to what Constance told Robert this morning, Edward handed her his drink after she spilled hers. It was the one which she had originally given to him."

"Hold! You're losing me," O'Brien muttered. "Start again."

"Okay. After they got out of the pool, Constance spilled drink number one, the one Janet admits she drugged on Edward's instructions. We can regard that one irrelevant since it ended up on the concrete. Drink number two was the one Constance originally gave to Edward. Remember, after she spilled drink number one, Edward gave Constance *his* drink, number two, and she downed it." I checked to make sure O'Brien stayed with me; at his nod, I continued. "I'm guessing that one was also doctored. Edward, who hadn't had a drink since they went swimming, went back into the water while Constance proceeded to get him a replacement, drink number three. I figure she drugged it before she gave it to him. It's not much, but the theory which fits what happened later. Edward, of course, drank number three."

"Why?" O'Brien's favorite word.

"Why did he drink it? She gave it to him. Why did she do it? Maybe she was trying to do the same thing to him that he was trying to do to her: make sure he was out of the way for an evening."

"Why?" demanded Mallory.

"You're beginning to sound like O'Brien," I grumbled to him. "Why did she want him drugged? She wanted to spend time with you."

Mallory groaned. "I shouldn't be surprised, I suppose."

"By the time they took their late swim in the Sound, they had each downed alcohol laced with drugs," I concluded. "Alcohol alone wouldn't have done it. We saw the results on the float and the beach."

"Wait a minute. Who drugged the one she drank?" Janet asked. "I mean, if she spilled the one I drugged, who drugged the one Edward gave to her?"

"She may have drugged it herself. Although," I pondered aloud, "it was grade-A dumb of her to gulp the one she spiked. I'm lucky I don't drink, or she conceivably would have slipped me something too, to further clear the way for her to be alone with Robert."

"What?" Arlene gasped. "But I saw you with a drink."

"Oh, I had a drink all right. I made a deal with George earlier that night. He agreed to make my special concoction and hand it directly to me or Robert Mallory. Club soda over ice with a twist of lime may look like a gin and tonic but it doesn't smell anything like one."

Mallory nodded. "Thankfully, I was drinking the same thing as you were."

"So was I, tonight," O'Brien said. He ran his fingers through his hair. "All right, you have it figured that

Constance drank the downer she meant for Thompson, and Thompson drank the one she got specifically for him." O'Brien looked like a confused motorist on an unfamiliar freeway at rush hour. "Say I buy all that. Then what?"

"I think they each had another drink and those may or may not have been spiked." I nodded toward Mallory. "We noticed by the time they swam out to the float— another grade-A dumb stunt—even Constance had over-run her tolerance. I doubt Thompson was used to anything like it. From his behavior, she must have handed him an upper in at least one of the drinks. He was giggling in the water and again before he passed out on the beach. Jim commented he was acting goofy, too."

"Uppers and downers? She has all that in her cabin?" O'Brien asked, astounded.

"I thought you saw her medicine cabinet." He shook his head and I apologized. "Sorry, you can check with Dr. James. There are multiple prescription bottles and I doubt they are all tranquilizers. The combination of drugs and alcohol overwhelmed Edward, and he almost drowned."

"But you saved him," Janet said, perplexed. "He told me you pulled him out of the water."

"I acted on reflex. I'm a lifeguard. He slipped on the float's ladder and I heard gurgling and flailing. I went over the side, pulled him up to the surface, and towed him back to the beach. To be honest, I didn't even think about it. Besides, I didn't want him dead."

"Fine, even commendable," O'Brien sarcastically remarked. "Now, what about the scuba gear?"

"Janet, tell him what you told me," I prompted.

"Edward tampered with the tanks. He told me that he fixed each tank so the diver would run out of air, but he insisted anyone used to diving would be able to surface. He wanted to scare Vera off. She was his wife, and she was going to make trouble for him with Mrs. Ambrose," Janet explained, sounding more matter-of-fact.

"You mentioned he agreed to go diving with her. When was that?" I asked.

Janet looked alarmed. "Does it matter?"

"Was it the day she died?" I probed.

Reluctantly, she nodded. "Yes."

"But he didn't go down with her. Why not?"

"He started to. I mean, they had all the diving stuff on and they were wading into the water when Mrs. Ambrose ran onto the beach and told him she needed him in the office. Edward told Vera to go ahead, and he'd join her. At least, I think he told her he would try to, but I'm not sure." Janet grimaced.

"How do you know all this?" O'Brien challenged.

"I started here as one of the housekeepers. I had just finished cleaning Cabin Five and saw it from the door. I don't think they saw me, but that's what happened. Edward promoted me to concierge a few days later. Please don't tell either of them I told you?" she pleaded.

"We won't." I exchanged glances with O'Brien and Mallory. "All along, we've been wondering why Vera went diving alone. It was the big question, and this explains it."

"She was already in the water," Mallory murmured while Arlene nodded.

"Edward only tampered with the valves. He told me he was shocked when the police said she drowned," Janet said. "He didn't kill her."

"I know he didn't," O'Brien confirmed.

I spotted a faint gleam of satisfaction in his steel grey eyes.

"You got a new autopsy," I said.

"After talking to you and seeing we might have missed something, I got a court order last night. Vera's body was exhumed early this morning for a more thorough study. At my request, the coroner ran a few additional tests."

"What did kill her?" Mallory queried for the rest of us.

"Arsenic. There was enough in her to kill two people."

"*Arsenic?*" Mallory, Arlene, Janet, and I pronounced the word like a chorus in an ancient play.

"We have some of her personal effects. She had an ear infection, and we found a prescription bottle of penicillin. The lab tested the remaining capsules and two had arsenic in them. She went diving and the poison hit her system while she was under water, a time gap of more than two hours. I asked the medical examiner why she didn't collapse sooner. He said the most likely explanation was she swallowed it with a meal, according to her instructions. Because of that, absorption and effects were delayed."

"Poor Vera," Arlene said. "She must have been trying to breathe and lost the mouthpiece. The first report said she drowned."

"The contorted facial muscles, initially assumed to be death throes of drowning, are part of the arsenic poisoning symptomology," O'Brien expounded. "The second report agreed that she drowned but cited the arsenic as the primary causal factor."

"Whatever that means," I mumbled. "Someday I'd like to meet a coroner who speaks plain English."

"Jargon makes it more official," Mallory absently noted. "However, if Thompson didn't tamper with the capsules, he's not Lauren's butler."

"Butler? What butler?" Janet wailed. "You mean there is someone *else* in this mess?"

"Not exactly. I got tired of saying things like 'someone' or 'whoever' when talking about the person causing all this grief," I clarified. "In honor of the old mysteries, I decided to refer to our unknown murderer as the butler, like all the plotlines when the butler did it."

"I hate to say this but that's the only thing I've heard tonight that makes sense," she agreed with a weak smile. "Edward isn't the butler."

"No." I took a deep breath. "I think it's time, Captain."

O'Brien nodded. "You or me?"

I opened my mouth; simultaneously the phone rang. Timing again. At his nod, I picked it up.

"Hello."

"Captain O'Brien has an outside call and the officer at Mrs. Ambrose's cabin just reported she's gone," Mrs. Abernathy reported.

"Oh, blazes!" I extended the handset to O'Brien. "Constance has flown, and you have a call."

"Put it through," he demanded. He listened for two minutes, fired an order for two more men to come out, and hung up. "Robert, we need to find her."

Mallory stood up. "I'll start—"

The telephone bell shrilled.

"Yes." O'Brien grabbed it before the first ring faded. "Evans, what in Hades happened? You were supposed—" Red-faced, he paused to give his man a chance, his fist rhythmically clenching and opening. "Okay. Get down to Cabin Four. Mallory and I will start a search, but I want you with Lauren Kaye and Janet Benedict."

"Hold, Danny! There's someone else we need to protect," Mallory interrupted.

"Hold it, Evans," he repeated to Evans, "there's more. Who?" he barked at me, which I thought a bit odd since Mallory brought it up.

"Carmella," I supplied. O'Brien looked blank. "She could also be a target," I offered. "How long ago did Constance bolt?"

"Stand by," he told me. "Evans? Is Randolph still around? I want you both down here. He can escort Arlene Hancock to the staff building and bring Carmella to Cabin Four." He hung up. "Constance Ambrose woke up, railed at Evans, got in a lucky shot with a book, and knocked him out. When he came to a moment ago, she was gone. He doesn't think he was out long." He looked at Arlene. "I know you'd rather stay here with Lauren, but I think you'd be better off in your own room."

"I'll do whatever you recommend, sir," she readily agreed. "I feel bad about all this."

"None of this was your doing, Arlene. You were right thinking there was more to Vera's accident, and for that I thank you. Robert," O'Brien continued without pausing, "you know Constance. What's your best guess? What will she do now?"

"First, she'd go to Thompson's cabin, which is sealed. Next, she'd try mine. Failing that, she'll come here. She'll be searching for Thompson and me."

"What about her vehicle? Would she try to run?"

"She doesn't have a license, or a car and I don't think she has keys to Edward's car," Janet informed us.

"Oh?" Mallory's quizzical expression asked the rest of the question.

"She lost her license in January after she wrecked her car. It was her third arrest for drunk driving in a year and with the accident, she ended up on probation. Someone has to drive her wherever she wants to go." The face she made indicated how much she enjoyed being a part-time chauffer.

"That would do it." O'Brien muttered. "Robert, go to your cabin. I'll wait here for Evans, and then join you. You are sure she won't run?"

"She doesn't have a reason to run," Mallory pointed out. His tone became somber. "Danny, be careful. She can be very wild and I'm not sure how well she's functioning. I've got to make a phone call." Mallory moved to stand in front of me. "You be careful, too. If anything happens to you—" He hesitated. His concerned blue eyes searched my face, as if he wanted to say more yet did not know what or how. "Well, I'd never be able to face Julie," he lamely finished. He gave my shoulder a squeeze and left.

"Janet," I turned to her, "you gave Edward a box of candy."

"Yes, I did."

"*Hold!* The box of candy in his cabin came from *her*?" O'Brien exploded, his face changing color again. "*Cheese and rice!* That puts us back on square one!"

"Don't jump to conclusions," I warned him sharply, waggling a finger of my own. "I take it the analysis turned something up?"

"It certainly did. That was the telephone call. The lab finished working on the candy. Surprise. Three of the remaining pieces contained cyanide mixed with arsenic."

24

"*Both?*" Stunned, I inhaled and slowly let it out in a low whistle.

"Arsenic? Cyanide? You mean Edward's *dead?*" Janet lamented, moaning. "*Oh my God!* I killed him! I gave him the candy! *NO!* Oh, no," she wailed in agony. "It's all my fault!" Rocking back and forth in her chair, hugging herself, she burst into hysterical sobs.

"This is precisely why I didn't tell her sooner," I told O'Brien. "She'll undoubtedly clam now." I started to sigh, and a yawn came out instead.

"But if she gave Thompson the candy and the candy killed him—" His statement hung in the air.

"I think we'll find there's a bit more to it," I told him. I felt sure Janet possessed the missing piece of that puzzle. "Meanwhile, I think Dr. James might be needed, especially if your men can manage to corral Constance." I went to perch next to Janet while O'Brien picked up the telephone.

Janet's sobs slowly subsided. By the time Randolph and Evans showed up, she only shuddered now and then. After Arlene left, I went into the bathroom to wash the small puncture on my neck. I grabbed a wet washcloth and the box of Kleenex for her. She wiped her face and blew her nose. Randolph returned shortly with Carmella, who looked as tired as I felt. She collapsed on the settee.

"Constance has vanished," she wearily announced.

"I know." I tossed the washcloth toward the kitchenette; it surprised me by falling into the sink. "Captain, I think Janet has one more thing to tell us."

"No, I don't," she sniffled, despondent. "I gave him that box of candy and it killed him."

"Yes, so you told us. Why did you give it to him?" Although he did not growl, O'Brien's tone lacked sympathy.

"He likes candy." She raised her head, woebegone. Her red nose, set in her blotched and puffy face, matched her bloodshot eyes. "He's dead. I killed him," she whimpered. "Nothing else matters."

"This isn't getting us anywhere," muttered O'Brien to me. "There were three sets of fingerprints on the box. One set belonged to Thompson, one belonged to Constance Ambrose, and I assume the third is hers."

"You found Constance's prints on the box?" I demanded, low-voiced. When he nodded affirmation, I hissed, "Back off a moment."

"But—"

"Will you let me handle this? Back off!" I snapped, remembering to keep my voice down. I planted myself in front of Janet, partly to block out O'Brien. "Why did you give him that box of candy?"

"I got it as a thank you gift and I knew Edward would enjoy it," she forlornly related. "Nothing matters now," she repeated, a portrait of crestfallen misery.

"Was the box open when you got it?"

Janet shrugged. "I don't know. Who cares? I didn't eat any of it."

"Janet, this is very important." I knelt, gripped her hands, and forced her to meet my gaze. "Was the box already unwrapped when it was given to you?"

"I can't remember," she replied in a dull monotone. "What difference does it make? He's dead. Is it really important?"

"Yes." I paused, groping for words to phrase what I wanted to say without scaring her. "Janet, close your eyes and listen to me. I want you to remember picking up the box of candy to hand it to Edward. Remember what it felt like in your hand," I quietly coached, letting go of her hands. "Think back to that moment. Focus on the box lying in front of you. Did the box make a crinkling sound when you picked it up? Was the cellophane wrapper on the box?"

Her eyes closed, she frowned in concentration. Her fingers twitched in her lap. "No, the box wasn't wrapped in cellophane when I got it," she finally murmured. She opened her eyes, tears welling in them. "I don't understand. What possible difference could that make? The chocolates killed him."

I turned to glance at O'Brien. No longer paying attention to us, he picked up the phone.

"Mrs. Abernathy? Any word on Mrs. Ambrose?" he asked. After listening briefly, he continued, "okay, I'm going to Mr. Mallory's cabin. Have the officer at the gate send the doctor to Cabin Four."

"Does it make sense now?" I inquired, punctuating the question with another yawn.

"All except the stabbing," he admitted. "Good call on this."

"I don't understand," Janet numbly repeated. "I gave Edward the candy."

"Did you put poison in any of the pieces?" I asked, resuming my place in the other easy chair.

"Of course not." A tiny flicker of indignation colored her subdued voice.

"Well, someone did. You told us you got the box as a thank you gift, and it was already open."

Carmella gasped; her hands flew to her cheeks. "*Dio Mio!*" she exclaimed. "My Lord! *Constance?* She couldn't have!"

"No, that can't be right. Constance wouldn't have killed Edward," Janet protested. "She wanted him. She was obsessed with him. She wouldn't hurt him."

"Who gave you the thank you gift? Was it Mrs. Ambrose?" I prompted Janet.

"Yes, she told me she wanted to thank me for my help the night Edward almost drowned—" She stopped, her voice trailing off. "*Oh my God!*" she sobbed through a fresh burst of tears, "Oh, good God! She meant the poison for—for—"

"You," I finished for her. I felt sorry for her; the man she loved accidentally died in her place.

O'Brien coughed. "If I may interrupt? I'll leave Randolph inside with you and take Evans with me. If anything happens, Mrs. Abernathy will find me." He turned to Randolph. "You're on guard. Be careful. If you need help, yell. Literally and loudly. Lock the door behind me."

"Yes, sir."

After O'Brien left, Carmella moved a chair next to Janet's and sat down. "Constance is not a well person, Janet," she said, her voice soothing, "either emotionally or mentally. Her family constantly worries about her."

"How do you know?" Janet asked, blowing her nose again. "You've only been here a month."

I surmised Janet did not mean to challenge Carmella; rather, I supposed she wanted to avoid dwelling on her narrow escape.

"Oh, bother!" I interrupted them. "You two need to be re-introduced. Janet, Carmella is Constance

Ambrose's cousin. Her family wanted her here to keep an eye on Constance. Carmella, Janet is Doug Ambrose's kid sister."

It took them a minute. I watched while they came to the realization of how they were connected.

"Oh, Janet, I'm so sorry! I really liked Doug. He was always kind to me, and it was a sad day for us when he died." Carmella glanced in my direction. "I told Lauren I thought Constance treated him very badly."

"It wasn't your fault, Carmella," Janet said, still sniffling. "All I knew was that he wasn't happy with her even though he adored her.

They sat quietly talking, trying to console each other. I took it as a good sign.

A small part of my mind focused on the taunt O'Brien handed me when he exited. *All but the stabbing.* I gnawed on the tangled knot for a moment and got nowhere.

To blazes with it, for now anyway. I decided if I wanted to make headway, I needed to leave it alone for a while. I also realized I needed a drink. I picked up my paper bag and went to the kitchenette for a glass and some ice. I sank onto the settee with a C&T, tucked my legs under me, and slowly sipped. I deliberately avoided checking the clock. I wanted to savor my calm moment because I knew, with absolute certainty, it would not last for long. I got less than ten minutes.

A wrecking ball slammed into the door of the cabin.

"Lauren!Where's Eddie? I can't find Eddie!" Constance yelled through the door.

Of all the luck. With the police scattered all over the resort searching for her, Constance showed up on my porch.

Randolph drew his pistol and positioned himself behind the door, approximately where Janet stood earlier. I jumped for the phone.

"Constance is kicking my front door," I rapidly told Mrs. Abernathy in low tones. "I need Mallory. *FAST.*"

"Patching you through." I heard her connecting to Mallory.

The onslaught continued. The window next to the door rattled under her fists.

"*Dannazione!* Damnit! I want to know what is going on around here! Where is Eddie? *Porca miseria!* A pig's misery on you! Damnit! What—" Constance continued her tirade in the language I heard her use earlier; her fury did not require translation. Carmella's face paled; she understood what to me sounded like incoherent jabber.

Mallory's voice came over the line.

"Danny's getting his men. *Don't open the door!*"

I heard a key in the lock. "She's using her key!"

"Blast it to Hades!" He slammed the phone down.

I told Randolph the cavalry would shortly arrive, jerked Carmella and Janet off their chairs, and shoved them into the bathroom.

"Sit on the floor, put your backs to the door, and lean with all your weight!" I ordered. "Crouch low and keep quiet!"

I made it back to the living room in time to see Constance burst into the cabin. She took two steps and stopped. Randolph, stationed behind the door with his eyes on me, raised his gun and reached to close the door. I gave him a slight negative head shake and he left it open. *One less obstacle for the cavalry.*

"Lauren, where is Eddie?" she demanded, wheedling. A small gun shook in her unsteady hand. "You know where he is, you want him," she badgered. She came closer and shrieked, *"Dannazione! Voglio delle risposte!"* Her weapon, pointing in my general direction, wavered wildly. "Damnit! I want some *answers*.

"Constance, please, you don't need the gun." I kept my voice low, calm, and even, trying to cue Randolph she had one. Over her shoulder, I saw Randolph's eyes widen in surprise. "I'm not going to give you any trouble."

"You already *have* given me trouble," she viciously spat. "Robert is *mine* and you're in my way. He likes you and that's not fair. I tried to warn him about you, but he won't listen. No one ever listens."

She paced across the room. Her eyes never left me. She kept the shaky gun constantly pointed in my direction. Her voice rose and she spat out her words, rapid fire, as if they were bullets coming out of a Tommy gun. "Robert is mine! He should have been mine eight years ago! *Mine!*" she screamed. Her black pinpoint pupils, constricted when they should have been dilated, made her brown eyes seem larger. "You and your *stupid* newspaper story! You've wrecked *everything!*"

She took two strides and gripped my arm, her fingernails digging into me like stinging, sharp needles. *"Where is Eddie?"* she clamored shrilly, her face inches from mine. I caught a whiff of alcohol on her breath while we stared at each other.

I drew a breath, groping for words. For once in my life, they would not come.

"Constance," Mallory's calm, steady voice broke the silence while he came up behind her. "We need to talk."

"Robert!" She swung around to face him, not heeding anything else. She raised her arms to embrace him. Her finger tightened on the trigger. The gun's loud report filled the cabin. The bullet hit a picture on the wall near the door. She jumped and dropped the weapon.

"I didn't mean to do that," she whimpered. "I didn't mean to." Her gaze sifted to Mallory's face. "Robert?" she begged. Putting her hands on his chest, she started to cry. "Please? Help me? You're the only man I ever loved. Help—" Her voice trailed off and she crumpled, slumping to the floor in a faint.

My ears painfully rang from the reverberation of the indoor shot. I decided fainting might be nice. Since I did not have the three minutes to spare, I skipped it and retrieved the gun. Mallory gathered up Constance and carried her to the settee.

O'Brien charged into the cabin. "I heard a shot!"

"Constance fired it," I explained, handing him the weapon.

He gave me the once-over. Seeing me unhurt, he scanned the room and barked, "Where are they?"

"Bathroom. Knock first and identify yourself. They're sitting on the floor with their backs to the door. I'm fine, thanks for asking," I told his back. I unsteadily crossed the room to get my drink and sat in my easy chair to see if I could stop shaking. Carmella and Janet emerged from the bathroom.

The telephone went off. It rang loudly or I never would have heard it over the ringing in my ears. I forced myself to answer it and exchanged information with Mrs. Abernathy. I hung up and relayed her update.

"Dr. James is on his way up from the gate. O'Brien's men are also coming up."

O'Brien nodded. "I have to run out for a moment, but I'll be right back. Can you control her if she comes around?"

"I think so." Mallory knelt beside the settee and tenderly stroked a stray hair away from her face. "Poor little rich girl, she's never been happy, and it's not entirely her doing."

O'Brien left, shaking his head.

"Mr. Mallory? I should call her father," Carmella said timidly, her misgivings evident in her voice. "She's going to need help."

"I spoke to him earlier, when I went to my cabin. I'm waiting for a call with instructions."

"You know her father? Are you the one she kept taunting Doug about?" Janet demanded, anger creeping into her voice. She stopped short and put her hand to her forehead. "I'm sorry, Mr. Mallory. You had nothing to do with this. I had no right to say anything."

"If you are asking if I'm the man she always held up to your brother as an example," he said, "I could be. There was another man whom she dated before she met me. Who knows? In her mind, she might have blended us together."

"She's that confused?" Janet gasped, astounded. "She's been so good at helping Edward run this place."

"She goes through ups and downs, and apparently the mood swings have been getting worse," Mallory said. "Her father hoped owning and running the resort would help steady her, but the least bit of strain set her off and things got out of hand." He smiled at me. "Danny told me you worked out that the candy was meant for Janet, rather than Edward. Good work."

I nodded. "He'll find Janet's fingerprints are the last set, but Constance gave the box to Janet, who passed it along to Edward." I glanced at Janet, sitting quietly with Carmella, and lowered my voice. "I don't think it has completely sunk in how close it came. That brings up a question. Does Constance know about Thompson? She was asking about him."

"No. I'm hoping to speak with her father again before she finds out."

O'Brien came back inside, followed by a new officer, Randolph, and Evans. I saw the oozing wound on Evans' forehead where the book hit started to bruise.

"Can I talk to her?" O'Brien asked, indicating Constance. He sat down in a chair.

"No." Mallory and I became the Greek chorus again. It occurred to me the situation, rife with tragedy, offered a good basis for the analogy.

"Danny," Mallory said firmly when O'Brien started to object, "I have called her father, and I'm waiting for him to call back with instructions on what to do next."

"*What?*" O'Brien yelled, forgoing restraint. "*No!* That woman has killed two people. I can't ignore that!"

"Think about it!" Mallory commanded, getting to his feet. He lowered his voice. "Can you prove she did? Can you prove it beyond a shadow of a doubt? Good enough for a jury? Can you tie her to the arsenic or the cyanide?" Mallory's voice, pitched at almost a whisper, carried authority. He stared down at the seated policeman.

"Not exactly," O'Brien grudgingly admitted. "We're going over every inch of her cabin. So far we've come up empty."

"Have you tried Edward's cabin?" Janet suggested. "She spent a lot of time there, too."

"Randolph, get on that," O'Brien ordered. "This is critical. You're searching for a source of the poisons, primarily arsenic and secondly cyanide. Any source, but especially one that can be tied to Constance Ambrose."

"Yes, sir. I'll take Evans and report back to you."

"Hold. Walsh, take Evans back to the station for first aid. Randolph, get Morse. Search Thompson's cabin and the office."

"Yes, sir." The three men filed out.

"Captain? Who stabbed Edward?" Janet spoke up.

"I'm honestly not sure," O'Brien admitted. "We're sure Constance Ambrose doctored drinks and the candy, based on what was seen and what you told us. I wondered if Miss Sharp-Eyes has any theories about the stabbing."

"Meaning me, I suppose." I punctuated my statement with a wide yawn. "Sorry, all tapped out at the moment." I stood up, stretched, and took my glass to the sink.

"Too bad," he muttered. "Robert, let's get back to why I can't do anything about—"

"Robert?" Constance groaned, struggling to sit up. "Where am I?"

"You're in Lauren's cabin," he answered, moving back to kneel by the settee. "You came here looking for Edward."

"Where is Eddie? I can't find him." Sitting upright for a moment, she put her hands to her temples, and rocked back and forth. "I don't feel good." She curled up on her side, her eyes half closed.

Someone knocked on the door.

O'Brien nodded to me. "It's your cabin."

"Oh, feel free," I told him, waving my arm in a bow.

Dr. James entered, bag in hand. "The officer at the gate told me to report to you, Captain."

"Thank you for coming so promptly, Doctor. I want you here while we talk to Mrs. Ambrose," O'Brien greeted him. "Mrs. Ambrose, if you can manage to sit up, Robert can sit next to you."

The police captain placed one of the kitchen chairs so the doctor could sit to one side of his patient. He took another one and sat directly in front of her. The rest of us gathered around the settee. Carmella, sitting on the floor, folded her legs so she could pop up quickly if necessary. Janet stayed in her easy chair and I took the other one.

I glanced around room. The stray bullet destroyed one of the pictures on the wall; I decided it might be an improvement with spidery cracks decorating the glass. The white dress and hair ornaments lay on the counter next to my loot bag where I put them after Janet jumped me. According to the clock on the wall, that happened a little over an hour ago. It seemed like days.

"What is going on?" Constance demanded in a weary and whining voice. "Why is Dr. James here? I don't *need* a doctor. I don't *want* a doctor. I *hate* doctors. I only want to know where Eddie is! Please, Robert, tell me," she begged, her voice quavering while she pleaded. "Why can't I find him?"

"Mrs. Ambrose, it is my duty to tell you that Edward Thompson died about two hours ago," O'Brien quietly informed her.

25

We all carefully watched her in the silence that followed the policeman's statement.

"No." She emphatically shook her head. "No. He didn't. He couldn't have." She sat up straight, moving so her feet rested on the floor. Turning to Mallory, her voice became matter-of-fact. "Robert, why is this man lying to me?"

"He's not lying to you, Constance. Edward died shortly before midnight. I saw his body myself," he confirmed.

"No. It's not true," she declared positively, shaking her head as if to clear it. "Dr. James, you told me Eddie was going to be fine, that Janet didn't hurt him badly."

Janet sat up straight. I reached to put my hand on her arm, mouthing 'no.' She nodded without speaking and sank back into the chair.

"He didn't die from the stab wound," Mallory told her. "He was poisoned."

"No, he wasn't." Constance gripped Mallory's arm, tight enough to turn her knuckles white. "He *couldn't* have been poisoned. Don't lie to me! Poisoned? No." She squarely faced him, her tone wheedling again. "Robert, please don't lie to me. If you'll take me back, I'll give up Eddie, but don't lie to me."

"I'm not lying to you, Constance. You know me well enough to realize I'd never do that," he reminded her, his voice gentle and calm. "Edward died because someone put poison in a few chocolate candies, and he ate one."

"Chocolate candy? Eddie loves candy. I usually give him a box for the weekend." She smiled. "But I didn't give him a box this weekend. I bought a box, but I gave it to someone else."

"Edward ate a piece of poisoned chocolate. It was one of four that had been doctored in the box that was found in his cabin," O'Brien explained.

"But that can't be right! I gave the box of chocolates to Janet, not to Eddie."

"You gave the box of chocolates to Janet?" Mallory reflected her statement back as a question.

"Of course, I did." Constance smiled at him. "Robert, you understand! I had to do it. Janet was annoying me, just like Vera did. She kept making a play for Eddie all the time. I got tired of watching it and she would not listen to me, so I decided I didn't want her around anymore. I gave her the box of chocolates after I fixed the candy, just the way I fixed Vera's penicillin. I even reminded Vera to take her pill at breakfast that day. Vera wanted Eddie to go diving with her, but I stopped him. It was all so easy, you know," she said conversationally, her smile broadening. "So simple, like this was. I told Janet the candy was a thank-you for her help the night Eddie almost drowned." She firmly nodded. "It's Janet who is dead, not Eddie. Yes, Janet's dead," she repeated, confirming it to herself.

She stared directly at Janet. "I don't know who you are, but you can't be Janet because Janet is dead. Eddie's going to be fine. I have it all figured out." She turned back to Mallory and beamed serenely at him. "Eddie can have the resort and I'll marry you, Robert. Yes, that's what we'll do. It's the best way." She smiled and firmly nodded her head.

I don't believe what I'm hearing! She's clinically insane. Flabbergasted, I shifted my gaze to O'Brien. His mouth hung open, speechless. Mallory, seated next to her with her hand still clutching his arm, exchanged meaningful glances with O'Brien. *There's that connection again. These guys have worked together. A lot.*

The stunned silence palpably built for what seemed like an eternity.

Constance suddenly exploded into action, catching all of us off-guard. Like a torsion spring released from pressure, she jumped to her feet, bowling O'Brien over sideways, chair and all.

"You killed him! That was *your* candy! You gave him the candy I meant for you!" she screeched, going for Janet with her manicured fingernails extended like claws. *"You killed him! YOU KILLED MY EDDIE!* I loved him. I had him. He was *MINE!* You're dead now! You died, not him! You're dead!" She screamed obscenities, half in English and half not.

Mallory attempted to grab Constance from behind. I tried to get between her and Janet. Carmella, on her feet, tried to pull Janet out of the reach of those long nails. Janet's chair toppled sideways, and they landed on the floor. O'Brien got himself untangled from his chair and used a shoulder block on the out-of-control woman. She ruthlessly fought the three of us, kicking and clawing. It took both men to get her back to the settee. Constance, writhing with inhuman strength, continued to shriek. Her arms flailed dangerously, swinging around our heads, forcing us to bob and weave.

I managed to grab the arm closest to me with both hands. I hung on to steady it while Dr. James jabbed it with a syringe and pushed the plunger. She screamed in wordless rage, twisting and biting us to get free. Mallory sat on the couch, legs apart. O'Brien and I pushed while Mallory pulled her into his lap with her back to his chest. Mallory tightly wrapped her in his arms and legs. Grimly, stone-faced, with lips pushed together in a thin line with effort, he held her until the shot took effect.

Slowly the tantrum subsided, although Constance continued to mutter in Italian for a few long minutes. We stared at each other, horrified and dumbfounded at the scene we witnessed.

"Janet, I'm sorry," Mallory apologized while he shifted the now-quiescent Constance over to the settee cushion, "I should have suspected something like that was coming."

"Holy Mother of God," O'Brien sputtered, aghast, groping for words. "I've never seen anything like—that. She—she's completely—flipped—" At a loss for words, he ran his fingers through his hair and whistled. "Dr. James, thank you."

"Sorry it took me so long to get it out of my bag," the physician replied, shaken and apologetic.

"Doctor?" Carmella, her voice shaky, spoke from her position on the floor. "Janet is hurt." She had the older girl's head in her lap.

We looked at Janet. Curled up on the floor on her side, she had her eyes closed. She sat up and winced. The scratches on her arms, with blood seeping from them, resembled long scarlet ribbons. Her face had one long scratch.

"I'll tend to those." Dr. James dug into his bag and pulled out a small green bottle with some cotton. "Bactine. It's a new antiseptic and doesn't sting." He got busy swabbing, taking her first.

Bactine did sting at first, although not nearly as badly as iodine or mercurochrome. One of Janet's arms needed bandaging. Carmella and I got by with swabbing. Mallory suffered a long gouge on one arm deep enough to require gauze. I took advantage of the lull to change out of my polka dot dress back into my sundress. The dance festivities felt like ancient history.

We held a conference at the kitchenette table. Dr. James maintained his vigil next to the settee.

"Are you convinced now she can't stand trial?" Mallory asked.

"After all that?" O'Brien, overwhelmed and stupefied, shook his head in disbelief. "I'll call the county hospital. They can admit her for observation and diagnosis. It needs to be official."

I wondered when Mallory would bring up her connection to the mob. I saw him take a deep breath and slowly exhale. He squared his shoulders.

Here it comes.

"Danny, did your background search on Constance turn up her maiden name?"

"Yes, it did. Hard to miss, seeing how it's the same as one of our more prominent family names, meaning with a capital F." O'Brien regarded Mallory. "So what?"

"Danny," Mallory's voice held a strange undertone, "that is her family."

"There are lots of families with that name," O'Brien wryly observed with a shrug. "Most of them are law-abiding citizens. It's only a few—" He broke off and closely stared at Mallory. "Hold! You don't really mean *that* family? Her father is—?" The police captain left the name unspoken.

"Yes. I'm waiting for him to call back." Mallory leaned forward on the table. "Ordinarily, I wouldn't suggest this, but I think we should let him handle this however he wishes. He has the money and the clout to keep her from hurting others as well as protecting her from herself."

"But she's responsible for killing two people!" O'Brien protested. He smacked his hand down hard on the table for emphasis. The rest of us jumped.

"No, she's not, and that is precisely my point. Legally, she *isn't* responsible. Period. If you need a certificate to that effect, I'm sure a fully qualified psychiatrist can provide one."

"You say you already called him. How do *you* know someone that high up in the rackets?" O'Brien bitterly challenged.

"I dated Constance about eight years ago." Mallory noted the puzzled expression on the policeman's face and answered the unasked query. "You were," he hesitated with a side-long glance at me, "out of town. Her father made a point of meeting me, and we have met a few times since."

"I don't like this." O'Brien stood and began to pace. "At *all*. How do I explain this in my report? You *know* I don't take any liberties with my position. I've been approached often enough, but you know I've stayed clean. Now I'm supposed to conspire with *him*?" He ran his fingers through his already unkempt hair.

The telephone rang. We all turned to stare at it, unmoving, too shell-shocked to deal with anything else.

I answered it on the eighth ring. "Mr. Mallory," I intoned softly, "I believe this is the call you are expecting."

From the day we met, Robert Mallory impressed me with his ability to handle any situation that arose. I recalled his anxious face the day Julie broke her arm falling off my bicycle; she constituted his whole world, yet he calmly reassured us both and insisted he did not blame me. I also remembered the way he guided my mother through the intricacies of military red tape following my father's death in Normandy, assuming much of the burden. Yet my respect increased to a new level during that long, traumatic night, especially when I heard him explain Constance's deteriorating condition to her distraught parent.

Mallory relayed the circumstances honestly, one father to another, ignoring the other man's position. His tact showed me, clearly, why his acquaintances in diplomatic circles sought his advice. He paused in his conversation and smiled at Carmella, who paid rapt attention throughout. He assured his caller she remained unhurt.

"Of course, Vincenzo. Carmella and I will stay with her until you get here," Mallory concluded. "I will notify the gate you will be arriving with an ambulance. We'll meet you in the owner's cabin." He replaced the handset and turned to us. "We need to get her moved. Dr. James, I'm afraid we need your assistance."

"It won't be the first night's sleep I've missed," the doctor dutifully replied with a small shrug, "and I'm willing to bet it's far from the last, too. How do we go about it?"

"Use the service road," Janet volunteered. "It's a narrow dirt road that runs all the way around the periphery. We use it for deliveries. Does anyone have a small car?"

I dug my car keys out of my shoulder bag and tossed them to Mallory.

He nodded and left.

O'Brien reached for the phone the moment it rang.

"Cabin Four." He paused to listen. "Okay, leave Morse at the gate. We're expecting a—visitor. Direct him to the owner's cabin and allow the private ambulance entry. I'll be over there momentarily." He hung up. "No source of anything in either cabin, which means at the moment we can't tie her directly to either murder. I haven't heard from the man I sent to search the office, but that looks dim."

"Captain? Are you going to close the resort?" Janet hesitantly asked.

"Thankfully, that's not my call," he admitted. "If I were you, however, I'd ask Robert Mallory. I know him. He's undoubtedly already working on a plan to keep this place in operation."

"How far back do you two go?" I gave the nagging question another try.

"A-ways." He gave me a non-committal smile.

"That's a big help." I returned a mock scowl, and his smile briefly became a grin. "Oh well, it was worth asking. Someday I'll get the story."

"Speaking of stories, how are you going to write this one?" O'Brien asked. I caught the glint of mischief in his grey eyes. "You can't mention the man who's coming."

"Believe me, I wouldn't dream of it. I thought I'd see what your press release looks like before I write my story," I shot back my rejoinder with a snicker that turned into a chuckle when he groaned. "I hear my car."

Mallory entered. "I'm parked on the service road behind the cabin. I already turned around. Dr. James, can she walk?"

"She's out. After her erratic display, I wasn't taking chances, so I gave her a stiff dose. If you can carry her, I'll help you get her into the car. I'll follow on foot."

Mallory paused for a moment, surveying the rest of us. "I'd like you to follow us over to Constance's cabin. Once she is in her father's hands, I'd like to discuss what is going to happen to the resort. Janet, I'd appreciate you being there if you're not too tired. I won't keep you long."

O'Brien sent Janet an 'I told you so' smug look.

"Certainly, if you want me there," Janet said, trying to smile.

"Are you including me in that invitation?" I thought I would try to weasel out, although I held no real hope of a reprieve.

"Yes." O'Brien supplied.

"You know, Thompson gave me this cabin so I could relax in comfort. It would be nice to spend some time here when I'm not fighting with someone," I complained.

Mallory gazed at me, assessing me. "I'm sorry," he told me, his blue eyes shadowed by an emotion I could not identify. He rested his hands on my shoulders. "I know you're tired but right now I need you. We can't have an official record of this and you're a valuable witness."

"I have to be honest with you: I'm out on my feet," I warned him.

"You wouldn't be my first choice, but you're all we have," O'Brien commented without sarcasm.

"I'll try not to feel too welcome," I mumbled.

26

A few minutes later, we entered the owner's cabin. Carmella and I got Constance out of the blouse and slacks she wore during her assault on my cabin. Dressed in a clean nightgown and robe, we left her lying down on her bed with Dr. James in attendance. The physician readied another syringe in case she came around. After the scene in my cabin, he did not trust her reactions or tolerance to drugs.

We joined Janet, O'Brien, and Mallory at the dinette table. Mallory finished briefing us on what to expect and we fell silent. All of us drained, we waited for whatever happened next, each of us lost in our own thoughts.

The anticipated knock sounded and Mallory opened the door. A large man, wearing a suit straining to contain his musculature, entered first. Silently he scanned the room, taking in everything and everyone. After nodding to someone outside, he stepped in and to the side. An older, distinguished-looking man, in a beautifully tailored three-piece light grey silk suit and pale blue silk shirt, followed him. Perfectly groomed from his neatly parted silver-grey hair down to a matching pale blue handkerchief perfectly folded in his pocket, he stood gazing around the room without saying a word. I recognized him from the wedding portrait on the desk and saw the family resemblance to Constance in his facial structure. Although not much taller than I, his formidable presence intimated the man should not be crossed.

"I'm sorry we are meeting again under these circumstances," the newcomer greeted Mallory warmly, shaking the offered hand. "Robert, I thank you for notifying me."

His slight accent reminded me of Gianello's. His gaze quickly darted around again, coming back to rest on Mallory. "Where is she?"

"In the bedroom," Mallory replied, indicating the partially closed door.

The older gentleman turned and gestured to someone outside. "My personal physician," he explained when a slim older man entered.

Carmella stood. "Uncle?" Uncertainty clouded her voice and she timidly approached him, understandably nervous. "I'm so sorry! I did what I could." She added something in Italian.

"Carmella, my dear child, please do not worry. I have no complaints about anything you have done." His words and voice soothing, he stepped over to her and lightly placed his hand under her chin, raising her eyes to his. "You are not accountable, my dear. Constance was more disturbed than I believed. It is I who now apologize to you for imposing such an unwarranted burden upon you," he reassured her in careful English with a slight hint of a smile. "Will you please show the doctor in to her?" He gave her a kiss on her forehead.

"Certainly, Uncle," she agreed, obviously relieved. "This way." She and the physician vanished into the bedroom.

Both physicians emerged shortly, agreeing the patient could be transported. The older physician nodded to the muscle man, who could pass for a professional linebacker. In turn, he summoned attendants with a stretcher. Dr. James hovered in the doorway until we heard the ambulance depart. The linebacker stayed at his post.

"Mr. Mallory, may I leave? You have my numbers if you need anything from me," James said.

"Dr. James, thank you for all your assistance. We've had a rough evening and you were very helpful." Mallory's genuinely warm tones reinforced his words while the men shook hands. "I'll see you are compensated for your services. Please be careful driving home."

The physician left.

Carmella rejoined us at the table, her sigh of relief accompanied by a small, shy smile.

"Excuse me, sir," O'Brien spoke to the newcomer for the first time. "May I ask where she will be taken?"

"Vincenzo, may I present Captain Daniel O'Brien of the Northwoods Glen Police Department?" Mallory paused to consider how to complete the introduction. "Captain O'Brien, this is Constance's father."

The two men nodded, one at ease in contrast to the other's wariness.

"Captain O'Brien, do you have any doubt that my daughter is mentally unstable?"

"Absolutely none, sir." O'Brien cleared his throat. "I ask only so I can close out my investigation by noting you are taking her into your charge."

"I understand. Robert, may we sit?"

"Of course." Mallory indicated one of the easy chairs placed near the settee.

The three men sat.

"Captain, I appreciate this situation is difficult for you," the visitor offered, gazing steadily at the policeman. "You want a tidy end to an untidy business. I can only assure you my daughter will be well-treated and carefully guarded at a private facility. The actual location is irrelevant to your purpose. Once obtained, a certificate will be forwarded to you."

O'Brien clearly did not approve of that at all. "You are placing me in a very awkward position." He ran his hand through his hair and carefully continued. "Even disregarding the two attempted murders, I have two dead to account for."

"Two murders and two attempted murders?" Constance's father, puzzled, turned to her former suitor. "Robert? Will you explain this to me?"

"Vincenzo, with your permission, I would like to defer to a friend of mine for further explanations," Mallory stood and beckoned to me.

My mouth fell open. In the guidelines Mallory laid out, which included the idea some names were not to be remembered or recorded, he made absolutely *no* mention I would be asked to join the anticipated conference. I assumed his deliberate oversight stemmed from his belief that I might walk out if I knew of it. That very notion flitted briefly through my mind. I closed my mouth and stood. I heard Carmella murmur something I did not catch, undoubtedly a warning. I wanted to assure her that "Careful" was my new middle name.

"Lauren Kaye is a reporter for the *Daily Gleaner*. She was assigned to do a publicity spread on the resort," Mallory informed his guest. He took my suddenly ice-cold hand and guided me to his vacated chair. "She also has a knack for seeking out solutions to questions of, shall we say, complicated events. I have employed her investigative talents and she has my full confidence."

"Please be seated, young lady," the man cordially addressed me. "I am not a monster."

"I assure you, sir, I never entertained such a thought." I sat, partly on my own volition, partly from the pressure of Mallory's hand on my shoulder, and partly because my knees would give way if I did not.

Mallory took a seat next to O'Brien on the settee and smiled encouragement.

"Are you aware a young woman named Vera Campbell died at the resort approximately three weeks ago?" I asked our guest. At his nod, I continued, "Mr. Mallory and I became involved when a friend of ours came to us, concerned there was more to it than a diving accident. I was asked to check into the matter to see if those concerns were valid."

"Were they?" His gaze, which seemed to peer inside me like an x-ray, never left my face.

"Unfortunately, yes. Vera's body was exhumed late last night and evidence of poison, specifically arsenic, was found." I took a deep breath while I unsuccessfully tried to gauge his reaction. "Immediately prior to your call to Mr. Mallory tonight, Constance stated unequivocally she deliberately put poison into prescription capsules Vera was taking and ensured the woman went diving alone. Constance also told us she fixed the candy which killed Edward Thompson, although he was not her intended target. She admitted she altered the candy to get rid of Janet Benedict. In Constance's own words, she decided she no longer wanted Janet around. The only accident was Edward Thompson died instead of Janet Benedict."

"Why would she do any of this?" He put the question to me calmly and factually, with no anger or challenge. For some reason, my wariness increased.

"In her mind, both Vera and Janet were threats to her relationship with Thompson. Jealousy appears to have been at the root of it."

"The other young woman at the table is Janet Benedict?"

"Yes, sir."

"Is there any direct evidence to link my daughter to the poison, other than her confession?"

"No, sir, no direct evidence has been found as of this moment. The police are still searching for a source of the poison." I swallowed and took another deep breath. I found his eyes required steady concentration to meet, not an easy task. "There is, however, some evidence to link her directly to the stabbing of Edward Thompson."

"Robert stated that Edward Thompson was poisoned."

"Yes, sir. Poison killed Thompson. However, earlier in the evening, Constance stabbed him."

"Hold a moment," O'Brien interrupted, pouncing on me like a hungry tiger going after its lunch. He treated me to a ferocious glare. I did not quail, although under other circumstances I might have. "You can prove that?"

"I think so." I started to sigh, and a yawn broke out. "Excuse me. We all saw it. Only after we got over here did I realize the proof was literally in front of me."

"Show me." O'Brien brusquely commanded.

I looked from Mallory to our visitor; both men nodded. I got up and walked to the kitchenette counter where the dress and towel lay. The three men followed.Janet and Carmella stayed at the table.

"We've been searching for direct evidence of any of the crimes," I explained to O'Brien while I undid the bundle. "I believe this is what you want."

I spread the dress and retrieved the long hair pick. Pointing to the blotch on the shoulder seam, I held up the jeweled hair ornament.

"We know the wound was caused by a long, thin, pointed blade. This ornament was designed to be inserted into a bouffant hairstyle. It is metal, long, and pointed, similar to a letter opener. You can see that the metal portion is stained. This and the spot on the dress should be tested for Thompson's blood."

Mallory motioned us to our seats in the living area. I saw Carmella's face relax when her uncle nodded his agreement.

"I think she drew the ornament out of her hair, drove it into Thompson's shoulder, and immediately pulled it back out. When she put it back into her hair, a splatter of blood fell on her shoulder. The test should tell us if I'm right." I swallowed again, took one more deep breath, and let it out slowly while I sat down. "I've been toting that bundle around all night. I didn't realize why until a minute ago, but something kept nagging at me from the first moment I saw the dark spot after the lights came back on."

"Blast it!" O'Brien frowned at Mallory. "You weren't kidding when you said she doesn't miss much."

"Lauren?" Janet spoke up from the table. "Why would Mrs. Ambrose stab him?"

"I don't have a concrete answer for you. That's probably why it took so long to sink in. There's no logical motive for it," I replied, twisting in my seat a bit to face her. "It doesn't make any more sense than downing the drink she herself drugged. It's as if she didn't remember doing these things." I frowned. Something I saw or heard nagged at me, but the memory eluded me. I turned back to O'Brien. "You have no real case on anything except the stabbing, and that's minor."

"I know she can't be charged with anything, but I'd still like to have a clearer picture of these events," O'Brien grumbled.

The phone on the desk rang. O'Brien jumped up to answer it. I surmised he needed some form of action, even if only to answer the phone.

"O'Brien." The police captain listened for about a minute and some of the tension eased out of his shoulders. "Good work, Morse." He placed the handset on its cradle.

"If I may say something?" O'Brien asked when he resumed his seat. At our visitor's nod, he continued, "We found the source of the arsenic."

"The office?" I ventured.

"One of my men uncovered a small jewelry box in the back of the top drawer of Mrs. Ambrose's desk. It has her prints on it, and when he opened it, he found a supply of a whitish powder. The lab says it is arsenic."

"Any sign of the cyanide?" I asked. O'Brien shook his head. "Maybe Constance used her entire supply of the cyanide to bait the candy."

O'Brien shrugged. "At this point, it's moot."

"Arsenic *and* cyanide?" the distinguished man repeated, astounded, his poise visibly shaken.

"The analysis of the candy which killed Edward Thompson showed both poisons in three of the remaining pieces." I stopped abruptly, not sure how far I wanted to push the explanation. I knew I certainly did not want this man as my enemy. I turned to Mallory for guidance. The gentleman forestalled the need.

"Young lady, please do not hesitate for fear of angering me. I respect honesty and will hold nothing amiss." The barest smile flitted across his face. "Miss Kaye, you have done well. Do not let unwarranted fears hold you back now."

"Sir, this new information places both deaths at the feet of your daughter," I gently told him. "Please understand she did not intend for Thompson to die. Janet was her target." I studiously watched his face. Although well-schooled in concealing his reactions, I caught the tiniest flicker of something for a second, possibly anger. It quickly faded, replaced by a deep sadness.

After a silence, during which we all tried to make sense of what we knew, O'Brien spoke.

"We have a major problem here," the police captain began. "The stabbing happened in full view of half the members of the resort. Thompson, the manager, is dead by Constance's hand, even if he died by inadvertence. She now owns the resort and yet is totally incapacitated. We can't even begin to explain what really happened." He shook his head in resignation, running one hand through his hair, the one nervous habit I had seen. "I hate loose ends," he groused.

"With respect, Captain, maybe we can use a distraction." I wanted to float an idea.

"Now what are you talking about?" O'Brien snapped. However much Constance's father intimidated him, I elicited no such effect.

"You know I have to produce a story for the *Daily Gleaner* or risk losing my job. You have to do some sort of official report and press release. In addition, we need to decide what is going to happen to the resort." I glanced at Mr. Mallory. "I can see a way out of this so most of the situation need not be made public."

"Meaning?" Mallory would not blindly support any idea until he understood it.

"Consider putting it simply. The resort's owner collapsed following the sudden death of her general manager and partner, which itself followed a fatal accident shortly after the summer season started. Although it's light on details, it's all true."

"You have an admirable way of marshalling thoughts and words," the older gentleman complimented me. "Have I seen your byline in the *Daily Gleaner*?"

"I doubt it, and unless I file a story soon, you won't." My reply popped out much more sharply than I intended. "I apologize, sir. I didn't mean to be quite so blunt."

He smiled again, warmly this time. "No apology is needed, my dear, I assure you."

It crossed my mind that this man could be extremely charming when he wanted to be. The thought scared me more than the power he undoubtedly wielded.

"It's a good start," O'Brien nodded with grudging approval, "but where does it go from there?"

"Does Thompson have any family?" Mallory asked O'Brien.

"No," Janet spoke from the table. "He told me he was all alone in the world."

"That's what Constance told me," Carmella confirmed.

Both girls rose and joined us, standing behind me.

Mallory cleared his throat.

"If I may, I would like to make a proposal, Vincenzo, with all respect to you. Constance owns the resort. She had a survival partnership agreement with Thompson, and now he's gone. Would you consider letting me take it over? I can have a manager here tomorrow." He glanced at his watch. "Rather later this morning. In an effort to keep as much continuity as possible, I would like to see Janet Benedict become the assistant manager."

The distinguished gentleman scrutinized Janet. "Young lady, do I know you?" he asked. "You seem familiar."

"No, sir, we have never met. You knew my brother, Doug Ambrose," she said, her chin slightly raised, not quite defiant.

"I see the resemblance. What is your name?"

"Janet Benedict Ambrose. I used my mother's maiden name when I applied for the job here."

"Robert, is she good at her job?" he asked with his gaze locked on Janet's eyes.

"I was told she was being groomed to become assistant manager."

"My family has hurt you, Miss Ambrose, which I regret. I would like to make amends." He turned to Mallory. "I will sign the resort over to you with a small share going to Miss Ambrose after a period of one year."

"I will accept only if there are no strings," Mallory stated, his voice firm.

"No strings."

"Your word?" Mallory insisted, ignoring Carmella's slight gasp.

"My word of honor." The older man rose and addressed O'Brien. "Captain, I would advise you to listen to this talented young lady and to your friend Robert Mallory. You are still seeking a tidy conclusion, yet the situation is too complex for one. You are both honorable men, sir, and I respect that."

Our visitor took my hand and bowed over it. "I thank you, my dear."

Making his way to the door, he put a hand on Carmella's shoulder and smiled. She rose on tiptoes and kissed his cheek.

"Again, I thank you, Robert, for your help," the older gentleman said, offering his hand. "I assure you Constance will be placed in a convalescent home, surrounded by caring people. My lawyer will be in touch with you." He left, followed by his rather large shadow.

"Facing him isn't easy, and I sure don't want him after me," O'Brien commented while the tension level in the room dropped by ninety-five percent. "Even knowing the answers, the situation is not as simple as I thought it would be. Robert, I'll need your help with my report."

"You'll also need Lauren's," Mallory pointed out.

"Yes, I suppose," the police captain admitted, reluctantly I thought. He glanced at me quickly, like he heard it. "No offense."

"None taken," I acknowledged. "The only reason I'm not shaking is I'm sitting down."

"Mr. Mallory, will he really do it? Sign over this place to you?" Janet sounded bewildered.

"He will. His word, when he gives it, is solid gold."

"He frightens me a little," she confessed.

"He should," O'Brien flatly observed.

Janet shuddered. "Why a year for my share? Not that I mind," she hastily amended.

"You probably won't see him again," Mallory assured her. "I'll handle the legalities. To answer your question, remember he's also a businessman."

"You mean, I need to prove myself." She gave a slight smile when he nodded. "I understand. That's fair."

"Mr. Mallory, I'm with Captain O'Brien. I'm going to need help with my story, which will now start with 'Under New Management'. Mr. Slater is going to have a fit about this," I finished with a bone-weary sigh.

"Not a problem. We can work on this later today." Mallory stood up and stretched. "I suggest we all catch four hours of sleep. There will be a lot of explaining to do when all the guests wake up."

O'Brien swore he personally escorted me to my cabin. I took his word because I slept through it.

27

Monday evening, one week after the dinner with my boss and Mallory at Susan's Place, the three of us agreed to meet at the resort for dinner. Mallory reserved the owner's table for the occasion. Danny O'Brien, also invited, phoned to say he would be late.

During the interim between the wee small hours conference on Saturday and dinner Monday evening, major progress occurred while we tied up some of O'Brien's loose ends.

O'Brien, grousing and grumbling non-stop, completed his paperwork with our help. We ignored any mob connection while we used some of what he referred to as my creative ideas. It proved to be a masterpiece of collaboration. All of us agreed to forget we saw Constance throw a tantrum or acknowledge we met her father. Carmella spoke privately with Jim, while Mallory and I briefed Arlene.

I phoned in a preview of my story Monday morning and gave Slater a brief explanation. Slater insisted on speaking with Mallory, who did not give away much more. Still demanding further explanations, he accepted Mallory's dinner invitation.

"Lauren!" my editor called, spotting me across the dining room once he arrived. "What the deuce is going on? And why didn't you show up to work this morning?"

"Mr. Slater, here is the full story and the exposed rolls of film," I explained, handing him the items.

Mallory entered and ordered for the table.

"I get the feeling that there's a lot more to this than you're telling me. I know I don't have the full story of what happened over the weekend," Slater complained after he read the article, "and I suspect I never will."

"Let it rest, Bernie. You have all you need. Accept it. Thompson collapsed and died. Constance Ambrose had a nervous breakdown when she found him dead," Mallory explained over appetizers.

"Lauren," Slater said, "I am going to schedule your story to run this Sunday, rather than waiting for the Fourth of July. I'll decide what photos to use once they are developed." He turned back to Mallory. "Robert, are you honestly telling me that you *own* this place?"

"Yes, I signed the papers this afternoon." Mallory appeared more refreshed and rested than I suspected he felt. "Who knows? I may enjoy this."

"Bernie may be angling for a free membership," O'Brien suggested, coming in and joining us. "I know if I ever want to stay here, I'll need a sizable discount."

Throughout the meal, I listened to the banter between the men and thought back to the very hectic Saturday following our all-too-brief four-hour nap.

Mallory brought in John Edgecombe from his office to take over as manager and Janet stepped up to assistant manager. The staff pitched in whole-heartedly; they were happy to keep their jobs. The members cooperated with the changeover, relieved that the resort wasn't going to close. We agreed the memory of the stabbing, the only public incident, would be a nine-day wonder and quickly fade.

My boss brought me out of my reverie.

"Lauren, I want you back at your desk tomorrow. No excuses. Now that I know you can do a full feature, I'll get you more of them." Slater put his napkin on his plate. "It's getting late, and I've got to get back to the office. Robert, thank you for dinner. The food here is good, although not quite up to Gianni's."

"Boss, I'll see you tomorrow." I did not get a reprimand.

Slater left the dining area, exchanging nods with Arlene who entered with Carmella and Janet right behind her. I glanced around the room. Thankfully, the clubhouse was empty. Jim moved a couple of tables together. Mallory sat at the head of the table, befitting his new position. Edgecombe arrived last and sat at its foot, notepad in hand.

Mallory engineered the meeting in three stages.

"This is the first opportunity I've had to thank all of you for pitching in the way you have the past three days." Mallory smiled at us. "That goes especially for Saturday. I know none of us got much sleep."

"I knew I occasionally talk in my sleep. I found out Saturday that I can also walk, think, and wait on tables in my sleep," Jim joked to general laughter.

"Seriously, there was a lot of confusion, rumors were flying, and I'm sure members were stopping you every five minutes to ask for details. I wanted to get you all together now as we officially start under new management; first to thank you, and second, to see if anyone has any questions. This will be the last time we'll answer concerns over what happened, so speak up now." Mallory glanced around the table.

"I wanted to ask if there is any word about how Constance is doing," Carmella shyly asked.

"According to her doctors, she has suffered a complete mental breakdown," Mallory replied. "She has become totally separated from reality."

"My office has been told there is no chance she will recover enough to be able to stand trial for what she did," O'Brien added, "which is why we withheld the events from the news."

"If anyone asks about her, refer them to John," Mallory instructed. "Don't speculate. Don't try to handle it yourself. That goes for the rest of the staff as well. John, you will pass the word."

Edgecombe nodded and jotted a note.

"Mr. Mallory, one of our members asked me if the resort would be staying open after Labor Day now that you own it," Jim reported with a smile. "Any plans like that?"

"With so much of our staff being college kids on summer break, it would be difficult. What I would like to consider is opening for the week of Thanksgiving and two weeks at Christmas," Mallory responded. "It won't happen this year. I've asked John to get estimates on installing fireplaces in the cabins. I'm hoping we can manage it for the holidays next year."

"Oooooh! Thanksgiving and Christmas out here! That would be terrific!" Carmella exclaimed.

"We'll have to see how things go. I am also considering some expansion. Thompson's idea about a local resort with day access was a good one, and I'd like to build on it. We have five acres and only about one-third is in use. Constance and Thompson had some tentative plans and I'm going to study them."

After a few more questions about new policies, the first stage of the meeting broke up. Edgecombe, Carmella, and Jim left. O'Brien asked Janet and Arlene to stay for a moment. I started to excuse myself; Mallory shook his head.

"I know none of this will ever be made public, but there are a couple of loose ends I'd like to tie off. I'd like to clear up one thing in particular, strictly for my own knowledge," O'Brien said. "Arlene reported that her office had been vandalized Thursday evening but when she went back the next morning everything was tidy."

"That's what you want to know? Who cleaned up?" Mallory asked, startled. "Is it pertinent?"

"Not really. I'm just curious."

"I know who. What I want to know is why," I said.

"You know who straightened Arlene's office?" O'Brien demanded, his voice sounding like an ominous rumble of thunder.

"Captain, only one person could have done it," I logically pointed out. "I was with Constance and Mr. Mallory stayed with Thompson. Jim and Carmella went off together to their quarters. Janet mentioned she wanted to swing by the switchboard office before going to bed. Of all the people involved, she was the only one who had the chance."

She gave me a shy smile. "Yes, I did."

"Why?" O'Brien tried not to bark at her. I hoped the effort did not hurt.

"Edward asked me to make sure Constance hadn't done anything stupid and gave me his keys. When I unlocked the door and saw the mess, I figured he would want me to straighten it up."

"That was my guess." I leaned back in my chair, "and it brings up something else. Captain, you might consider assigning a detail to search the boathouse, to make sure the cyanide isn't hidden there."

"Blast it!" O'Brien frowned at Mallory and turned to regard me. His grey eyes bored into mine for a moment.

"We didn't check there because we didn't think she had been there. Easily done. Meanwhile," he addressed Arlene, "please be careful if you find some sort of container you don't recognize. Don't touch it. Notify me immediately and I'll send someone over to retrieve it."

"Certainly," she agreed.

"Arlene, have you spoken to your grandmother?" Mallory asked.

She nodded. "I called yesterday. She would like to invite you, Lauren, and a few others for a Sunday afternoon thank you dinner. I know someone has to stay here, but could something be arranged?"

"I'll have John work out a schedule so those involved will be able to attend," Mallory told her. "I'll be happy to let her know how many there will be."

Arlene smiled and left.

"Janet, some of your actions may have been questionable, but in view of the way it ended, I think you've been through enough. I'll call it square if you will," O'Brien offered, surprisingly gentle. "You helped towards the last, and there would be no point to prolong this."

"Not to mention the fact that if you did bring charges against her, you'd have to explain them, and that would blow the whole story open," I tossed out.

"Well, yes, there is that aspect," he conceded, aiming a glare at me.

"Captain, thank you. I was prepared to face the consequences, but at the same time I've been hoping you wouldn't charge me with anything. It's going to take a while to get over this." Janet tried to smile while her eyes welled with tears. "I feel responsible for Edward's death. He was good to me and he didn't deserve to die."

"Maybe not. However, there was more to him than you're aware. I made some inquiries through official channels and the final report came in today." O'Brien dug into his inside jacket pocket, pulled out an envelope, and handed it to me. "Open it and summarize it." While I read it, he spoke to her. "There are a few things you should know."

"Janet," I began, skimming the pages while I spoke, "I'm holding an FBI report on a man named Alexander Charles Talbot. Born in Illinois in 1912 and orphaned at age eight, he was placed in an orphanage run by a theological seminary. Arrested for theft in 1929, the judge went easy on him because he pleaded for understanding and affirmed he wanted to enter the seminary attached to the orphanage. Talbot was expelled at twenty for cheating. He was the prime suspect in a murder in Chillicothe but vanished ahead of arrest. After changing his name, he moved to a town in Indiana and proclaimed himself a preacher. He charmed and married a rich woman, who died in a scuba accident shortly after the wedding. Unfortunately, she hadn't signed her new will, and everything went to the church. He left Indiana and came to New York."

I looked up from the report. "There's more. However, that's enough to give you an idea of the man's character."

"What has this got to do with Edward?" Janet asked, baffled.

"Alexander Charles Talbot was the man we knew as Edward Thompson," O'Brien informed her. "We finally got a line on his real name with his fingerprints."

"Janet, you don't need to feel guilty," Mallory told her. "He was charming yet totally unscrupulous, without conscience. He would have used you the way he used everyone."

She turned pale under her tan. "That's a lot to take in but thank you. I'll always remember that he was kind to me. The rest will take time. On another matter, I want you to know I appreciate the opportunity you are giving me here, Mr. Mallory. I promise I won't let you down."

"I know you won't," the new owner said. "Run along."

Her exit ended stage two.

"Heaven help us," I commented when the door closed behind her. I handed the report back to O'Brien.

"He was as nuts in his own way as Constance was. Good grief." Mallory sighed, his fatigue showing.

I gasped as an elusive memory sprang to my mind.

"What?" both men asked.

"I can tie off another loose end," I told them. "I think."

"Don't stop there," grumbled O'Brien.

"Friday, when I returned to our lunch table," I expounded to Mallory, "you and Constance were standing and she told you, 'I promise I'll make sure we have a chance to talk tonight.' I wonder if that explains the stabbing."

"Cheese and rice!" O'Brien exclaimed, shaking his head.

"I remember the comment and you're probably right. In her mind, that would have made sense. Thankfully it's over." Mallory heaved a deep, tired sigh and looked at O'Brien. "Okay, Danny. I know there's something else you want to bring up. Let's have it."

O'Brien aimed a penetrating stare at me. "Lauren is everything you said she would be when we first spoke about the case last Thursday. I admit to being skeptical, but she proved herself." The stare evolved into a glower, belying his praise. "Now, although I admit you were helpful getting this contorted havoc straightened out, I do *not* want you sticking your nose into any of *my* investigations."

"Captain O'Brien, I promise I won't seek them out. However, if circumstances conspire to involve me, I won't back down," I countered. He did not intimidate me any more than I did him. "You heard what I told Constance's father. I came here to do a story and nose around to see if Arlene's fears had legs. Don't blame me for the fact that she was right, and the original investigation missed a couple of things."

"I'm trying to remember that," he tersely acknowledged.

"Are you always this cantankerous?"

Mallory laughed. "She has your number, Danny."

O'Brien glared at the two of us.

"I'll make a deal with you. If you don't snap and bark at me, I won't ask what big secret binds the two of you," I bargained. "I have seen people work as a team, yet most of them are dilettantes compared to you. You two are like a well-oiled set of gears meshing together. When the lights went out Friday night, you took charge. Together. It happened again when Thompson's body was discovered, and I saw it when we were dealing with Constance. That kind of teamwork is only honed with practice."

"An explanation for another time," Mallory contributed.

"Right. Absolutely. I get the feeling that your 'another time' is years away. Fine. Swell, even. I'll let it slide for now. I warn you, though, if you two don't come across, I'll start digging for answers. You both should realize by now I'm good at that."

"Fair enough," Mallory grinned.

"You're going to start getting bigger stories now, right?" O'Brien asked.

"In theory."

"If you come up against criminal activities, let me know. I may be able to teach you a few tricks," he offered, giving me what he thought passed for a smile, "so you can gather information without damaging our evidence. If you're going to be a pest, I want you properly trained. I also want your word you will pass along what you get."

"That sounds reasonable, leastways on the surface. Agreed." I glanced at Mallory. If his smile got any broader, his ears would fall off. His eyes danced with merriment while he enjoyed watching the scene playing out in front of him.

"One more thing. Your name. Lauren." O'Brien scowled like the name itself tasted sour in his mouth.

"What's wrong with Lauren? Mrs. Bogart likes it," I objected, although I smiled. "Mine is genuine. My parents gave it to me. She got hers from the studio."

"It sounds phony. According to your driving license, your middle name is Elizabeth." He thought for a moment. "Beth? Nah, too bland. Betsy? Ugh, no. Too syrupy. How about Lizzie?"

"Sorry, I have dibs on that one," Mallory informed him, snickering.

"Figures." O'Brien made a rude noise. "Would it offend you if I called you 'Kaye'?"

"You already have."

"I did? When?"

"After the discovery of Thompson's body, you told Evans to take me to the clubhouse and escort me to my cabin. You referred to me as 'Kaye' when you gave the order." I smugly grinned. "I can furnish your exact words, if you want them."

"Uh, no thanks." He looked torn between scowling and laughing. "I'll take your word for it. Did it bother you?"

"I can live with it. This way, if I hear someone bark 'Kaye!' I'll know it's you."

Mallory threw back his head and laughed. "I'm going to enjoy watching you two," he announced once he could speak. He chuckled and winked at me.

I exchanged looks with O'Brien. He rolled his eyes in response to my grin.

"You aren't helping me here," he mumbled sourly to Mallory before turning back to me. "As for you, I will make allowances." He got to his feet and made his way to the exit without a backward glance.

I stood and Mallory rose with me.

"Are you staying here or going home now?" I asked.

"I want to go over some details with John before I head back," he replied. "Lauren, Danny didn't thank you for your help, so I will."

"No need."

"Will you be going to the dinner on Sunday?"

"Try and stop me!" I took a few steps and paused. Looking back, I grinned at him and added, "Next time, I hope I can manage a story assignment without a crisis."

"Knowing you, I wouldn't count on that," he commented. His laughter followed me out the door.

Find more Exciting Titles from

JUMPMASTER PRESS™

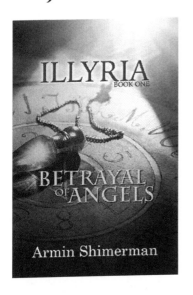

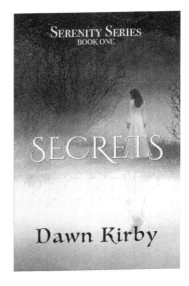

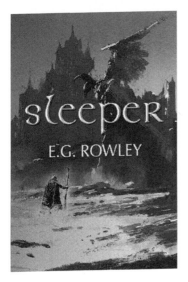

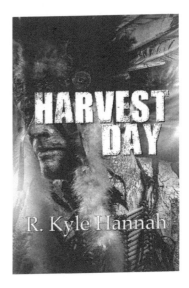

About the Author

Dale Kesterson

A native of NYC, Dale is a writer, actress, singer, and character voice artist currently living in a small Kansas town. Although a science major in college, she enjoys the creative side of life.

Her first science fiction short story was in the award-winning, *Tales of the Interstellar Bartenders Guild,* and she is the co-author of the time travel series, *Time Guards: The Devil to Pay*, released in 2020.

Besides writing, Dale performs with local community theater groups; recent roles include Cinderella's Stepmother in *Into the Woods* and the store psychologist in *Miracle on 34th Street – the Play.*

A professional photographer, Dale lives with her husband and their hairless cats, and if she's not busy doing something else she does handcrafts – she hates being bored!

Made in the USA
Columbia, SC
03 July 2021

41208802R00178